JT ⌐⌐

The City That Barks And Roars

J.T. BIRD
AUTHOR

First edition

ISBN: 9781838047900

This book was professionally typeset on Reedsy.
Find out more at reedsy.com

To Hao,
who saved my life

Contents

Acknowledgement

To my Wife and Child, who allowed me to write, and scream, and ponder.

To my Mum, and Dad, and Sister, for unwavering support of my dreams.

To the Birds and the Bushes, for continually backing my barmy ventures.

To Erika, Kestutis, and Raisa, for kindness and servings of cepelinas.

To Latte, Roisin and Mr.Adams, for constant help and invaluable assistance.

To Friends, Fellow Clowns, Minions, and Anyone who patted my back.

Thank You

1

The Penguin Who Wore A Fedora

I t's 1952, which is one thousand nine hundred and fifty-two years since
mutiny aboard the ark. Sunbeams coat the land as melting icicles trickle
off leaves warmed up by their welcome shine - which is curious given
that January's usually bleak for its entirety. Yet sadly for one unfortunate
soul, there's a dark cloud looming ominously overhead.

Detective Lucas Panda lays slumped on a riverbank, cradled by the thick
sticky mud so often present at the eerie heart of Old Buck Forest. Life seeps
from a cut to his belly - his fur now a mixture of black, white, and speckles
of red. He has a pulse, however it's faint and each breath is an uncomfortable
struggle. A tatty cotton shirt, loose cream tie and ripped silver trousers do a
poor job of keeping him warm, as icy cold waves gently splash his helpless
body. But still the bear clings to hope of a rescue, though hours and darkness
have passed, and the river delivers no saviors - no hero steps forth from the
background of lanky pine trees.

'Help...somebody...anybody...please!!' he wails, raising his head to inspect
the damage, but it's hazy and flops to the sludge. Trembling mucky paws
fumble around trying to block the wound, but they only trigger a gasp. As

he rattles his head with frustration, the soothing sound of rushing water and insects singing within the marshes, are interrupted by a formidable howl. Evil lurks in the forest, and it's scuttling with haste towards the bank.

Lucas lays still, his teeth firmly gritted for he dares not breathe or whimper. Knees begin to wobble and each hair on his neck immediately stands to attention. His tiring eyes gaze up at the clouds, half expecting a glimpse of heaven; he takes comfort in the knowledge that when animals pass, their spirit departs and drifts up high, to a better land, a pleasant land – happiness beyond the sky.

A stork flies past, delivering the morning post, but she's oblivious to the trouble below. Paradise Mail is printed in bold on her satchel, which is bursting with parcels and letters. The panda's reluctant to shriek for help, fearful of alerting pursuers, but he attempts to flaps his paws. His efforts are futile; staff at Paradise Mail are notoriously slick and efficient. Only a miracle could prize them away from the task at hand.

On the vastly diminished plus side, there's a bamboo shoot tucked in his pocket; he plucks it out and gnaws with silent delight. What he'd give right now to be sipping a meal at The Bear Pit with all his family and friends – what he'd give for their honey grass soup.

Then suddenly but inevitably, the haunting clatter of footsteps. They creep closer and closer, hurriedly crushing twigs, and leaves, and pine-cones. Lucas winces at the sound of a growl, an oink, and a heart-stopping mighty roar. Three ghastly beasts now gather immediately behind him. Light on the bank turns to shadow.

'Well, you sure don't smell like the cavalry…' he whispers resignedly.

An overwhelming stench of pungent hunters tickles his soggy nostrils, as all hope of evading capture withers away. And the last thing the panda sees before he's plunged in a sack of darkness, is bedraggled white fur, a wide-open frothing mouth, and eyeballs red as the devil.

Heaven will have to wait.

****

A fleet of rusty police cars approach with speed in the distance, tearing down a thin muddy path; they're black at both ends and white in the middle, like big mechanical zebras. Sirens are furiously whirring; the flashing red lights sit atop the roofs like horns, while they unleash their piercing blare. A cluster of motors hurtle towards the site, each one screeching to a halt as it spots the water.

They swiftly circle the scene of a crime.

Enter Detective Jake Bear; the furry white giant clambers out of his ride. He's wearing a neat white shirt, with the sleeves rolled up to display his numerous scars. Like most detectives he opts for a wide brim hat in darkish brown, with braces to hold up the caramel trousers. There was a nice pair of polished shoes but they're ruined by the muddy surroundings (don't mention his beloved red tie because he gets a little touchy – and by touchy I mean he lifts you by the scruff of your neck and shakes you like a rag doll). With a look of both urgency and concern he makes his way down to the river, trying not to slip as he does so.

Numerous pigs in uniform exit their vehicles, each of them officers, with equally despondent looks upon their faces. Anxiously they wait for the bears response. Jake removes his hat before kneeling to inspect the cordoned area. He strokes a patch of claret stained grass and sighs.

'Looks like they dragged him off the bank,' says the bear, carefully studying all the marks on the ground. He scratches an ear and gawks at the tight parade of trees, each colossal and prickly, hovering over the cluster of police cars. 'Maybe took him through the forest towards the Widows Road.'

Bingo - Jake spots a wallet. He flicks it open and skims through the wedge of receipts; they're all for groceries, which in Lucas's case means copious amounts of greens. There's also a crumpled photo stuffed inside a pocket; it's a black and white shot of Lucas out fishing with panthers - one an adult male, and the other a stroppy young female. Jake taps the snap on his knee while he ponders and scans the river, hoping for a sight of his friend.

Detective Hudson Rhino arrives - fashionably late as always. He's crammed in a corn yellow shirt struggling to cope with his size and it's smeared with fragments of breakfast. A cigar drapes from the side of his jaw, where one usually spots a doughnut. He steps out his car and slams the door shut with his pointy horn.

A nervous piggy clutching a notepad approaches immediately; there's visible beads of sweat on his head which he keeps trying to wipe with a trotter.

'Errr…factory worker called it in, sir. Heading back from a shift, heard some commotion. She said…ummm…she said the noises sent a chill through her bones, sir.' The pig decides it's considerably less nerve wracking if he just mumbles and stares at shaky notes.

'Species?' replies the rhino impatiently, tightening and straightening his tie.

'Ummm, she was a raccoon, sir. So, it's safe to say she probably isn't a suspect,' bumbles the increasingly sweaty officer.

Hudson tilts the officer's head so there's eye contact while he scolds him. 'I'll decide what's safe to say, piggy. Now where's the divers? We need to search the river *pronto*.'

'On their way, sir. Four of our best seals. Sir.'

'Be sure that they are, pig, be sure that they are.'

A tarnished badge is poking from a mound of mud: *Kingdom Police Force*. Jake immediately retrieves it and wipes the gold clean with a paw.

'What happened, Luc?' he mumbles to himself, while his eyes scout for additional clues. A couple of coins and a ticket for the nearby racetrack is the best the ground can offer. After a moment's pause the bear rises and turns to face the mournful crowd; his high hopes for a year of peace and calm, have quickly been laid to rest.

'Looks like they took him rather than dump him in the river, so there's a fair chance he's still alive. Fetch some more pigs and hit the woods,' says the polar bear, addressing the crowd of officers. Then he turns to the cigar touting rhino. 'Hudson, check his apartment and speak to some neighbors. And get on the phone to Frank. If anyone can solve this thing, it's the penguin.' Jake returns his hat to his head, curses the filth on his shoes, and slowly trudges

4

back to his car.

****

Noah's Kingdom: home to nearly two million walking talking animals. Behold a buzzing concrete jungle bathed in bright lights, forged at the feet and mercy of a towering dam. A thriving metropolis packed with all the good, bad, and ugly creatures you could possibly imagine. Some call it 'the city that never sleeps', yet for many, it's where dreams are lost or found.

Thick grey clouds have been weeping for hours, and streets are approaching submersion. The donkey behind the wheel slams on his brakes, right outside the Arctic Cafe. You'll struggle to find a bleaker street in all of Noah's Kingdom; it's dark and murky even on the sunniest of summer days and riddled with crumbling buildings.

Chico Monkey hops out the taxi and wishes he'd packed an umbrella. Up until last night he was locking up small timers for the West Bay Police Department in a sleepy town at the middle of nowhere. Then, without any say in the matter, he was promptly re-assigned; much to his dismay he was chucked on the earliest train destined for 'Kingdom' and told to aid in the search for a panda.

Chico's young and energetic but cursed with a fondness for sarcasm which often leads to trouble. If he gave as much thought to his choice of words as he did to his choice of outfit, then he'd have avoided a few black eyes. Today it's a crisp grey suit, matching hat and light blue shirt – closer to crooner than crime fighter. Technically he's a 'red howler' monkey, hence the reddish fur, but the lengthy tail and trendy beard make him reasonably easy to spot. Normally you smell him before you see him though, thanks to the bucket of cheap fruity aftershave he insists on bathing in every morning (today's scent: *Eau De La Nana by Franco Chimpo*. The perfect choice for any gent wishing to smell like ripe bananas).

He tosses the driver some coins, pats the roof, and spins around. The ink on the note in his hand is washing away, but the message is still pretty clear: *Arctic Cafe*. He scrunches the reminder into a soggy ball and stuffs it back in a pocket.

'You gotta be kidding me,' he groans, looking through the window of the dingiest diner in town. It's an ill-kempt cozy joint, and in desperate need of a lick or two of paint, but popular for those seeking coffee and breakfast fresh from the ocean.

Bells chime above the door as the monkey dives inside to escape the relentless downpour. He shakes a few drops off the soaking wet suit and dries his eyes with a sleeve. It's a pit of chaos: animals queuing for breakfast, trying to eat breakfast, and serving breakfast, all within an inappropriate amount of space.

A pack of sailor seagulls are babbling loudly at their table beside the doorway - typical noisy gulls.

Squidged behind a table in the corner and facing foggy windows, sits a hard-boiled penguin devouring a plate full of scrambled eggs and mackerel. He's a 'King' penguin, so shorter than an 'Emperor' but stout with a sharp beak and orange fur at the back of his neck which closely resembles a collar. Meet Frank - the only bird in town wearing a beige crumpled rain mac and chocolate colored fedora (the hat of choice for any true detective). His coat looks a shade too big and the hat's tilted too far back, but he's never been one for fashion.

Chico takes a seat opposite Frank, but the penguin barely flinches, such is the desire to finish his breakfast as swiftly as possible. *Vote Spots* – the monkey can't help but notice the bold wilting poster of current mayor, George Leopard, overlooking their greasy table.

'Ahem'. Chico tries to catch his attention. Frank licks the plate clean, before taking a long sip of pitch-black coffee. As the cup returns to the table, he finally sets eyes on his latest partner, and breaks the awkward silence.

'You must be the chimp? Hot shot from West Bay. They tell me your good,' he says, tapping the table with a cheap knife and fork. 'I thought you'd be taller.' By the sound of his voice you'd think he owned a pizza parlour, as opposed to being the city's most experienced sleuth.

'I'm a monkey. We tend to be short. And just for the record, I thought you'd be younger,' says the monkey, inching closer to deliver his taunt.

'To be honest, kid, at first glance I could swear you were a drowned rat.'

'Well, they never warned me I'd be working with a fish.'

Franks turn to lean across the table. 'I'm a flightless bird, Frank Penguin. Welcome to Noah's Kingdom.'

'Charlie Monkey, people call me Chico.' They shake hands firmly, but with minimal eye contact.

'What's with the fancy schmancy suit, kid? Looks like you're here to sell me insurance,' says Frank with a hint of smirk. 'Anyways, you're late and you nearly missed breakfast. Speak to the walrus - he ain't too friendly, but you won't find a tastier way to start the day, in this or any city. And that's a fact.' A plate of squid on the table beside them catches his eye; if the platypus who ordered it leaves a few scraps, he'll undoubtedly be first to pounce.

Chico slumps back in his chair and glances at the blubbery walrus; he's stroking his whiskers and trying not to gore favored regulars with his prominent tusks, while he takes the orders and yells at the poor rabbit in the apron and chef's hat. 'You know what, I'm not too hungry.'

'Coffee?'

'Mmm not big on caffeine. More of an OJ kinda monkey.'

'You sure you're a cop?'

'I like to keep in shape. You should try it sometime.'

Frank ignores the cheap dig, licks his lips, and wipes down his precious mac. 'Ok, look, just so you know it ain't no picnic being a cop stuck in Kingdom. This place has a habit of wearing you down, till all you got left is despair. And things can get a little rough. But hey, stick close to me and follow my lead, you'll be fine.'

Chico's eyebrows raise and his head jolts back with slight disbelief. 'Appreciate the warning, but I'm no boy scout. I made detective two years back. No hand holding required.'

Frank holds his wings up as if to apologize. 'Jeeze, relax. All I'm saying is, this ain't no city of angels. Plenty of devils prowling these streets and chances are you'll meet 'em. Trust me, you're a long way from West Bay, kid.'

'Read my lips, I can handle it. Devil shows up, I'll be ready,' says Chico, sliding out his chair to stand over his newest partner.

Frank wields his fork as a toothpick before wagging it at the hovering monkey. 'You got spirit I'll give you that much, and I know you never asked for a ticket to the party, but we could sure do with some help.' He drops a copy of the Kingdom Chronicle on the table; 'Detective Feared Dead' is stamped across the top in a thick bold font. 'My partner. Week shy of retirement. Snatched off a riverbank, down in Old Buck Forest.'

Chico looks down at the breaking news. In a flash he tastes regret and curses himself for giving the penguin a hard time. 'I'm sorry...I didn't realize he was your partner-.'

'Every morning he'd collapse in that seat you got right there. Never a second late neither and always the prawns on toast. Not a fan of variety,' says Frank, remembering the good old days.

'Any leads? Ransom note?'

'No notes, no leads. Divers came up with his mac though. Slashed up real bad, so that's something to go on, I guess. Oh, and Detective Bear found this at the scene,' says Frank, passing Chico the photo from Lucas's wallet.

'Fishing with panthers. Any idea who they are?'

Frank is quick to snatch it back once his new partner has taken a peek. 'I got no idea who the cat is, or the kitten with the face like thunder. Never heard Luc mention no panthers. Anyways, I got some pigs looking into it.'

'Ok, so, when do we start?'

'After breakfast, kid. Always after breakfast.'

'You've had breakfast.'

Frank prods the platypus. 'Buddy, you gonna finish all that? I'm still a bit peckish.'

'Beat it, penguin!' snaps the hungry customer.

'Ok, i'm done. Let's get to work.' Frank buttons up the mac, pulls up the collar, and nudges the fedora forward – ready for an onslaught of drizzle. He gives Chico a friendly slap on the shoulder before slipping through the crowds to the exit. 'Tomorrow, walrus!' he yells, yanking open the door. Again, the bell chimes, as the caffeine-fuelled penguin fades into a mist of raindrops. Chico takes one last look at the Chronicle upon the table: a picture of Lucas Panda standing proudly in dashing uniform.

2

Brothers, Where Art Thou?

F rank and Chico dart from the cafe to a black and white rust bucket parked across the street - but still get drenched by the rainfall. Chico manages to climb inside however he's guaranteed an unpleasant ride; the pint size police-mobile was designed to accommodate stumpy penguin drivers rather than monkey passengers.

'I hope we don't get into a chase with this thing. We'd be better off pursuing on foot,' quips Chico, writhing around trying to find a position of comfort. His head presses firmly against the roof.

'Quit complaining, kid, or you can pursue me on foot all the way back to the station!' snaps Frank, slamming his foot on accelerate. Pungent smoke pours out the exhaust, which is further evidence that this car's best days are over. Somehow it commences a brief drive back to police headquarters over in central Kingdom.

'Can I ask some more about your partner?' quizzes Chico, adopting a serious tone for once. He wipes condensation off the window to catch a peek of rush hour; the streets of Noah's Kingdom are crammed with hordes of workers, fighting their way to early morning meetings. A trio of elephant businessmen stampede across the road like warriors charging to battle.

'Lucas Panda, great cop, we joined the force together. He was my partner for nearly five years. Never married though…no kids, family, nothing. And tonight was meant to be his big retirement party over at The Bear Pit. Instead he's vanished cause I wasn't there for him,' explains Frank, tightening his grip on the steering wheel and trying to hold back the rage. 'I don't get it, kid. We weren't running heavy cases…just small fish, couple of bank jobs, some gang trouble, but no major crime. So, either it's crook with a grudge from the past, *or* Luc was up to something on the side.'

'Did he owe someone money? Mixed up with the wrong crowd?' prods Chico, carefully trying not to overstep the mark.

'When I say great cop, kid, *I mean* great cop. Clean as a whistle, one of the nice guys. A law-abiding panda.'

Chico whips out his flashy new notebook, a birthday gift from his aunt, and flicks to a fresh new page. He scrawls one word at the top with a flashy pencil that came with the book: *Lucas*

'What do we know so far?' he asks, pencil primed.

'Worker heard hell breakin' loose around six am. She was on her way back from a shift at the nearby milk factory. Checked her out, she's clean. But we got no actual witnesses,' says Frank, trying to get his new partner up to speed. 'Pigs found a trail of blood…led from the Widow Road down through some woods and ended up at the river. Looks like he was attacked by the roadside and made a run for it.'

'*Widow Road*. Up by the racetrack, right?'

'That's right, kid, up by the racetrack.'

'What about the cuts to his mac?'

'Can't be certain, but our boys down in the lab reckon they came from some kinda dog.'

Chico squeezes one last word in the bottom corner of his first page of notes: *Dog?*

Frank smashes his horn and angrily waves at the driver up ahead. 'What are you… a camel?! Get moving buddy, jeeze!!'

'You're pretty angry for a bird.'

Frank huffs and wags a wing at the cocky passenger. 'When you get to my age, kid, you're not angry…you're just grumpy, there's a difference. I say what I think, I'm a penguin, we're a passionate species. I mean *wow* you should meet Mrs Penguin, jeeze Louise…now that's one scary animal right there. Last week I forgot to pick up her groceries from the store, *boy* she hit the roof, nearly tore my beak off. I always said my wife should've been a cop.'

Chico grins and feels a sudden warmth towards the cranky old penguin – maybe he isn't so bad after all.

'So, tell me about *Chico* Monkey. Crime solving run in the family or what?'

'Nope. Mother was a teacher, father put out fires. But they passed away not long after I was born. So, I grew up with my Aunt Sally, and *no*, she's not on the force either. She's a prickly head chef at The Leaping Lobster. Comfortably West Bay's tastiest restaurant.'

The penguin takes his eyes off the road for a second to twist and face his passenger. 'I'm yet to meet a great chef whose temper wasn't short.'

'She's pushy, terrifying at times, but she means well and keen to see me prosper. Just trying my best to not disappoint her. I'd give anything to be a hero like my dad and do Aunt Sally proud.'

'I'm sure if your aunt were here right now she'd tell ya she's proud already.'

'Oh, I wouldn't be so sure. Fishing for compliments from Aunt Sal's like squeezing blood from a rock.'

'What about a dame? Got yourself a dame yet, kiddo? Charmed any gorgeous gorillas, a cute miss chimpanzee? Or maybe you're still too young for all that jazz and heartache.'

'Not yet, but I'm working on it,' responds the monkey bashfully, staring into the distance and reflecting on his life; there was a pretty monkey back home that lived across the street, and he'd promised her a dance and milkshake (probably a trip to Mickey's Diner, the most popular haunt in West Bay) - but those plans had been scuppered by his assignment in the city.

'Plenty of time, kiddo, plenty of time. You're still a young buck. Who knows, maybe you'll meet a lucky lady on the job?'

'Yeah, maybe,' mutters Chico, clearly not convinced.

'I mean, we pinch all kinds of dealers, thieves and nut jobs. Maybe one of them will take ya fancy hey, kid,' yaps Frank, honking the car horn to celebrate another attempt at humor. Chico smiles, nods and gently shoves his grumpy partner.

****

'Spare a gold coin for a struggling ostrich, could ya sir? It's my birthday.' A beggar is camped outside headquarters with a collection tin rattling on his feathery lap.

'Jeeze, big bird, every week you say it's your freakin' birthday,' snaps Frank, marching past and reluctant to part with donations.

Chico's heart is better positioned but there's nothing to share in his pockets; the best he can do is a shrug. 'Hey grouchy, why can't you chuck him a coin?' remarks Chico as they charge towards the entrance. The building is truly unremarkable; just ten levels of brown brick planted on the corner of Tail Street. Pockets of officers are mooching around outside, inhaling fresh air and gossip.

Frank pushes open the door and gestures his partner to enter. 'Charity starts at home, kid. Bills to pay and a lady to spoil.'

Chico is slightly taken aback by Frank's reluctance to demonstrate kindness. 'Wow, it's like working with a ray of sunshine,' he utters, striding into the tower. 'You should try lightening up a little. Life's more satisfying if you're generous and carry a smile.'

Frank sniffs and scoffs at the cheeky attack. '*Lighten up* he says. One more wise crack, kiddo, and it'll be lights out for *you.*'

Neither had noticed the bench across the road; the young panther with crossed legs in the long pink dress and floppy blue sun hat, watching their every move. She had perfectly feigned curiosity in a trashy fashion magazine, when really her eyes were latched on the pair of detectives. Her paws, sheathed in red silky gloves, slide into pockets till one comes across costly sunglasses. She delicately pops them on despite the gloomy weather and hails a passing taxi.

14

Frank and Chico exit a packed elevator and stroll onto the busy fourth floor of Kingdom Police Headquarters. *Rat-a-tat-tat* - the sound of busy typewriters fills the air. A sea of officers caked in navy blue are hunched over desks writing reports (officers tend to be pigs but there's a mixture working today and even a few detectives – just look for the cheap suits and tired bloodshot eyes).

'Ok, teams of two. We search every inch of forest and Widow's Road. Knock on door, twice if you have to. We need clues and witnesses. And don't head back till we have one or other,' harps Officer Yuriko Wolf from the corner, huddled with eager pigs and a disinterested looking rat. A crinkled map of Hare's Forest is pinned to the wall behind her and a red dot marks the spot where Lucas was stolen.

A short-sighted mole races passed, both squinting and nodding in the general direction of Frank as she does so. 'Morning Frank,' she says hurriedly, before darting back to her desk via a collision with various colleagues.

Officer Thelma Eagle swoops in through an open window; she has the wonderful advantage of avoiding morning traffic (birds of prey are extremely valuable to the police force due to their flair for surveillance. Tracking criminals from the sky is an invaluable talent).

Hudson Rhino is leaning back in a swivel chair with both arms folded behind his head. He's had a smile from ear to ear ever since the penguin arrived. '*Hey*, Frank the Mac, what time you call this?!' hollas the rhino loudly. 'Vulture wants you in her office pronto and she don't sound happy. Enjoy.'

Frank nods to acknowledge the beefy rhino and promptly responds. 'We still on for poker tonight, big boy? I fancy some more of your coins.'

The rhino laughs. 'Tonight's *my night*, penguin. Feeling real lucky. I'm gonna win cash, your precious mac *and* your wife.'

Quick as a flash the penguin returns fire. 'Hey, I'll pay you to take Mrs Penguin, how about that? Trust me…twenty-four hours and you'll be paying me double to take her back.'

A speckled pig in uniform looks up from his desk and spots Chico inspecting the office. 'Hey Frank, who's the new guy?' asks the pig, pointing her head at the newest recruit.

Frank turns to Chico, puts an arm around him, and makes an announcement to the entire office. 'Everybody listen up, this is Detective Chico Monkey. Drafted in from West Bay to help on the panda case. First day on the job, so let's try and treat him with a bit more respect than you show me. And *yeah*, that includes you ya chunky rhino scumbag.'

Chico gives a small wave to the crowd, most of which have already returned to doing their work. He clears his throat, pretending he wasn't offended.

Chief Vultures den. The stern looking bird is perched behind an extremely tidy desk; she takes great pride in her ability to avoid hefty piles of clutter. Her eyes are sunk behind a thick pair of spectacles and she's packed in a tight black dress, which only adds to her intimidating presence. She's stubs her fourth cigarette of the morning into a glass ash tray shaped like a nest.

'Thought you quit smoking, chief?' jests Frank, picking his seat. The frosty vulture lets the spectacles slide down her beak to reveal her beady eyes. She prods her head forward and studies the uncomfortable visitors.

'I quit having insects for breakfast, that's enough quitting for now. If I quit smoking, you'd probably all be dead by now,' responds the vulture. 'And *you* must be Detective Charlie Monkey. Welcome. And my sincerest apologies you're stuck with this incompetent penguin, but there we go, that's life, deal with it. Any questions?'

'Actually, they call me Chico, ma'am.'

No response. Only silent eye contact.

'No questions, ma'am,' says Frank, butting in to save the day.

The monkey gulps, prickling with discomfort - but incessantly tapping his feet and stroking his beard seems to help with calming the nerves. 'Err yeah, Charlie's fine, no questions ma'am. Just keen to get started.'

'Splendid. *Well*, there's a beaver waiting downstairs and he's itching to speak with someone about some missing friends. See if you two can help,' says the chilling boss whilst reading the notes on her desk. 'Oh, and any word on Lucas? Do we have any leads? I've got a meeting with Mayor Leopard in an hour and he's bound to push for an update.'

Frank sits up and straightens his back. 'Nothing major yet, chief, but we're working on it. Apartment was clean, and nothing from friends or neighbors. Fat Chinchilla might have something though. I'm meeting the greasy snitch at the palace later today and we'll shake him down. But hey, we'll catch this guy, ma'am, don't you worry.'

'Glad to hear it, good luck, and keep me posted. And do make sure you get this monkey a badge.' The vulture's quite done with looking up from her desk. Frank and Chico take the hint and quietly depart her lair like a pair of dismissed naughty schoolboys.

****

LeRoy Beaver manages the Shepherd's Dam which protects Noah's Kingdom from flooding; he and a small army of other creatures (mainly beavers) work both day and night to ensure the dam never cracks nor crumbles. Currently he's sat quietly in an empty interview room at police headquarters and has been for over an hour. Two cups of cheap coffee, both of which arrived in feeble thimbles, have helped him pass the time. LeRoy's stocky for a beaver and easily recognizable thanks to a shiny gold tooth and the chunky gold medallion hanging around his neck; the shredded denim, dusty boots, and muck infested t-shirt suggest he's come straight to HQ from a shift. He crushes the cup and bounces if off the wall.

Frank and Chico burst into the room. Before either can say a word, the furious beaver propels to his feet and slams both fists on the table.

'Where have you been, fools? Unbelievable. Been sweating here all day and I got three beavers missing!!'

Chico jumps but Frank barely moves a muscle – fear's not in his DNA.

'Take a seat goofball, it's been a busy day,' snaps Frank, failing wonderfully to calm the situation.

LeRoy shakes his head, clearly still upset, before finally sitting down. 'Johnny, Chuck and Benny, all missing. Now that ain't right.' He's a mixture of tense, angry and twitchy – not the healthiest of cocktails. Spit fires from his lips as he vents sheer irritation. 'Something going down ya feel me, and

17

I'm wasting time. Sat here sippin' cheap ol' coffee all day.'

Frank and Chico finally grab a chair while they pull out pencils and notebooks. Eager to impress his partner, Chico sets to work scrawling down details. 'When did you last see them?' he asks.

Leroy sniffs and cocks his head. 'Been three days now man, *three* days. That ain't like them. They ain't never been late to work, not one single time since I laid my eyes on 'em, not one time. Even their cousin been calling me, asking if I seen the boys.'

His claws tap furiously on the table but there's no more cups to launch, which might explain the vein throbbing on the side of his head 'Something ain't right, ya here me, and you know who they run with? That *damn* dog, that's who.' He takes it out on the table again with all his rage and fury. 'They're hungry for money cause working the dam ain't enough. So they go to *him* for a few extra nuggets o' gold.'

'Damn dog, what damn dog?' asks Chico, scribbling furiously.

'*The* damn dog brother, yo, there only one dog in town. You livin' in a cave or summin' fool?' snarls LeRoy.

'Salvatore Bulldog. Runs a nightclub down in the dog district. Real goon with paws in plenty of dirty pies,' answers Frank calmly. Chico shrugs and sketches a quick doodle of a dog with podgy cheeks on a fresh page. He jots the word *'Salvatore'* just below it.

'They ever mention a panda? Lucas Panda?' asks Chico, munching the end of his pencil.

LeRoy scratches his twenty-four-carat tooth. 'Panda from the papers, the cop? Nah, they ain't never mentioned no cop. Doubt the beavers be friends with any creature packin' a badge.'

'Anything else you can tell us, LeRoy? They talk of any problems? Mention what they do for the dogs?' probes the penguin.

LeRoy's on his feet again and pacing around the room, battling to control his emotions. The sleeve of his crumpled t-shirt takes the place of a tissue as he runs it across his face. He clears his throat and shrugs his shoulders, shaking himself back to macho mode.

'Look, they never told me about no extra work 'cause they know I wouldn't be happy. But I'm LeRoy Beaver, I know things and I sure ain't stupid. I let it slide ya feel me, figure they need the money, so I let it slide. But they close as brothers, they like blood to me. *Yeah*, they get on the wrong side of the law few times, but they're good boys and religious nuts too - just holla Father Goat. They wouldn't miss church for all the gold in Paradise Valley. So, you track 'em down ya hear, cause if harm should come their way, then *damn* boy I'll find who done it and drag them from the land of the living. You hear me, fool?'

It was clear this strapping beaver wasn't one for joking, clear from his eyes that he was genuinely concerned for his friends, and equally genuine when he promised repercussions. The Kingdom Police Force was now under pressure to find a panda *and* discover the whereabouts of three unscrupulous beavers. Chico pined for his Aunt's blueberry pie and relaxing nights on her porch, but he kissed those plans goodbye; he knew deep down that this city was far from done with him.

3

Bon Appetit

Reports of a disturbance: 5th floor, 135 Carnival Boulevard - a rundown apartment block out on the lower east side (it's a medium block where 'medium' sized animals live. The building to the east is half the size and accommodates short creatures like hedgehogs and mice. To the west is a gargantuan tower; home to monsters such as hippos and elephants). Ruben Rat and Yuriko Wolf's turn to draw the short straw; two officers in no doubt they're heading for trouble. Cops try to avoid stepping foot in the hellhole that is New Carnival because it's mainly a hideout for dirtbags, but it's close to the riverbank where Lucas was kidnapped so needs to be investigated immediately. It's neither a safe nor a pretty neighborhood; even the air tastes hazardous and the sunlight appears to be faded. Just row upon row of derelict towers of grey, waiting patiently to meet a bulldozer.

Ruben's winding tail swirls out of the police vehicle long before his furry grey body hops out to join it. He doesn't strike you as a typical cop, with his diminutive stature, constantly unbuttoned shirt, and comical oversized cap – not to mention the squeaky voice. Despite his size and lack of respect for the uniform, the rat's been in the game a long time and certainly has experience on his side; if only he had a grip of his nerves and behaved less like a mouse. He peers up at the frail looking building lurking over him: old, dirty, and falling apart. A strong gust of wind would probably finish her off.

'Why can't we get a disturbance in Paradise Valley, just for once?' he groans.

Yuriko calmly steps out the vehicle next. A quietly spoken grey wolf with piercing white eyes and long bushy fur. This officer certainly wears her uniform with much more pride; the cap neatly placed on her head and a shirt perfectly ironed. Even her badge has been thoroughly polished. She doesn't say a word - just stares at the mumbling rat and prepares for duty. Ruben stops gawping at the hideous architecture and they make their way inside.

Both rat and wolf climb the mucky steps all the way up to the filthy fifth floor. There's nothing to greet them except a long empty corridor lined with flickering lights (the maintenance guy's on holiday).

'Any luck on your hunt for a new apartment?' enquires Ruben, unable to keep his mouth shut for more than a handful of seconds. 'I gotta cousin who could help ya find somewhere and a brother who could help ya move.'

'My father still looking. Find something soon, I hope. Living with four sisters, *big* nightmare.'

They exchange glances before slowly proceeding with caution, constantly checking their surroundings for strange behavior. Each step is met with a prolonged unhelpful creak as they shuffle along the ancient wooden floorboards. Suddenly, from the corner of their eyes, they spot a door reluctantly opening gently. Ruben holds his breath. An elderly sheep reveals herself and points towards a room at the end.

'Last door on the left. Be careful,' she whispers, with a trembling lip, before sinking back to the safety of her dreary apartment. She pushes the door shut and slams multiple sturdy locks.

Phew. Ruben breathes again.

'Should've been a hairdresser like my father, not sneaking round creepy dark buildings looking for trouble,' spurts the rat quietly, trying to settle his nerves through sarcasm. It doesn't work.

'You have no style rat. Me think you find plenty of trouble as hairdresser,' responds the wolf with a wry smile, her gaze fixed on the end of the corridor. They finally arrive at the door in question: apartment 58.

Ruben slides one of his thin round ears against the rotting wood. 'I think I hear something.'

Yuriko knocks three times. They take a step back and ponder the terrors that might imminently confront them. The sound of footsteps. Then nothing. Yuriko, like always, is a shining example of how to remain calm during a tense situation (she learned most of her skills abroad from a reputable police force, before her family moved to a new home in Noah's Kingdom). Ruben on the other hand, looks well positioned to run for cover the second he needs to.

'Why you hide behind me? You always coward, rat.'

'I'm not hiding, it's tactical.'

The door swings open. Surely a raging venomous python? A furious bloody thirsty croc? Or an unstoppable rampaging tiger? Not quite. It's a fox in a green tweed coat, yellowy knitted jumper, and tartan golf trousers that now stands before them; he's trying so hard to smile it must be hurting his cheeks.

'Officers, how can I be of service?' he gleams.

'Officer Rat, and this is Officer Wolf. Kingdom Police Department,' snaps Ruben, his heart rate sliding back to a regular beat. 'Complaint from one of your neighbors. Some kinda disturbance.'

'We come in *now*,' adds Yuriko with a louder more confident tone than before.

'Have I done something wrong officers? I'm just a harmless car salesman. And I've been home alone all afternoon, I swear.'

'Did you know Detective Lucas Panda, sir? Ever meet him?' asks Ruben.

'Is that what this is about? The missing detective. I never met him, why would I?'

'Ever sell him car?' adds Yuriko.

'No, not that I recall. Look, if that's why you're here then you really are wasting your time. I had nothing to do with it. And anyhow, I've been out of town and only got back last night. There's tickets and friends to prove it.'

'Yeah, well, we're gonna come in and take a look around now, just to be on the safe side. If you don't mind?'

'Why would I mind, Officer Rat? I've done nothing wrong?'

Ruben makes his way past the fox and into the home. Yuriko follows his lead.

'Take a look around, you won't find anything,' squirms the fox anxiously.'I sell cars and that's all. I'm a good citizen.'

They commence their tour of the property. There's a smell in the air and not a delightful one, but the cops can't be sure of its source.

'Aww boy, what's that hum?' mumbles Ruben. His itsy-bitsy eyes dart around the bomb site of a living room. Clothes, junk, and unfinished anchovy pizza line the dirty carpet. There's a black and white telly in the corner trying to display *The Perry Zebra Show* – but it's in need of a good old whack. The curtains may have been chalky white at some point, but now they're unpleasant yellow and permanently closed.

Yuriko can't resist pulling a face as she casts her eye over the gloomy decor; evidently the fox has not acquired expertise in interior design. The damp walls are ruined furthermore by the ghastly brown paper that hides them - though in numerous patches it appears to be peeling away. There are minor attempts at decoration: a couple of cheap ornaments and a dozen family photos. With great haste and tightly pinched noses, the curious officers make their way to the kitchen.

Miraculously his kitchen manages to pull off a dirtier and *even more* neglected feel than the adjacent stinky living room (the rat looks unimpressed and you should smell his cheesy apartment). 'I'm gonna be honest, Mr Fox, this is disgusting,' yells Ruben, wading through sticky flooring. He skips past piles of rotten pots and manky pans, to inspect a cauldron bubbling over a fire in the corner. 'I hope those cars you sell are in better condition that your home?'

'Cooking something?' asks Yuriko, spotting the bubbles.

'Oh yes, just a spot of lunch. Soup,' replies the bag of nerves.

'And what type of soup would that be, Mr Fox?' says Ruben, sniffing his way around the room.

'Fish, fish soup of course.' The suspicious tenant wipes his clammy palms down the tweed jacket, followed by another cameo from his utmost smile. Sweat trickles down his head and into his furry brow. 'It's extremely hot in here, isn't it,' he remarks, finding an excuse for his sudden perspiration.

'You seem nervous'. Yuriko can smell fear racing through the fox's veins.

'I just sell cars, I'm a good citizen, this is madness. In fact, I really think you should leave now.'

'Mind if I try the soup?' replies the rat, stirring the cauldron slowly with a long iron ladle. Ruben peers into the steamy liquid, slightly concerned by what he might find. 'I don't believe it.' The rodent shakes his tiny pointed head with disbelief.

Nothing. No boiling bunny, no victim left to simmer, and no crime committed in the kitchen – unless you believe the cooking of haddock to be a sin. The cauldron reveals nowt but a stew of fish and carrots. Maybe the fox was innocent after all?

'Are you happy now?' asks the fox, with hands on hips and a brief burst of confidence.

Thud. It came from the bedroom.

'What was that?' Ruben scampers across the syrupy floor of the kitchen and heads for the noisy bedroom.

'I didn't hear anything. It's nothing. Can you *please* just leave?' insists the fox.

The bushy tailed salesman dashes after the rat in a state of panic. Yuriko calmly follows. Ruben bursts into the bedroom with his claws both primed and ready. He spins around, checking the area's clear; thankfully, there's no unwelcome scoundrels hiding behind the door. Fox and wolf promptly join him, barging through the door simultaneously.

'There's nothing to see in here, this *really* is madness.'

Yuriko doesn't waste time dragging open an old mahogany wardrobe which is stood beside the Fox's messy bed. Inside the decrepit piece of furniture, much to the shock and horror of the officers, lays a frightened postman pig. He's tied up with rope and there's a juicy apple stuffed in his mouth to prevent any screams for help (it's illegal in these parts to eat someone that talks. Stick to fish, veg, nuts and seeds to avoid the local jail).

'Wanna explain why there's a postman in your wardrobe, Mr Fox?' asks Ruben bluntly.

The fox looks set to attempt an excuse but swiftly abandons the idea in favor of running away. He shoves the wolf into the wardrobe, before taking the rat in his mouth and flinging him against the wall. Ruben slumps to the ground while Yuriko leaps to her feet and gives pursuit.

The guilty fox bounds down the corridor with the route to freedom locked in sight. What he can't see however - is the grey wolf rapidly chasing behind him. As the vermin reaches the top of the staircase and prepares to jump, Yuriko buries her teeth in his tail. He lets out a howl as he's helplessly dragged back to his festering home; his hopes of avoiding punishment have been dashed - and met a painful end.

Yuriko lets go of his hindmost part, but only once they've arrived back at the doorway of apartment 58. She pins the whimpering creep against the wall.

'Now you go prison,' she declares firmly, still catching her breath. The fox spins around, his head slapping against the wall while he's secured with Yuriko's handcuffs.

'I'm a good citizen, truly I am!' cries the fox. 'But he smelt *so* good. His belly, *oh please* let me taste some boiled belly. Or a juicy leg, mmm the legs, at least allow me a nibble on a leg. It'll be our little secret– .'

'Rule number one,' shouts a dizzy Ruben, wobbling out to the corridor. 'Thou shall not eat thy neighbor.' He rubs the nasty new bump on his head.

'I'm a good citizen,' mutters the fox to himself, as Ruben leads him away.

'Good citizens don't cook their postman–.'

'You ok?' asks Yuriko, hitting the stairs.

'Fine, I'm fine. Possible skull fracture, blurred vision, can't walk straight. But yeah I'm fine.'

'Aww come on, just little bruise. You always drama queen.'

'I am *not* a drama queen. But I get a little miffed when cannibals try and put my head through walls.'

'Moan moan moan, always rat moans.'

'You know which job doesn't involve regular brain damage? *Hairdresser.*'

A sly fox caught red handed and looking at years behind bars - but innocent where the panda was concerned. The slippery salesman had eyes for pigs, *not* bears, and a watertight alibi. Whoever it was that attacked poor Lucas Panda, was sadly still at large.

4

A Kingdom's Pride

Emzara's Palace stands nearly as tall as the Shepherd's Dam and lies at the heart of the city's most affluent area, Paradise Valley. It's a white colossal playground, rectangular in shape but topped with three emerald domes. A towering wonder of the world with a face of a thousand windows, each one glistening in the sunshine and glowing with amber light. Few can resist the urge to gaze in awe at its magnificent beauty, or the craving to experience its luxurious rooms. Prosperous animals flock from lands afar merely to pamper within the gates; from kings and queens to movie stars and sporting greats, each has relished the chance to sample its lavish delights.

We have lions to thank for such a marvel for it was their riches that paid for this grand creation. In fact, Lioness Annabella is probably the wealthiest creature to ever have walked these lands, thanks to good fortune in the trade of precious metals (it's amazing what creatures will pay for gold, silver and platinum). Yet Annabella enjoys an unsociable existence, hidden away in the penthouse suite of her greatest and priciest achievement. Not many have had the pleasure of her company, or at least, lived to tell the tale.

The entrance to the hotel sits beyond banks of leafy palm trees and a courtyard of extravagant stone fountains in shallow mosaic pools. Its doors are twenty feet high and only opened by loyal guards – four humorless Komodo dragons. The dragons of Noah's Kingdom have been faithful servants to this pride of lions for numerous generations. Patiently and silently they wait. Each guard stands neck to toe in ancient silver armor, a distinctive lion's head painted in red across their chest plate, and a lofty spear clasped tightly with a claw. Only the richest and luckiest of creatures are granted entrance to the utopia within. Unwelcome visitors such as *Chronicle* journalists digging for tales of Annabella, face the wrath of a sizable lizard.

Frank Penguin needs no introduction; the dragon's pull open the huge doors before he gets a chance to flash a badge. That's not to say he's a popular visitor - the guards look far from ecstatic that a detective has waddled into the luxurious lobby, and they look equally unimpressed by the monkey casually strolling behind him.

The lobby is a marble hall of treats under a gold encrusted ceiling, showcasing a selection of the priceless art purchased by Annabella. There's a timid lamb strumming a harp in the corner while wide-eyed guests admire sculptures and valuable ornaments. A two-hundred-year-old oil painting of Emzara, wife of Noah, takes pride of place; the beautiful brunette is dressed in a flowing peach robe, looking down on all who dare to enter.

'Welcome to Emzara's Palace, kid, what d'ya think? Not bad right?' asks Frank, stroking a priceless piece of pottery, despite multiple signs around the lobby which say: *Do Not Touch*.

'It's something else,' mumbles Chico to himself, twisting his head to admire the eye-catching checkerboard floor tiles.

'That it is, kid, that it is.'

Hospitality manager Omar Tiger spends much of his time prowling around the swish reception area, welcoming swish new guests, before charming them into parting with lots more cash (spa treatments and time with a masseuse don't come cheap at the palace!!). You won't find a more impeccably dressed tiger this side of the ocean and today he's strutting around in a navy three-piece suit. A large percentage of guests actually *gulp* when they first meet the tiger, and hope for the best, as they make for rather imposing figures - yet Omar would consider it terribly improper to gobble you up for lunch (the same can't be said for some of his acquaintances though). He's currently engaged in conversation with a family of jolly deer but concludes the exchange after spotting Detective Penguin.

'Pedro, can we have some sparkling lemon juice for these wonderful deer's please.' Omar clicks his fingers and a lemur swoops over to serve the family of deer a complimentary glass of fizz (a lemur is a mischievous form of grey furred monkey with a short snout, black and white tail, and freaky bright eyes).

Frank and Chico approach the reception desk which is manned by a busy hen; she's furiously chewing a wad of gum and counting down the minutes till home time.

'Hey lady, we're here to see the chinchilla,' says Frank, sliding one elbow across the desk (whenever Frank's desperate for info or gossip he always seeks out his favorite chinchilla, because there's nobody better at providing the word on the street).

The hen reluctantly and momentarily quits her chewing to stare at the penguin. 'Room number?'

'No idea. Said meet me at the Palace, that was the message...meet me at the palace.'

Rolling her eyes and continuing to churn the gum, she runs her wing down a clipboard. 'Sorry, no chinchilla.'

Omar quick steps over to deal with the situation, his head held high at all times like he can smell something strange in the air. 'It's ok, Patricia, I've got this. And *please* stop chewing dear, dreadful habit, extremely unprofessional darling.' The tiger locks arms with the detectives, much to Frank's discomfort, and shuffles them to one side where they can discuss the matter discreetly. 'Tenth floor, room five five five. He's waiting for you,' whispers Omar. He pulls a key from his waistcoat pocket and passes it to Frank via a nifty handshake.

'I'll grill the chinchilla. You wait here and make friends,' says Frank, patting Chico on the back.

'Wait, *what*? You want me to wait here?'

'Look, he gets in a panic if I don't come alone. Chinchilla's a snitch, they're all the same.' Frank shrugs to suggest he's helpless and heads for the lift, with an unhappy partner left behind to twiddle his thumbs or count sheep -a whole herd had just walked in with a trolley full of suitcases.

Sammy Davis Hippo, the bell boy, leaves limited room for anybody else wishing to slip in the elevator. Tiny red hat with a black ribbon chin strap and a matching red uniform full of shimmering golden buttons– he certainly looks the part. The elevator is a typical box of mirrors fitted with patterned carpet, except this one has ninety-eight floors to choose from. Frank steps inside as the hippo squidges into a corner and tries to create ample space.

'Hit number ten, big guy,' cracks Frank without needing to make any eye contact.

'Sure thing,' yells the hippo with a beaming smile. He tries not to press four buttons at once with his clumsy hoof of a hand. The doors slide shut and after a mild jolt starts rattling to its destination.

'Maybe this thing would move a little faster if we weren't hoisting the world's biggest bell boy,' remarks Frank impatiently, briefly inspecting Sammy through the mirrors around them.

'I'm on a diet as it happens, sir, trying *real* hard too. Just vegetables for me now, sir, veg veg veg, and I've kissed goodbye to blueberry pie. Omar said I should shed some weight and mother agrees, but personally I think it's genetic. Anyways I run to work three times a week now too, and I think it's working wonders.'

'Jeeze, you always yap this much hippo?' replies Frank to the chirpy porter, adjusting his hat in the mirror.

'Omar says I should talk less, mother agrees. Maybe he's right, sorry sir, I get a bit flustered you see. Have you had the tour? I can give you the tour, I'm a great tour guide so they say. I recommend the spa sessions, value for money and great for the skin. Mother, she tried the hot stone massage, and *oh* boy how she loved it, yes siree.' Sammy clears his throat and loosens his neck strap, realizing that his tongue is getting the better of him. He promptly reverts to silence. Another slight jolt and the lift finally comes to a halt.

'See ya around, big guy,' chirps Frank as he hops through the sliding doors and heads to five five five.

'Yes, see you again soon, sir. Have a great day now. Don't forget to check out the casino, oh and the pools, and the restaurants– '. The hefty bell boy smiles and prods the button for ground, still babbling as the doors slam shut.

You may not be all that familiar with the animal known as 'The Chinchilla'. Imagine an inflated rat with dense fur – the densest fur of any mammal in fact. They tend to live in herds on high ground: their diet is mainly plants, fruit, and insects. Oh, and they can't be trusted. Fat Chinchilla is no exception: his family live in the mountains just west of Paradise Valley, his fur is impressive, and he most certainly isn't trustworthy.

Frank twists the key in the lock and enters the room. One overweight rodent is sprawled across a king size bed in a fetching white silk dressing gown, enjoying a glass of mango on the rocks. A couple of female chinchillas in bikinis emerge from the bathroom.

'Ladies, hit the pool for a while, I got some business to deal with,' snaps the chinchilla, pointing his half empty glass at the exit. The giggling duo duly oblige and promptly leave the room. Fat Chinchilla hops off the bed with a spring in his step and shakes the penguin's wing. 'Frankie, my favorite bird, how's life?'

'Not bad chinchilla, not bad. How's the king of the snitches?'

'Life's good my friend.' The chinchilla grins and tops up his glass with plenty more juice and ice. 'They don't stock mackerel, but I can offer a drink?'

'No thanks. Just information.'

The chinchilla stirs the glass and raises it. 'To the safe return of Lucas Panda,' he says, taking a short sip.'

Frank blinks and bows his head. 'What's the word on the street?'

'Nothing, Frank, not a zip. Believe me, I been asking every crook, wise guy and whacko in town. Nobody knows who done it.'

Frank looks around the room. 'Then why am I here in a hotel with a half-naked chinchilla, when I could be talking to someone more helpful, *and* fully dressed.'

'Hey Frankie, come on, you know me, I wouldn't invite you if I didn't have gossip.'

'Start talking fur-ball.'

'You got coins? Mango juice and rooms at the Palace ain't cheap you know?'

Frank grabs the chinchilla by the scruff of the neck; his drink flies through the air before shattering against the window. Fragments of ice and a puddle of orange colored liquid trickle down the glass. Time for small talk appears to be over.

'First I get the word on the street. Then I decide whether to pay you, or drop you five floors for wasting police time.' Do not mess with Frank Penguin.

The big rat wriggles free and holds up his paws. 'Frankie, when have I ever let you down? I'm always true to my word but *hey* I'm a businessman, survival of the fittest and all that jazz. Said I got news and I do. Little birdie tells me that Salvatore's running something out of a bookstore down in San Shem, tight operation. Old Badgers Bookstore. Trust me.'

'Little birdie? You mean Kurt Sparrow?'

'Try Tommy Robin.'

Frank strokes his chin, intrigued by the tip off. 'So, what's the operation?'

'Tommy wasn't certain, but the dogs are keeping it real *hush hush*, so I'm guessing it's something big. He's seen Leonard Weiler take a trip to the bookstore three times, and that meat-head can't even read.'

'And what's in this for you? Besides the gold.'

'Let's just say I got *friends* who'd love to see Salvatore behind bars.'

'Wouldn't we all, damn stinkin' dog. I been chasing his tail for years.' Frank grabs an envelope stuffed with cash from his coat pocket and chucks it on the bed. The chinchilla doesn't even look.

'Not gonna count it?' asks Frank.

'Trust, Frank…trust.'

The penguin tips his hat and slides his wings in pockets. 'Sorry about the drink.'

'Waste of good mango.'

'Hear anything on the panda, you let me know.'

'Will do, Frank, will do. And send the pooch my regards.'

Frank pinches his beak and taps his head, having forgotten a vital question. 'One other thing. *Beavers?* Anything?'

'What about 'em?'

'Brothers from The Swamp. They're missing.'

'I ain't heard nothing about no beavers, sorry Frankie. But I know a little birdie who might be able to help.'

'Tommy Robin?'

'Sonny Boy Falcon. Used to run with the brothers. I'll pay him a visit.' The chinchilla slips off his gown to reveal a tight pair of ruby red swim shorts. He slides into a hot-tub bubbling in the corner.

Frank doesn't quite know how to react. He opts for a simple raised eyebrow. 'Yeah, I'm outta here.'

Chico has done two laps of the lobby already and mulling over starting a third, when he's joined by Omar Tiger. Together they stand and admire a splendid watercolor of Lioness Annabella. It's a framed depiction of her sitting upon a throne; she's swathed in a purple robe and the epitome of fearsome.

'A striking portrait wouldn't you say?' purrs the tiger, arms folded and clearly enchanted by the image. 'She didn't pose of course, no, she'd never pose. Merely the impression of a fabulous artist. And between me and you, she looks *far* more frightening in reality.'

'Looks kinda cold if you ask me,' replies Chico. 'She ever smile?'

'It's not really her thing, *smiling*,' replies the tiger. 'But then you don't need to when you reach the top, do you darling? But I'm with you, I much prefer a smile, frowning leads to wrinkles and we can't have that now, can we.'

The monkey turns to the tiger and leans towards him slightly. 'So, where is she today? This rich lioness I keep hearing so much about. She going to swing by anytime soon?'

Omar smirks and strokes his whiskers. 'Oh, I very much doubt you'll catch a glimpse, even on as pleasant day as this one. Bright blue skies and cozy warm air, still won't tempt the cat from her lair.'

'And why's that? Shy or something?'

'*A shy lion?* Oh, imagine that.' The tiger can't help but plant a paw on Chico's shoulder as he holds back an impulse to chuckle. 'I assure you, Annabella is *quite* the opposite, and anyone that's had the fortune of her company will certainly vouch for that. *And* she doesn't suffer fools so if you're foolish in nature detective, you may wish to keep your distance.'

'I'll tell you what's foolish, sitting on a fortune but hiding in a tower all day. Now that's foolish.'

'She simply relishes solitude my dear monkey. And I for one believe that her reclusive behavior breeds more respect, in fact I'm certain of it. A lioness that catches the eye each passing day, eventually becomes a bore, just part of the scenery. But a lioness that only roams the streets on odd occasion, shrouded in mystery, is far more intriguing…wouldn't you say?'

Chico steps away from the paw on his shoulder and slides face to face with the hotel manager. 'I would say…far more suspicious, *darling.*'

The tiger opens his jaw and reveals a perfect set of glistening sharp teeth – he must brush three times a day. For a second Chico wonders if his head is about to find its way into this big gaping mouth. But then, the posh orange cat just smiles politely. False alarm and loss of head avoided.

'I better get back to work.' Omar twists around like he's stuck on a dance floor and marches back to address another group of excited arrivals.

'Let's go, kid.' Frank shouts and points at the exit as he jumps out the lift. Chico takes one last look at the painted lion, then heads towards the dragons.

5

Recipe For Purrsecution

Jake the Bear is slouched on a wooden stool in the corner of a primitive
boxing ring, with a skimpy white towel draped around his neck and
sweat dripping from every pore. He's struggling to focus, let alone
breathe, and awaits the sound of a bell for round number five. Yuriko Wolf,
his coach and principal source of motivation, struggles to stem the bleeding
from a cut to his bulging left eye.

'Raging Bull' in the opposite corner looks confident, fresh, and in far less
discomfort. Puffs of steam erupt from his nostrils as he stuffs a mouthguard
over his sloppy gums and thumps his cheeks with the gloves; the powerful
black beast looks eager to crush his rival. Herds of detectives and officers
have surrounded the square shaped battlefield, enthralled by a bruising
encounter. It's only a fight between two cops and it's only taking place in
the police force gym, but pride and honor are up for grabs, and they aren't
prizes taken lightly.

Ding Ding. Hudson Rhino leads the cheers, encircled by pigs in uniform,
as the two fighters exchange a combination of jabs. Jake taps his protective
head guard with his glove; he's kitted out in a star-spangled vest and long

blue shorts while the bull went for no vest and red. Frank and Chico arrive in time to witness poor Jake take a pounding – only his tight guard preventing clear strikes to the head.

'Give 'em hell, Jake,' yells Frank, taking ringside seats with his partner.

'Which one's Jake?' enquires Chico over the loud cheers and jeers of the rowdy crowd – all totally gripped by the bout.

'Jake the Bear, kid, Jake the Bear.'

A fine uppercut sends Jake stumbling to the canvas. The referee immediately starts her count (Thelma Eagle tends to referee most kingdom police force sporting events, due to her deep love for rules and regulations). Raging Bull skips around the ring in celebratory fashion, lapping up the applause from his backers. Jake's no spring chicken, he's not far off retirement, and his best days as a boxer are far behind him – but he's also a polar bear, and an extremely tough polar bear at that. Jake grabs the rope and drags himself back in contention. The ecstatic audience *roars*!! It's not over yet. Even the bull seems surprised by his opponent's robustness.

'Finish him, bull!!' bellows Hudson - the only other heavyweight in the hall. However, the raging fighter is now an exhausted one: his breaths are heavy, his movements are sluggish and the punches left in his tank are going astray (the last place you want to be if you're tired, is in the ring with an angered bear).

Jake can barely see out of one eye but it doesn't prevent him launching a flurry of punches to the bull's sore ribs. His opponent reels and tries to retreat but Jake's found a second wind and moves in for a merciless attack. The feet of the crowd are bouncing and fists all pump in the air. Even Chico applauds the excitement of this nail-biting duel.

Raging Bull makes a last-ditch effort to conquer the bear with a couple of futile swings, but Jake 'Honeypaws' Bear ducks and dives with ease before landing a thunderous blow to a formerly solid jaw. The defeated black minotaur crashes to the ground as pandemonium ensues from delighted spectators. Jake raises a glove to acknowledge the show of support, before helping his dizzy opponent get back on his feet.

Two fine warriors embrace.

Once the satisfied mob has dispersed, Frank and Chico climb into the ring to congratulate the champ.

'Still need to work on that defense, buddy,' quips Frank, shaking Jake's paw.

'I'd like to see a penguin fight a bull sometime,' replies the bear, patting his face again with the flimsy towel. 'This your new partner?'

'Chico Monkey, nice to finally meet you detective. Great fight.'

'Any leads on the panda? Chinchilla got much to say?' enquires Jake, still coughing and spluttering following the grueling contest.

'All quiet on the leads front,' says Frank, shrugging his shoulders. 'Chinchilla threw me a tip though. Something cookin' down at Old Badger's Bookstore which could be related, so we're checking it out. Gonna hit South Shem right about now as it happens.'

'Need some backup?'

'Jeeze, why you think we swung by, *Honeypaws*? Course we need some backup,' says Frank.

'Yeah, that right hook be much appreciated,' adds Chico, trying to make a new friend.

'Room for one more?' asks Yuriko, poking her head through the ropes.

Frank flings his wings above his narrow head. 'More the merrier. I'll grab some pigs and meet you out front.'

****

Old Badger is twenty-four years of age and that's particularly mature for his species. He requires a wooden cane whenever he hobbles and spectacles whenever he reads (animals can walk and talk but they're yet to discover a fountain of youth. Some creatures are blessed with centuries to sample the joys of life, while others have barely a decade or two before it's time for eternal rest). Even older than the badger though, is his precious bookshop; 'Badger Books' was run by his father, his grandfather and even his great grandfather. It's located in Sam Shem (the southern section of Noah's Kingdom) down a secluded alleyway, and practically camouflaged by thick green moss; if it weren't for the pile of dusty books that sit in the window, you'd assume it was empty and likely haunted.

The first visitor to the store that afternoon was a young studious pelican looking for something to read on her forthcoming travels abroad. Old Badger was kindly guiding the bird around his library, introducing her to all sorts of thrillers she might enjoy. The store is starved of light, extremely cramped, and there's plenty of sticky cobwebs; it's also crying out for a brand-new carpet, extra shelves, and alphabetical order.

'Ah, here's another one,' says the elderly book dealer, flicking his pointy face through another classic off the 'Adventure' shelf. 'The Count of Turtle Bay, do you know it?'

The pelican takes the book and has a quick skim. 'No, no I don't believe I do.'

'Pirates, gold, mutiny, romance, it has the lot. I thoroughly recommend it.'

'Ok, I'll take it.'

'Wonderful, let me add it to the pile.' The badger staggers over to his desk and drops the book on top of a stack, while the pelican hovers from section to section looking for one more story. Her shorts, t-shirt, and backpack suggest she's already on a holiday. Like all pelicans she has a long orange beak but also an odd pouch around her throat (when she scoops up fish from rivers and oceans, it helps to drain out the water before she swallows). They are without doubt peculiar looking birds, but they tend to be intelligent, well-educated, and eager to broaden horizons.

'How about this one?' queries the bird, pointing her prolonged bill at a chunky piece of fiction. 'Jane Bear.'

'Oh yes,' beams the badger as he looks to the ceiling, recalling the first time he enjoyed it. 'Another classic and a fine choice, you'll simply adore it.'

The pelican probes her lip with a wing as she scans the blurb on the back. 'A love story, perfect, this'll do nicely.' The book passes to the elderly badger as she raids her pockets for coins.

'Six books, ok that's twelve please young lady.'

Old Badger packs the novels into a brown paper bag; he exchanges them for a smile and the correct amount of money. 'Enjoy the trip.'

'Oh, I will, I most certainly will,' says the satisfied customer before skipping out the door to explore the world.

The second visitor that day was a penguin, followed by a monkey, a bear, one grey wolf, and three little pigs – which barely left room to breathe.

'Police!! Don't move!!' shouts Frank, scanning the shop for potential danger. Old Badger just about manages to avoid a heart attack as he grabs his chest and breaks into panic.

'Where is it, grandpa?' blasts Frank, trying his hand at bad cop as per usual.

The badger tries to calm his nerves enough to reply. 'Wh…where is what?'

'We know you're working for Salvatore Bulldog,' explains Chico, in a more reasonable tone than that of his flappy partner.

'What is it, laundering, stolen goods, harboring known criminals?' adds Jake, who's probably the most intimidating member of the team, yet the least likely to hurt a fly (unless absolutely necessary). Yuriko leaves all the squabbling to boys; she's discovered an antique cookbook and is hunting for inspiration.

The badger tries to wave away accusations. 'Gentleman, this is Badger's Bookstore *not* Badger's Money Laundering Service. Maybe that's down the street?' he says with a sudden bout of bravery and sarcasm.

Frank is not amused.

'I got something!' yells one of the pigs. One of the bookshelves is suspiciously planted on top of a short steel track. Frank tries to peer behind the shelf but it's far too close to the wall. Chico pulls out all the books, but none trigger any sort of reaction.

Yuriko is more intrigued by the bust of a three-eyed elephant which sits on a plinth beside the shelving; she inspects the bronze exhibit, strokes her chin for a moment, then prods the middle eye with a paw. The eyeball, sat within the forehead of the elephant, sinks back into the bust. A tiny whirring sound is followed by the bookshelf sliding along the track - revealing a hidden door. The badger's giddy mind is unable to conjure convincing explanations, so he simply closes his eyes and sighs instead.

The pigs step aside, allowing space for a charging bear. Jake promptly solves the door issue with a firm use of his hefty left foot.

'Maybe try the handle next time?' remarks Chico, bemused by Jake's impatience. The doorway leads to darkness. No sign of movement. But everyone's tense, nonetheless.

'Pigs, grab some light,' snaps Frank. Three porkers snap into action and scamper out the shop to fetch some torches.

'I had no choice. I needed the money. You must believe me,' begs the badger, fearful of spending his remaining days locked away in a cell - without a book in sight.

'There's *always* a choice,' responds Frank. 'And you chose to help Salvatore store all his blood money, stolen treasure or whatever else he's stashing in your damn basement.'

The jittery old badger looks confused and stumbles over to Frank, till they're face to face. His lips begin to quiver. 'You keep mentioning stolen items detective penguin, but it's not the spoils of theft you'll find down there, oh no sir. For my sins, for the sake of money and greed, I've allowed something *much* worse.' The suspect slumps to the ground, his head between his paws and overcome with guilt.

Frank drags him back to his feet. 'Worse? What do you mean...*worse?*'

The badger grabs the penguin with both paws, weeping uncontrollably. 'I had no choice, I'm sorry. I *had* no choice.' He eases his grip, sinking once more to the ground. Frank steps back, shocked by the creature's peculiar breakdown. What could possibly be hiding under a bookstore that would bring an aged badger to his knees?

Pigs burst through the door and they come baring torches. The gang light up, brace themselves, and carefully invade the unknown. Bumping, tripping, yelping and apologizing - the troop of coppers crouch through a pitch-black tunnel.

It's no surprise that Jake takes the lead and is first to reach light on the other side. Having tackled the passage on paws and knees, he arrives at a spacious room. Bleak white walls, wooden floors, and a ventilation fan rumbling on the ceiling. There's a pyramid of unlabeled crates stacked in the center and another door on the opposite side, waiting to be opened (or kicked off its hinges). The rest of the team emerges from darkness while Jake sniffs the heap of boxes - and instantly regrets it.

'Woo– wee, what is that smell?!' gasps the bear, tightly gripping his little black nose. One by one they react the same way as they catch a terrible whiff - except for Frank who simply can't understand all the fuss.

'Smells fine to me,' remarks the smug penguin. 'Reminds me of home.'

Even the officers appear a tad uncomfortable (you know something's wrong when a pig finds a pong unpleasant). 'Gonna be honest boss, that's pretty grim.'

'I'm gonna be sick, I'm gonna be sick,' chokes Yuriko. 'What you wait for Honeypaws? Open other door!'

'I got it, I got it– ,' says Chico intervening.

'Wait monkey, wait!' yells Frank, but it's too late.

The cheeky monkey grabs the handle, pushes open the door and prances through another passage – leaving common sense firmly behind him. Big mistake. The second that Chico tumbles into the next room he's greeted by five ferocious dogs, each of them wearing the standard attire for henchmen. There's a cage beside the door hosting a dozen captured cats, and a table in the corner where the dogs were playing cards. A tough Dalmatian wrapped in leather garments, swings the monkey against the wall. Some of the trapped cats grab the bars and desperately scream for help.

'Get us out monkey, please, you gotta get us outta here!!'

The three pigs are next to shuffle into the scuffle, and pandemonium inevitably ensues. Fists fly, dogs fly, and low and behold - pigs can fly too. Yuriko joins the mayhem in time to bash a husky against the cage and render him close to unconscious (up until that point he'd been happily throttling Chico).

'You owe me one, monkey boy,' she says with a wink, before a scruffy terrier in a string vest yanks her by the legs and drags her along the ground. Chico scrambles to his feet and prepares to save the damsel, but he needn't have bothered. Jake ducks his head below the doorway and finally makes an appearance - which heavily shifts the odds in favor of a law enforcement victory.

The terrier spits out the cocktail stick he'd been chewing, releases Yuriko immediately, then holds up his paws to surrender. All the other dogs take one look at the size of Jake's claws and decide it's wise to follow suit; they even cue up against the wall and wait for bracelets.

'Good boy,' says Yuriko as she moves along the line, shackling each of the pesky pups.

'Please let us out, let us out!!' The cats are still trying to break free. Most of them haven't the strength to stand or beg, but those that do, plead with the cops to find a key and set them loose.

'Just…just hold on a second. Just hold on *one* second!!' demands Chico, trying to hush the mob of desperate kittens. 'You need to answer some questions first. *Then* we can see about letting you go. Alright?'

'Was there a panda in here at all? With a badge. A detective,' snaps Jake, clutching the bars - but the kitties say nothing and are far more concerned with freedom and daylight.

'What about beavers? Any of you seen any beavers? Brothers?' asks Chico half-heartedly. He assumes the prisoners will provide no response.

He was wrong.

'Beavers. Yes. I heard talk of beavers.' A ginger cat with a puffy face and an eye patch limps forward.

'He's lying. They ain't heard nothing,' barks the terrier, before Yuriko elbows his ribs.

The one-eyed cat is starving, thirsty, and struggling to speak but finds the strength to share his tale. 'Only whispers in the dark mind, and I can't be sure who was talking, though I'm certain one was a rottweiler. But they were angry, and beavers was on their mind. Heard the word '*traitors*' used, and not just the once.'

Frank waited behind to inspect the smelly crates a little closer; he's quite happy to leave any brawling with dogs in the hands of younger cops. After a short snoop he stumbles upon a crowbar, hidden among a clutter of tools and mess.

'Jackpot.'

He jams the bar into a crate and tries his best to lever it open. Following a bit of straining and various sounds of struggle, the lid snaps free. The penguin peers inside. His face changes from one of curiosity to one of disgust as he slams the crate shut and shuffles backwards in horror. 'Jeeze, you gotta be kidding me?!' He blows a sigh of disbelief before taking one more peek, just to be one hundred percent sure his eyes weren't playing tricks. They were not. He thumps it tightly shut and wipes his forehead with a silky hankie. 'Damn, the old badger was right…this is worse…*much* worse.'

A creamy ball of fluff with orange eyes moves forward. She decides to speak on behalf of all the fellow cell mates, as their nominated leader.

'Detective, we've all been kidnapped against our will, by those hideous hounds. So, we'd appreciate it if you let us go home now. We're tired, frightened and haven't as much as smelt a meal in days.'

'Why did they do this? Why are you here?' asks Jake.

'Don't you say a word,' shouts the leathery Dalmatian, turning his head to scowl at the cage.

'One more word, I knock your spots off,' replies Yuriko, slapping his snout back towards the wall.

'I don't know. We don't know,' says the cat sincerely. 'But when they take you in *there*, you never come out.' She's almost shaking as her paw points towards yet another door; there was so much kerfuffle that nobody really noticed it before.

'Wh..what's in there?' asks one of the pigs fearfully.

'None of us can be certain, but we know it's nothing wonderful.' She looks to her fellow cats who all shake their heads in agreement.

'Key. I found rusty key!' exclaims Yuriko, swiping it from the pocket of a dopey basset. She chucks the key to Chico who it catches perfectly - but he's in no rush to twist the lock. This time he's siding with caution.

'Please can we go now, we've suffered enough.' The impatient creamy cat shakes the bars and hisses.

'Why are they locked in a cage?' Jake lifts the terrier off the ground, hoping it will inspire some speedier answers. 'Tell us why you gotta cage full of cats?'

'I…ain't saying…nothin',' boasts the terrier proudly.

'He won't say nothing and nor will any of us,' yaps the husky. '*You know who*, would have us for breakfast.'

'Salvatore?' asks Chico, his ears pricking up.

'*You...know...who*,' repeats the husky, but slower and firmer this time.

'I want answers, dog,' growls the polar bear.

'Well you won't hear them from me. I'm done talking. We're all done talking. Shake us all you like, we ain't spittin' one more word.' The husky's lips are sealed.

'Alright, let's sweep this other room,' says Chico, heading hastily towards the door.

'Don't go through that door monkey...and I mean it this time,' orders Frank, arriving just in the nick of time. 'I think I know what's through there...and if I'm right, it won't be pretty.'

'What are you talking about, Frank?' probes Jake.

'I got answers, Jake...that's what I'm talking about.' Frank whips something out of his pocket and chucks it across the room. Another flawless catch from Chico; the detective finds himself holding a round pie wedged in a foil tray.

'Cat pies, kid...cat pies.'

'Eurghhhhh.' The moment Chico hears 'cat' and 'pie' in the same sentence, he throws the pastry to the floor and tries not to heave up his lunch. Jake, Yuriko, and the pigs cover their mouths with sheer surprise, while the fluffball leading the cats decides to faint. The rumbled line of mutts stare at their feet; they know the cat's out the bag (or pie in this case).

'I'll bet that's the kitchen,' says Frank, looking at the mysterious final door. Yuriko huffs and moves everyone aside as she marches into the room.

They briefly wait in silence.

Almost immediately, the wolf slowly and wistfully steps out backwards, then turns to face the crowd. She puts her fist to her lips and fires a tiny cough. Then only needs to share a single word.

'Abattoir.'

Frank wastes no time in arresting the dogs and freeing the cats. Old Badger is whisked away, along with the five feisty pooches, and taken for further questioning. The purring dozen are close to tears as they leave their prison behind them and step out into moonlight; for many it's been weeks since they last enjoyed odorless air.

Yuriko twists the 'Open' sign in the bookstore window, till it simply reads as 'Closed'. No cases were solved today, but lives were saved, and further tragedy averted, so the cops walk out with heads held high and applaud a job well done. Now it was time for a drink.

6

Red Valley Blues

I f you're seeking the best jazz club in town, then look no further than The Blue Crypt - an intimate swinging joint just south of city center and right in the heart of San Shem; it's hard to miss the neon blue sign flickering above its entrance. Lights are dim inside, and space is tight, but what it lacks in style it certainly makes up for in sound. All the greats have played here at one time or another, from Sonny Buffalo and Smooth Jack Cat to Wilson Panda and Smokey Joe Flamingo. However, as Frank and Chico walk through the door, there's a wombat on the stage failing miserably to warm up a boisterous crowd with his cringe worthy excuse for a comedy act. At the very least he knows how to look the part: red velvet waistcoat, black bow tie, and repulsive baggy green trousers.

'My girlfriend said to me, she said you need to grow up. I said *get the hell*...outta my tree house,' yells the hairy nosed comic, desperate for a chorus of laughter. Those still listening to the comedian smile out of politeness – but they're eager to see him give way for the headline act. 'Ahem, I broke up with a girlfriend once. I probably shouldn't have got down on one knee.' The wombat, now sweating with failure, taps the microphone to check it's still working.

Frank and Chico wade through the crowd and make their way to the bar; a relaxed cow in a honey leather vest and brown bandanna waits for their order (she used to work at the milk factory down the road like a lot of the other cows in town, but she fancied a complete career change).

'Large salt-water for me. What can I get ya, monkey?' says Frank, patting his partner.

'Banana Paradise,' replies Chico without a second's thought.

Frank stares at the monkey for a moment, clearly not impressed with his strange choice. 'Ok, and one banana paradise for the lady.' The slick cow glides back and forth behind the bar grabbing the required ingredients, then swiftly prepares the drinks. As Frank snatches his glass of salty water, the banana paradise lands before his eyes: a bright yellow jug of banana, soda, fruit juice, and cream. Frank tuts and shakes his head. 'Kid, there's parts of the city where you'd get whacked for drinkin' this mess. And rightly so if you ask me.'

Chico ignores the sarcastic remarks and swallows a sip of his refreshing yellowy beverage. He leans against the bar and takes in the vibe of the crypt; he can't help but notice a female gorilla giggling with a friend and looking in his general direction. Chico straightens up and raises his glass. The gorillas giggle some more and respond with a bashful wave. Frank's busy swapping war stories with a bunch of ex-cops so he won't mind the monkey schmoozing. Chico makes his way through the tight knit hoard of jazz fans and approaches the sniggering pair.

'I take it you weren't laughing at the wombat?' he says, trying his best to play it cool.

'Him? Oh no chance…we've seen him before. Such a drag,' says the one who caught Chico's eye. She's out for the night in a nice purple dress, which matches the lipstick and heels. Her friend has made similar efforts to look beautiful but prefers to be pretty in pink.

'I'm tempted to arrest him.'

The sparkly eyes of the purple gorilla light up instantly. 'You a cop?' she says, both impressed and intrigued.

Chico clears his throat, before proudly dazzling the two glamorous gorillas with a flash of his new gold emblem. '*Detective*, Chico Monkey.'

'I'm Nancy and my shy little friend here, she's Cynthia.'

'Lovely to meet you, Nancy, Cynthia.'

'And lovely to meet you, *detective*.'

'Can I get you ladies a drink? I hear they make a nice melon soda.'

Suddenly Nancy spots a familiar face in the audience and the laughter abruptly halts. She grabs Cynthia's arm. 'You didn't tell me *he* was coming?'

'Everything ok ladies?' says Chico, confused by the rapid change in behavior. He takes another swig of juicy bananas and cream.

'I thought he was working tonight, I swear,' pleads Cynthia sheepishly. Chico has another question on the tip of his tongue, but before he gets to say it there's a tug on his collar and someone spins him around. He's face to face with a wide hairy chest, poking out of an ill fitted short sleeve shirt; the top three buttons are undone to cope with this sweaty venue. The monkey looks up at the cone shaped head of a furious silverback – one mean looking gorilla. Chico *gulps*. The gorilla takes Chico's drink and passes it to a buddy, then grabs him by the tie and holds him up real close.

'You talkin' to my girl, gibbon!!?'

'Which one's your girl?' asks the detective, concerned that his tie is getting tighter and tighter. 'Cone head' doesn't say a word; he just points a meaty finger at Nancy. Chico *gulps* again.

'Smasher, leave him alone! You always do this!' screams Nancy, standing up to try and prevent a tragedy.

'Wait...your name's *Smasher*?' There isn't enough phlegm left in Chico's mouth to gulp for a third time. He's on to begging higher powers for help now.

'Yeah, I'm Smasher. Gotta problem with that ya little punk?'

'Not at all, great name...suits you.'

'Why you lookin' at my girl?' The crypt regulars turn their back on the comedy; they'd much prefer to see what unravels between a monkey and touchy gorilla.

'*I said*...why you lookin' at my girl?'

Chico has to get smart and think quick. 'I wasn't looking at your girl, I wasn't looking at your girl. I promise.' The silverback lets go of the tie, and it looks like the sly monkey from West Bay might live to see another day. 'I was looking at her friend, I was looking at Cynthia.'

The silverback twitches and grabs the tie again. 'That…is my *sister*.'

Chico closes his eyes and prepares to die.

'Smasher, drop him. That's my partner, and I can't lose two in a week.' Frank slaps the gorilla on the leg. Smasher lets go and puts his hands together for an apology.

'I'm sorry, Frank, I'm so sorry. Rush of blood to the head, that's all.'

Chico can't believe his luck as the hot-headed mountain sets his tie straight. Nancy breathes a sigh of relief. The unsatisfied crowd grumble among themselves after such an anti- climax and resume their endurance of comedy.

'Get yourself a drink, and one for the lovely ladies.' Frank slips Smasher a few coins.

'Too kind, Frank, too kind. And sorry again, monkey, misunderstanding that's all,' beams the silver beast, before dragging his knuckles towards the bar.

The monkey stares at the penguin.

'Smasher?' says Chico, almost laughing.

'Yeah, kiddo, Smasher. Used to be a cop.'

'I need another drink.'

'Same again?'

'Something stronger. Gimme some lime…*straight*.'

'Ok ladies and gentlemen, enough jokes, time for some music,' announces the wombat, finally receiving a round of applause. 'Let's give a warm welcome to the one and only, Miles Skunk and the Zebras!!' The wombat now makes a hasty retreat towards his dressing room so he can reflect on where it all went wrong. Wolf whistling, loud clapping, and plenty of clinking glasses follow as three zebras in sharp suits take to the stage. On piano we have Big Bo Stripes, Aretha Zee picks up the double bass and our drummer for the evening, is none other than Scat Zebedee.

As the band begin to play, a skunk casually emerges from the shadows beside the stage. His tail wags to the tempo as he takes his place behind the microphone, armed with a glistening golden saxophone. No suit for the main man – just trousers, a white shirt, and the funky pork pie hat resting upon his head. Further cheers are unleashed by the huddle of bustling jazz fans as the remarkably cool skunk wets his lips, closes his eyes, and blows the sweet sound of sax.

Your regular crowd at the crypt usually work for the police force; it's a popular spot for cops winding down after a hard day's beat and tonight is no exception. If you topple an operation run by Salvatore Bulldog, then you've earned the right to a drink - or *two*. He's unlikely to be dragged before a judge, unless Old Badger spills the beans, however his business has taken a major blow so there's cause for celebration.

Even Chief Vulture has made an appearance; she's happily tapping her talons and enjoying the music, accompanied by Ruben and Yuriko. The chief rarely drinks anything sweet or strong, but the same can't be said for her officers; Yuriko is cradling a glass of fizzy apple while the rat holds a bottle of peach soda in either paw, to save on trips to the bar (it's usually difficult for rats to get served, unless they can stand on a stool). Jake is propped up against a wall sipping his pint of blubber, calmly enjoying the music. And in typical fashion - Hudson Rhino has engineered a drinking contest at a thriving corner table (quickest to finish their Pineapple Fizz is the winner). He's beaten one sailor and now he's onto the next.

Frank and Chico have found themselves a shaded spot at the back, away from the noise and dodgy dancing. They raise their glasses to a job well done and enjoy a sip of their tipples.

'Not bad for a first day, kiddo. Not often we get to stick it to Salvatore,' chirps Frank. '

'You really think the dogs kidnapped Lucas?' replies Chico, staring at his drink before his partner. 'I mean, there was nothing below the bookstore which linked the panda to dogs. Can we really be sure they're involved?'

'Something's going down, kid, that's for sure.' Frank stares at the band of merry colleagues now hogging the dance floor without an ounce of shame. 'Anyways, we know the beaver case is linked to the dogs. So that's something, I guess. What did the cat say? *Talk of betrayal*. We know they was on the doggie payroll, so if they messed with Salvatore, well, no wonder they disappeared.'

'I won't be eating pies for a while either, that's for sure,' says Chico, trying to block the bookstore basement out of his memory forever.

'You know, you should have listened to me back there, when I said wait. Running off with your eye on the prize, could've got yourself killed. Can't do your aunt proud if you're dead, kid.'

Chico tenses up. 'There's that daddy talk again. I'm not an officer, Frank. I'm not some dozy pig. I'm a detective just like you and I know what I'm doing. West Bay has crime and nut jobs, just like Kingdom.'

'Crime? Ok, kid, tell me about these *terrible* crimes you get over in West Bay?'

The monkey can't help but grimace as he pours another drop of lime down his throat. 'Well…you know…*loads* of crime, like the errr, the big one we had, that terrible terrible crime…'

'Someone pinch a donkey's purse? Cause that's *big* news in West Bay.'

'*Alright*, alright, we don't get much crime. It's a great place, great people, and i'm hoping to retire there one day. But still, whether you like it or not, I'm a detective, and I don't need constant guidance from the fountain of wisdom that is *Frank Penguin*.'

'I'm just saying, if you to listen Frank Penguin more often, you might avoid getting jumped by Dalmatians and choked by gorillas.'

Chico tries to hold it in but can't help but laugh at himself and the crazy day he's had.

'Alright, enough squabbling, we're meant to be celebrating,' says Frank, trying to lighten the mood again. 'How you end with a schmutz like me as your partner anyway?'

'Finished school, didn't know what to do with my life, so Aunt Sally dragged me by my ear down to Chief Owl at West Bay HQ. Rest is history. How about you? How you end up with a hot shot glorious partner like me?'

Frank pretends not to hear the last comment. He digs deep into his memory and tries to remember those days long since passed when he wasn't wearing a badge. 'Well, kid, I served in the army for a year or so, did my bit. Then when I got back, buddy of mine suggested the police force, so we joined together. And bless him, that buddy was Lucas Panda.' Frank shakes his head, determined not to ruin the mood again. '*Anyways* I think I made the right choice, so does my wife, I love what I do. Sure, there's good days and bad days, some very bad days, but hey that's the life right. Somebody's gotta stop these scumbags, might as well be Frank Penguin and his plucky chimp.'

'Hey, nothing wrong with a plucky chimp. And just so you know, Frank, monkeys and chimpanzees…completely different animals. But *hey* whatever.'

They clink their glasses one final time before swallowing what remains of their drinks.

Sat in the shadows behind them sits a lonesome mysterious panther - stirring apple juice, cream, and cinnamon. She's still tracking the detective's footsteps. Discretion is the name of the game, yet she insists on a fetching blue dress. She licks the fruit and cream off her silver spoon and places it down on the table, while listening to the penguin ramble.

****

A tiny apartment in the murkiest corner of New Carnival; the kind of area where it feels like the rain falls forever, and you sleep to the sound of sirens. The cold wooden floor is littered with banana skins and a few bits of festering furniture. A clock hooked to the wall is ticking and tocking, but it's been stuck on midnight for days. The only other sound to be heard is that of a snoring cop. Chico lays collapsed on his couch, still fully clothed having failed to make it to bed (one too many jugs of sour fluid). And barely four hours from the moment he waved goodbye to his colleagues, through the back window of a departing taxi – there's a very loud knock at his door. Followed by another. Then several knocks - each more urgent than the last.

'Mmph, *alright*…alright!' mumbles the monkey, still half asleep and glued to his makeshift bed. He manages to slide off the couch and onto the chilly floor, then drag himself close to standing – but his eyes are reluctant to open. Another knock at the door and this one nearly breaks it; somebody is desperate for immediate attention. The dazed detective yawns and stretches both slender arms as he shuffles across the room. Who would need assistance at such an hour? The door swings back to reveal Frank Penguin standing in the hallway, scratching the pointy carrot that is his nose.

'Grab your fancy coat, monkey. Looks like the beavers were kidnapped.'

****

It's not ideal visiting a crime scene before breakfast; Frank for one, isn't a fan of commencing duties till his belly is lined with mackerel and a barrel of coffee. But today is no ordinary day. They head out west of the city, knowing it shan't be good news that greets them. Barely a word is said as Frank's rusty banger plods along the empty stretch of road as fast as possible, which isn't that fast at all. A mixture of fatigue, lack of caffeine, and trepidation makes for an exceedingly quiet journey.

The Red Valley Motel is nothing special. In fact, the poor service and terrible rooms are infamous, but it's situated in a position which is perfect for visitors venturing to and from the city. There's also little competition in the way of other motels open for business around the area, and little of anything really. It's just desert, dust, and danger.

The decaying 'Red Valley' sign flaps in the howling sandy wind as Frank and Chico pull into the motel car park. Three other police vehicles got there first. They immediately spot Ruben heading towards the reception desk with a notebook and pen tucked under his tiny arm. Yuriko is crawling around on her paws and knees, thoroughly inspecting a trail of suspicious tire tracks. There's also two other vehicles present: one is a filthy green truck which belongs to Maggie Mule who runs the motel, while the other is a black pickup truck which belongs to the beaver brothers; they've been arrested so many times, that every cop in Kingdom knows these wheels. There are five rooms up for grabs at the Valley, and the third one is cordoned off; two pigs are guarding the door while another pair question Keaton Mule - son of the motel owner.

54

'I didn't hear or see nothing, sir, I swear. Mama told me to check on the room, cause them beavers been *real* quiet and all,' says Keaton, the only creature present who's comfy in stained dungarees. 'So, I did like she asked, and had myself a peek this morning, just shy of daylight, couldn't be later than six.'

Frank marches into 'Room Three' fearlessly; the penguin's done this before. Following the fiasco at Badger's Bookstore, Chico makes this entrance with a touch more vigilance. Both are startled by a flash of light as they step inside; a toad with a camera is taking numerous snaps of the scene. There are gaping rips down the cheap red curtains, a ruined bedside table laying on its side, and spots of blood on an ancient cream carpet. There's an empty bed where the beavers had slept and the covers are now torn and shredded (when a beaver is in the water they have the advantage of broad tails with which they can splash and raise alarm, warning others of imminent danger – but sadly it's a less effective strategy when you're cornered in a grotty room).

The detectives trample over broken glass to reach the bed; a big crate shaped television had also been destroyed amid the chaos. Frank makes his way through a door into the bathroom to hunt for more clues. Chico leans over the bed to get a closer look. Remnants of plants and twigs are sprinkled across the pillows.

'Sign of a struggle, but we can't find bodies. Slim chance they're still alive,' says Yuriko calmly as she enters the room. 'They put up good fight.'

'What's all this mess on the pillows? Food?'

'Probably gnaw on snacks while they watch telly in bed.'

'What about these?' Chico points at three wooden pendants lying beside the bed.

'They're arks, symbol for the church up in North Beach. Gotta buddy who wears one,' says Frank. He drops to his knees and peeks under the bed, hoping to find some answers. Nothing.

'Why rip off the pendants?' asks Chico, scratching his head with confusion. 'And there must be more than one attacker, right? I mean, grabbing three beavers, that's no stroll in the park.'

'There's numerous slash marks across sheets and curtains,' replies the wolf, with her usual soothing manner. 'Look to me like work of dog, or something bigger. And note damage to the door frame, like monster barge their way in.'

Chico nods in agreement, running his fingers down a busted wooden door-frame.

'Slashes on the curtain look similar to those on the panda's mac,' remarks Frank as he paces around the room, his back arched and head facing downwards as he scans the floor. Then he stops. There it is. *Finally*. Something. The penguin delicately picks up a tuft of white fur and holds it up to the light.

'Jackpot. Looks like fur. White fur,' declares Frank passing it to a wiser mind.

The wolf holds the evidence an inch from her eyeballs. She squints and stares for a moment. 'Again, could be dog but I can't be sure. Needs to go back to lab.' Yuriko frowns with frustration that she can't be more helpful.

Ruben is having much less success over at the motel reception. Maggie Mule insists she neither heard nor saw anything that would be of any use to the investigation. A counter with the word '*Welcome*' ironically printed on it, separates the unhelpful mule from the tired rat. Ruben is scrawling notes while he tries his best to obtain at least a single grain of useful information from the moody motel manager.

'I should have stayed in bed,' mutters the rat under his breath.

The mule, wrapped up in a flowery dress and apron, puts a hoof to an ear. 'What was that, officer? Speak up for heaven sake…I'm hard of hearing!'

Ruben puts on his best fake smile. 'Nothing ma'am, nothing. Tell me about your son, Keaton? Where was he last night, Mrs Mule?'

The lady of the manor produces a walking stick out of thin air and points it with menace at the rat. 'You leave my Keaton out of this,' roars Maggie, shaking her stick at an officer of the law. 'He's a good boy and he's done nothing wrong. He found their room empty is all, like I told ya before, and he damn well phoned you boys the moment he did so. We're good people, and we don't snatch beavers while they sleep. We're church folk don't you know.'

'Well, we need to question your son some more, Mrs Mule. If he's clean as a whistle like you say he is, then there's nothing to worry about, mam.' Ruben scrawls a few more notes, while keeping a close eye on the stick.

'I told you, we saw nothing, we heard nothing. The beavers had the room booked out for a week. They were quiet for days but that's their business, we don't snoop on our guests. When they didn't check out, I sent my Keaton to take a look. Ten seconds later he's standing here before me, with a face pale as the moon. Now leave me alone and get out, ya damn vermin!'

Big Mama Mule continues to yell and express her feelings of outrage, long after Ruben's getaway. He escapes the motel reception, unscathed but none the wiser as to who attacked the three poor beavers. He totters across the car park to join Yuriko, who is deep in discussion with Frank and Chico.

The wolf points at tire tracks for all to see. 'Fresh, not police car. Something bigger.'

'Blue van!' shouts an eager pig now joining the group. The tone of his voice suggests extreme excitement at having the opportunity to share his info.

'Keep talking piggy?' replies Frank.

'Errr, ok yes…well, we just questioned a gentleman, errr Mr Elliot Sheep. He was in the room adjacent to the beavers you see, and, well, he said he saw a blue van, blue van boss, early evening. Between seven and eight.'

'Early for a hit, why not wait till midnight? 'What about the lady? And the son? Any mention of blue vans?'

The pig looks nervy. 'Ahem, Keaton Mule, the son, no mention of a van. Stumbled upon the crime scene this morning but doesn't recall seeing anyone suspicious on the premises. We're still working him, sir, but he looks clean.'

'Good work.' Frank nods to thank the pig, before turning his attention to Ruben.

'Mrs Mule saw nothing,' spurts the rat, anticipating he was about to be nudged for an update. 'No mention of vans, and she needs to work on her customer service.'

'I can't listen to a word you say, Ruben, you're too cute.' Frank takes great pleasure in teasing the little officer.

'Funny, Frank, very funny,' replies Ruben, looking around for better company.

'Pat him on head, Chico, he loves that,' says Yuriko, feeling it necessary to join in with the mild mockery.

Chico to the rescue. 'Ah come on guys, leave him alone. Ignore them, Ruben.'

'It's ok, Chico, I've told them before. No patting, stroking or cuddling...not while I'm on duty anyway.'

Yuriko can't help herself and ruffles his head with her paw.

'Just messing with ya, rat, just messing,' chuckles Frank. 'Anyways enough goofin' around, case won't solve itself. Piggy, check the phone records, see if anyone made some calls from here yesterday. And check the sheep's story again, see what else he remembers, same goes for the mules.'

'Draw straws for the mother,' quips Ruben, raising his claws immediately to apologize for the interruption.

'Rat, wolf, swing by the brother's home and look for clues. Oh, and find that sulky boss of theirs, LeRoy Beaver. He reported them missing so check his alibi. Make sure it's watertight. Monkey, you're with me... we're off to church.'

7

Dread, Beavers, Goats, And Woes

Johnny, Chuck, and Benny Beaver - like so many beavers - worked up at the Shepherd's Dam. All three of them were experienced engineers helping to preserve the humongous barrier between Noah's Kingdom and the Scarlet Ocean. This was not, however, their *only* source of income. The trio were notorious criminals; the 'Beaver Brothers' as they were more commonly known had spent their entire lives drifting between cells and a shack by the river, which they called their home. The father had also been a criminal, *but* it was their mother who was comfortably the least pleasant; very few of us have a mummy with the nickname 'Knuckles'.

It therefore came as no surprise when they chose an unlawful path. Before they'd learnt to build their first bridge, they were mastering the art of pickpocketing and how to pull a con. Not many childhoods are spent pinching just to pay for hot meals, but this was sadly the case for three unfortunate beavers. Father often took the boys along if he planned to relieve a mansion of valuables; their ability to slide through a letterbox or sneak through a window was extremely beneficial. As they crept into adulthood the crimes became considerably more serious, and associates became considerably more wicked. The taste for burglary and lifting money from strangers, was soon replaced with an unquenchable thirst for robbing delivery trucks, raiding banks, and importing stolen goods.

At the point of their disappearance they were connected with crimes committed for every slimeball in the city, including Salvatore Bulldog. Head honchos at the dam would surely have fired them had it not been for their crucial expertise, and the fact that all the managers are just as corrupt and deplorable.

The beavers also had another passion - The Church of North Beach. Rule number one: *we never work on Sunday.* No matter what the job, no matter the coins that slid across the table, the brothers would simply refuse. It seems strange that criminals would frequent a religious institution with absolute devotion, but this was a triplet of poorly educated rodents, all of which had little grasp of right from wrong. The church gave them a sense of belonging, somewhere they had purpose and roles to play. Sunday was a time where they could escape the woes of their troubled lives – and the only time they would ever feel slightly 'normal'.

Every Sunday was the same: like clockwork the beavers would rise at dawn for breakfast and once the feast was over, they would make their way through the woods to the church on the other side, in time for morning service. They would sing, they would read, and they would pray - but never confess. At the end, each brother would happily drop half his week's earnings into a donation jar beside the entrance. If ever a member of the congregation was in need, they would support. If ever the church took to the streets to feed the poor and needy, they would lead the way. If ever the church was in trouble, these three beavers would always be there. One can only guess whether these occasional kind deeds will be enough to grant them a seat alongside Noah and their lord in the afterlife, or if a sorry life of constant wrongdoing will mean a trip down to fiery surroundings.

The sun is gradually waking. Ruben and Yuriko make their way into the heart of the Barro Forest so they can inspect the beaver's property. City folk refer to this area as 'The Swamp' due to the soggy ground and umpteen rivers snaking through it. You won't find a more popular spot for creatures at home near water: otters, ducks, frogs, and even a family of hippos live nearby.

Yuriko's head slams painfully against the roof of the car as it hits another bump on the hazardous winding road. The wolf lets out a yelp, struggling to steer the transport through rough terrain. Ruben is jolted into air before landing back on his seat with a thud; he's not enjoying the 'pleasant' cruise through the countryside either.

'I told you we should have walked. Hit one more bump, and I'm off the case,' moans Ruben, staring out the window. Yuriko has learnt to ignore the constant negative thoughts emitted by her little partner; she focuses on driving and protecting her skull from further damage instead.

The journey is far from ideal, but the route is unquestionably beautiful. Ruben leans out the car and rests his arm on the door; he admires the endless queue of tall trees, the calm twinkling river that follows the road and the soothing freshness of air.

They pass a crocodile out with his son for a spot of fishing - most likely catching breakfast; the rat nods and winks as the car slowly trundles by. Both crocs smile and tip their floppy 'fisherman hats' to acknowledge the passing officers, before promptly casting rods. The bright lights and chaos of the city suddenly feels worlds away.

Three bumps later, Officer Ruben and Officer Yuriko arrive at a wooden shack; it has a rusty tin roof and overlooks the river. The car, now coated in mud, comes to a standstill and two dazed creatures gladly fall out. Ruben is instantly up to his waist in muck and not best pleased; just last week he'd had this uniform cleaned at Herbie Chipmunk's 24-Hour Launderette.

'You gotta be kidding me, you have *got* to be kidding me. These are my best shoes!' yells the diva at the top of his voice. The bog starts to rise up and touch his chest. 'Hey, hey I think I'm sinking!! I'm sinking here!!...Quick, wolf, gimme a hand will ya, oh man, don't let me die like this. I wanna die in a blaze of glory, not drowning in sludge. Tell my mother I died in battle would ya? *Bravely.* Tell her there was ten dogs...yeah...big dogs with long fangs, and I went down fighting. A hero to the bitter end!' Ruben prematurely hits the panic button and not for the first time. Maybe this isn't the best occupation for such a nervous wreck? Yuriko is quite familiar with his tendency to overreact. She squelches through the bog and casually drags the wailing rodent away from the 'pool of doom'.

'How many times I save your life now? You owe me *big* time.' Yuriko's arm carries the rescued party like a crane and drops him off at drier land.

'Hey, try being my size for a week, it's tough!! And you may have saved my life, but these stains are *never* coming out in the wash.'

Hand in hand they wade through treacherous ground until they reach an 'Unwelcome' mat at the doorstep of the shack (the ground is undoubtedly firmer and safer for rats here).

It's hardly the prettiest of homes and not much bigger than a caravan but you can't beat the view from its doorway - a true work of art from dear old mother nature. Everywhere you look is luscious shades of green or streams for a morning dip. There's even a rocking chair parked out front so you can relax and take it all in.

The same can't be said for the scene inside the shack. Dark and dingy is the most accurate way to describe this humble abode. Truly little in the way of furniture: just a messy bed, circular table, and unsophisticated fireplace. Both officers hold their noses; the ghastly smell is overpowering.

'Smell so bad,' gags Yuriko, stepping inside. 'Nearly worst than your place.'

'Hey, don't start that again wolf. You canines just gotta strange sense of smell,' replies Ruben, defending his stinky home. 'This place does whiff like a junkyard though. Beavers never heard of a vacuum cleaner?'

Yuriko inspects the tiny bed in hope of discovering vital clues, but only stumbles on grime and crumbs. Ruben's attention is drawn to the windowsill, and all the miniature arks that sit upon it. 'They sure love Mr Noah,' mumbles the rat, fondling the weenie polished sculptures. He gazes upon a black and white photo on the wall beside the window, of the ever-bitter mother beaver; she's stood in front of the family home, arms folded across a cheap blue gown, offering a scowl where there should be a smile. Ruben widens his eyes with disbelief that this horrid creature was ever a mother, then joins Yuriko to inspect the dinner table. Four small bowls are still laid out, but there's an absence of cutlery.

'Why four bowls? Not three?' ponders Yuriko, circling the table with intrigue. Ruben peers into the first bowl and finds the remains of a typical beaver's supper: pieces of twigs and leaves. Yuriko grabs the second bowl, but only finds more of the same. Ruben grabs the third, and again, it's leftover greens.

'Lucas,' whispers Yuriko, clasping the fourth bowl. Her eyes are locked on its contents. '*Lucas,*' she says, handing the bowl to the rat.

'What do you mean *Lucas*?' snaps Ruben, snatching it away. His eyes light up and his mouth drops open. Another bowl full of leaves, but this time, accompanied by chunks of bamboo shoot. The beavers last guest, it would appear, was a panda.

'How…how do you know it was Lucas? Maybe it was another panda?' asks Ruben, placing the bowl gently back on the table, his mind racing to make sense of the clue.

'It was Lucas,' replies Yuriko confidently and calmly (Noah's Kingdom isn't rife with black and white bears in truth. It's uncommon you meet one, and you could count on one hand those of any importance. There's Peter Panda of course, the local author, and Amadeus Panda the basketball star, but neither of these would accept an invitation for grub with dirty beavers).

Ruben wanders over to the fireplace and gathers his thoughts. Yuriko notices a rainbow painted on the ceiling of the beaver's unkempt residence; she glares at all the colors, gently rotating on the spot.

'What the heck?' squeaks Ruben. Something rather peculiar, something buried in the ashes, something that was meant to burn in the evening fire. Officer Rat crouches down and runs his claws through mounds of cinder. He pulls out a tiny piece of burnt blue paper, then another, and another. Yuriko kneels beside him. Together they try to deduce the relevance of charred remains. There appears to be words on the paper, and parts of a diagram - all drawn with white ink.

'I think it's map,' says Yuriko, taking one of the charred fragments to investigate closely.

'More importantly, why burn it?' asks Ruben, looking his partner dead in the puzzled eyes.

****

As one reaches the tip of The Swamp, you kiss goodbye to trees and find yourself in the tranquil fields of North Beach, where you'll come across a crumbling church. An ancient building close to ruin, but a popular spot for the believers of Noah's Kingdom. Rather more eye catching, is the cumbersome apple tree which guards this house of worship, standing proudly in its shadow and bearing a full complement of ripe delicious goods.

Frank and Chico approach the entrance on foot; all roads and access for police cars had come to an end a long way back. The warm weather has forced the penguin into a welcome change of appearance and he now looks close to professional, modelling a bright white shirt and braces for tailored brown trousers - though it's hard to recognize him, strutting across the grass without his mac. Chico on the other hand, is undeterred by the temperature and stays loyal to his new grey suit.

'What this church really needs is a gigantic apple tree rooted on its doorstep, *oh*, well whaddya know,' remarks Chico, with a giant dollop of sarcasm.

'Let's get this over with, kid, I hate churches. Make me uncomfortable,' replies Frank, as the pair arrive at a broad open doorway.

'Anything to confess, Frank?'

'Trust me, kid, wouldn't be fair on *any* creature of the cloth to endure my list of confessions. They'd have to do it in shifts.'

A whiff of incense lingers in the air. Candles flicker, burn, and melt. The deafening notes of a busy organ echo around a towering ghostly chamber. Frank and Chico stride unhurriedly past rows of empty pews, their eyes darting between toad-faced gargoyles perched on ledges and the intricate stained-glass images of Noah on numerous windows.

Everywhere they look is another tribute to the holiest of creatures - the tortoise. This is the animal held in higher regard than any other (Antonia Tortoise, or The First Tortoise as she's more commonly known, is believed by the Church of North Beach to be a gift from the heavens, who fled the ark to share wisdom and spread the word of 'peace' for a lifetime of three hundred years. They believe that every tortoise since, descends from she and must be treated the same – as a demigod sent from above). The few tortoises still alive in Noah's Kingdom reside at the 'Temple of Hope' just beyond Paradise Valley, and only 'come out of their shells' for the annual parade.

As the detectives reach an altar, the organ falls silent; only the tapping sound of the visitor's footsteps on archaic wooden flooring can now be heard. They gaze at the setting like tourists exploring a gallery. A short lectern is overshadowed by the intimidating statue behind it – that of Antonia Tortoise rising onto her feet.

'Who enters the house of our lord?' A question posed from the shadows.

'We're here to see Father Goat. Police business,' replies Frank bluntly.

'And why is it you seek a discussion…with the master?'

'Hey, we don't answer to strangers,' says Chico, trying to figure what lurks out of sight. Seconds of silence are followed by a shuffling sound as a ferret steps into the light. The haggard critter moves gradually, hampered by a terrible limp. He's cloaked in blue rags with a black handkerchief tied around mangled eyes, to prevent discomfort from those who stand in his presence. Frank drops his gaze to the floor. Chico merely winces with pity.

'Don't be afraid, do not feel sorrow. For I am Enoch, and truly I am happy. The master took me in when I thought all hope was lost. He gives me duties, he gives me shelter, and he gives me food. What more could a blind ferret desire?'

'No offense, but what are the duties exactly? Don't strike me as security,' asks Chico, abandoning the more polite approach.

'Quite right, sworn protector of the master I am not. Yet I can play the organ, I can sweep the floors, and I can help prepare the sermons. And you… *you* are a monkey, am I right?'

An impressed monkey. 'So, you're not completely blind then?'

'Oh, but I am, all I see is various shades of darkness. But *smell*, I can still smell. Just ask the quiet bird beside you.'

'I'm a penguin ya festering little rat, now where's the goat? Before I remove your other five senses!' yells Frank, his words reverberating around the hall.

The ferret remains composed and refrains from confrontation. 'Father Goat is teaching up at the orphanage, I will take you to him. But you may wish to show him more respect than you've shown me, if you expect many answers.'

'Sorry about the penguin, he's just a bit grouchy cause we've not eaten. We'd be grateful if you would show us the way,' says Chico, with a touch of guilt.

'Very well,' declares Enoch as he hobbles towards a slender passage at the back of the Church. 'This way gentleman, we must climb the hill.'

'Chico, I think you need to carry me. This damn mountain's close to vertical,' admits Frank as he wheezes and ceases climbing to catch his breath. Chico puts his hands on his hips, a sure sign he's not best pleased with his partner's fitness.

'Come on, Frank, we're nearly there,' he pleads, waving his arms with impatience.

'I am a limping ferret without vision, yet it's the penguin begging for mercy. Surely it can't be so,' announces Enoch with great delight; it's been a while since he had company for a journey up the hill to the orphanage, and this unexpected twist to the schedule has likely made his day. Frank inhales, focuses on the finishing line and reluctantly proceeds to march onward and upward, towards their destination.

Strong gusts of wind welcome the trio of climbers as they finally reach the top and approach the North Beach Orphanage. A giant white home with a tiled sloping roof and the biggest chimney you ever did see. Perhaps an orphan's life wasn't so bad after all? Beyond the dwelling is a view of the Shepherd's Dam in all its glory - a perfect spot to observe the city it shields. Chico's breath is taken by the sights; howling gales brush his thick fur as he cherishes the spellbinding canvas.

Father Goat sips from a cup of tea - his fourth cuppa of the day already and we've barely touched noon. He's comfortably slumped in his favorite walnut armchair - or the 'story chair' as it's referred to by the little ones. The fireplace crackles behind him, with enough fresh wood to comfort the creatures for hours. This is the main living room of the orphanage; walls are dotted with photos of children past and present - and works of art or craft produced throughout the years. The floor is a sea of toys, blunt crayons, and half-finished coloring books. It appears to be a place of joy and happiness, far from the dingy and cruel environment you encounter at other such places around the city. The area is also packed with young chirpy creatures: from lion to mouse, from tiger to pig, from gangly to short, and slender to big. Each is without family but taken in and cared for by the old and wise vicar now addressing them. The younglings sit patiently on the floor in hushed silence, listening intently with legs folded and eyes fixed forward. Bulkier orphans such as the hippos and elephants must stand at the back though; there isn't the space to accommodate them on the ground.

Sister Aurelia Turkey enters the room, her head slightly bowed and at a pace that suggests she was late. A tray loaded with rainbow colored cakes and currant buns has arrived with her. 'As you requested, master,' mutters Aurelia into the ear of the goat. He nods, smiles, and helps himself to a cake.

'Usually children, I'd stick to grass of course. But there's no harm in treating yourself once in a while. Just don't tell my doctor,' says the goat, with a wink. The obedient turkey now passes the tray to the listeners, and they waste no time in grabbing and consuming the sweetest treats on offer.

'That will be all, thank you, Sister Turkey,' says Father Goat as he wipes the crumbs off his scruffy beard. His most loyal assistant leaves the room and makes her way below deck to check that other young tenants aren't up to mischief. The goat clears his throat as two detectives quietly make their way into the room, just in time to catch his latest speech. The aged priest smiles at his guests, before turning his attention to the audience surrounding his feet. Frank and Chico exchange a quick glance - a silent agreement not to interrupt proceedings just yet. They wait patiently.

'God said to Noah,' announces Father Goat, staring directly at the captivated audience of listeners making up the front row. 'Come out of the ark, you and your wife, and your sons, and their wives. Bring out every kind of living creature that is with you, the birds, the animals, and all the creatures that move along the ground. So they can multiply on the earth and be fruitful, and increase in numbers on it'.

Father now focuses his gaze on a timid looking hedgehog sat closest to his feet; the goat leans forward until the spiky orphan can touch his dangling scruffy beard. 'But Noah was not first to come out, nor his sons and his wife, and his son's wives.'

He rises back up and throws his fist to the air. 'First were the animals and all the creatures that move along the ground and all the birds. Everything that moves on the land came out of the ark, one kind after another,' bellows the goat, now raising his voice as he looks to the heavens. 'Now was the dawn of the animals, mankind finally our slave, and we were fruitful, and we did increase in numbers, and then...we *evolved.*'

The goat may be old but there's still passion coursing through those veins. None of the orphans move an inch; each and every one of them is mesmerized by their mentor. 'The birds they learn to speak, the fox's paws now hands and feet. The goats became wise, the lions stood tall. God bless the animals. God bless us all. Amen.'

'Amen,' reply the enchanted orphans.

Frank takes a step forward – time to break up story time. 'Sorry to disturb you, Father Goat. Would it be possible to ask you a few questions?'. Usual routine - both detectives whip out the pencils and notepads. 'It's about the beavers,' he adds, flicking through his previous scribbles.

'Children, run along now, we'll finish story time later. Join the others down in the hall,' says Father Goat, ushering the animals towards a door. The youngsters climb to their feet and dash off to join their friends in the dining hall down below.

'Would you care for a cup of tea while we talk?' asks the goat, gingerly treading closer to his interrogators. 'Sister Aurelia makes a splendid brew.'

'We're ok thanks, Father. I'm not big on hot drinks and *wings* here, only sinks buckets of coffee. But we appreciate the kind offer,' replies Chico, keen to steer conversation towards the topic of missing brothers.

'I heard it mentioned on the radio, dreadful news, though not totally unexpected I might add. Suppose you've come to see if I have vital clues to share? Crucial answers to the mystery?'

'If you don't mind, goat, *sorry*...I mean Father Goat. We know the brothers were fans of your church, never missed a meeting, ceremony, service, whatever you call it. You know any reason why they might have been kidnapped? Aware of any problems, enemies? They mention anything to you, that might help our investigation?' enquires Frank, scratching the side of his head with a pencil.

Father turns his back on the cops. 'I was sad to hear they'd disappeared. I don't recall a Sunday service where they weren't first to arrive and last to wave goodbye.'

He now turns to face them once again. 'But I'm not a fool, *old* yes, foolish no. Deep down I suppose I knew this day might come. You speak of enemies and problems, each of us here is fully aware of the demons that cursed the lives of these poor souls. From Monday to Saturday their lives were nothing *but* enemies and problems.'

Father breaks momentarily to address his dry throat with a sip of tea. 'Yet I can offer no name, nor reason I'm afraid,' he says, taking another slurp. 'Just know that I tried my best to lead them along a better path, truly I did, but my efforts were fruitless.'

'Anyone else we can talk to, the turkey lady maybe? She able to help at all?'

'I imagine Sister Turkey will be equally unhelpful, if not more so. She knew the brothers of course, but only by reputation, and by their frequent appearance on Sundays. Let's just say, she had reservations about the church allowing their involvement, given their...well, their lifestyle.'

'You didn't mind their lifestyle, Father? Surely it raised a few eyebrows with the congregation?'

'Their unlawful habits upset me, of course. So many creatures choose a life of crime these days, it troubles me deeply. The church has been robbed three times this year already, and I myself was recently attacked by a mob. This used to be such a wonderful city you know, now look at it...*crippled* by crime and greed.' The Father stops himself from carrying on, aware that he is starting to rant. He looks at his sandals, shakes his head, and composes himself with a grin. 'Forgive me, I'm rambling. Too much tea. My point is this, I never felt the beavers were evil, just lost, and I wanted to help them. Plenty of my flock felt the same. If only the legions of other lost souls would seek my aid, then maybe Noah's Kingdom would be the haven of tranquillity it once was.'

While the goat waffles on about the Kingdom falling apart, Chico steps away to explore the room; he inspects a couple of toys which brings back fond memories of his own. He then examines the gallery covering the wall, with arms crossed but a finger tapping his chin. The competency of the artist varies from picture to picture: some are good, some are bad, some are inexplicable. There's also a running theme - it's either a painting of a rainbow or a painting of animals leaving an ark.

'Thank you for your time, Father,' says Frank.

Chico returns to his partner's side. He's pretty confident that his mind had wandered for the last five minutes, while he lost himself in orphan artwork - yet all he had missed was a string of dull anecdotes recited by the goat. Neither detective has put pencil to paper since walking through the door, and North Beach Church was yet to reveal any clues.

'If you think of anything, or one of the church group, congregation, they mention anything…be sure to let us know. We'll catch the goons that did this, Father, don't you worry,' blurts Frank. 'Oh, and this orphanage, very nice but you might wanna build it again at the *bottom* of the hill. Just saying. My heart nearly packed his bags climbing the damn thing.'

'A valid point detective and very apt. We intend to re-locate soon in fact. I recently acquired a much more appropriate home for the children. It's perfect and not to be found atop a hillside.'

'Great. Well I hope you've moved before we meet again.' Frank offers his wing.

The Father smirks and shakes with the departing guests. He steps outside and watches them stroll away down the path. As they drift out of sight, four white rabbits appear alongside the Father, hooded in dark brown robes and each with thick golden rope tied around the waist - The Rabbits of North

Beach. A group of silent bunnies, loyal servants to the church, and staunch disciples of the elderly horned mammal they call their master.

8

The Orangutan's Dungeon

Police HQ is buzzing; detectives, officers, and clerks of every breed are zipping around the office, hard at work on an endless pile of cases. Hudson Rhino is slouched on his chair yelling at some poor witness down the phone. Everywhere you look there's busy pigs in navy blue with a hint of gold. Thelma Eagle - bird of prey and first class officer - is stood on a chair while she pins a garish poster against the wall: *'Annual Kingdom Parade 2nd February'*. A bold reminder that the annual parade is fast approaching. The second day of the second month is always the date for the magnificent Kingdom parade where the city comes together for fun, frolics, and wild celebrations. It's also a great way to earn further cash, but most choose to skip extra hours and enjoy the festivities instead.

Frank is sat behind his desk for once but there's no desire or time for paperwork. He's mulling over stacks of photos: black and white snaps of motels and riverbanks. Frustrated mumbling is loud and clear as he guzzles a hot mug of caffeine. His desk could do with a tidy; it's a messy collection of newspaper clippings, ancient stains, and pictures of female penguins (all from the family tree). There's also a photo of Frank and Lucas standing outside The Blue Crypt – back when they were young, happy, and the glass was half full. It draws his attention and he ceases the moans for a second - to wish that his buddy was still by his side.

'Might wanna see this, Frank,' blurts Officer 'Squinty' Mole, cutting short Frank's journey down memory lane. She has a short pink nose poking out from a black furry face which appears to be missing eyes - but they are definitely in there somewhere. A respected officer but limited in capability given her lack of vision, and rarely involved with surveillance. 'It's a statement from two witnesses. Both claim that LeRoy Beaver was threatening the beaver brothers outside a bar. Two weeks ago.' She drops the papers on the penguin's lap.

'That's around the same time they checked in at Red Valley,' says Chico. He had been spinning round and round on his chair while he awaited the team's next move, but the dawdling now ends abruptly.

'Great work, Squinty. Take a pig and speak to some beavers up at the dam again. One of them must know something.'

'Sure thing, boss,' says the mole, with a firm salute. She spins around, trips over a chair, and grabs a pig to hit the road with.

Ruben and Yuriko burst through the door, eager to reveal their findings.

'What you got?' says Frank calmly.

'Bamboo, Frank. We got bamboo,' replies Ruben, still waiting for his breath to catch up.

'Lucas?' Frank looks again at the photo of his previous partner, then back at his animated officers.

'We think so. Bamboo. Must be Lucas,' says Yuriko, chipping in.

'Why would the beavers meet with a cop?' asks Chico, resisting temptation to take another spin on his chair.

'We find blue paper in fireplace. Maybe clue. Left it downstairs with lab.'

Ruben hops onto a desk. 'Maybe a map or some kinda plans, we couldn't be sure. Nothing else but foul smells and a whole heap of religious stuff.'

'Arks and rainbows. Very empty. Incredibly sad home.'

'Good work. Me and the kid hiked up to north beach church, and the orphanage.'

'Any luck?' asks the wolf, pulling up an empty chair as a spot to rest.

'Zip, zilch, and nothing. Unless you count sore flippers.'

Ruben throws his hand up like a schoolboy with something to share with the class.

'We picked up LeRoy Beaver as well, if that's any help. Spent Friday night at the flicks watching *Street Cat Named Desire*, with three buddies he says can vouch for him. No alibi for the panda attack though, just home alone. And he's not happy, Frank. Still got him sweating in a room down the hall. You might wanna walk in with some kinda riot shield, cause I ain't kidding…that's *one* angry beaver!'

'Perfect, I'll speak with him, he's still got explaining to do. And I'll try to calm him down,' says Frank, sliding off his chair and ready for action. 'Chico, hit the lab and gimme some answers on the blue paper. Ruben, Yuriko…grab Jake and tell him about the bamboo. Everyone back here in *one* hour. If I'm not here…I've been eaten by a beaver.' Frank finishes his coffee, grabs his pile of photos, and swaggers through the exit.

****

Chico finds himself in a drab cramped lift. An irritating combo of flute and xylophone spews from a rusty speaker, as it drops down to the HQ basement. After a lifetime it comes to a halt. The doors try and open but fail miserably; they need helping hands from the monkey. He stumbles into a bleak windowless room known as the 'Kingdom Police Force Crime Laboratory'. Given the intriguing title you'd expect something a little more glamorous. The lab is a creepy mix of tables, chemistry sets, microscopes, and books (should you acquire a whole load of evidence from your crime scene and it needs to be properly examined, then you bring it straight here, and pray forensic science can provide the answers). Plenty of colorful liquids are happily bubbling away; you half expect to hear the sound of lightning or wicked manic laughter from a hysterical loony scientist.

Chico strolls across the ice-cold concrete floor, inspecting an array of gadgets. If there was a window and cozier feel to the space, then this would probably be a neat team to work for. He picks up a fresh mold of teeth and presses the incisors with a finger.

A gangly orangutan with a beaming smile looks up from his messy desk; new visitors are always welcome sight in a lonely dungeon. Checked trousers, lemon shirt, and glowing red bow tie are a strong giveaway that he shall not be crippled with shyness. He flops off his stool and hurriedly waddles to greet the guest.

'Hyena.'

'Beg your pardon?' says Chico, looking first at the loud choice of clothes, then up to the pan shaped head.

'*Aye* the set of teeth laddie, wee gnashers from a hyena, so they are.'

'I'm impressed,' replies the smaller of the two simians, with a nod and raised brow.

'Ah now what do we have here, a wee detective come to pay me a visit. Am I right? Aboot time someone came a knockin', I'll tell ya that for nothing laddie. I'm Ness.' This is no shrinking violet and wastes no time in offering a firm sweaty handshake.

Chico smiles and immediately feels at ease, despite the eerie surroundings. 'Pleasure to meet you. Nice to see an ape with a badge.'

'Argh, too many pigs on the force, not enough monkeys, chimps, and apes. Am I right? Aye, anyway what can I do for ya on this fine afternoon?'

'Blue paper,' says Chico.

'Oh right, wee penguin's case aye. Take it you're the wee new partner?'

'That's correct...monkey and a penguin. Your typical partnership.'

'Aye he's a good one lad. Wee bit crabby, but if you ask me, a right fine copper too.'

'Yeah, crabby's about right.'

Chico spots a pair of spider monkeys in grey lab coats, both fixated with test tubes. One of the monkeys looks up for a second and presents a subtle smile.

Ness McRangutan makes his way over to a microscope in the corner of the lab and waves his hand, gesturing Chico to follow. 'Come, take a wee peek at this, laddie.'

Chico peers into the microscope, carefully adjusting the lens until the blur is clear as day. It's a piece of blue paper, burnt around the edges but there's text which is clearly visible: *The Swamp*. Chico drags his eyes away from the scope and looks at the bubbly orange scientist - who is now standing a bit too close for comfort. They are practically touching eyeballs.

'Do you mind backing up a bit there, Ness. Look like your about to plant a kiss.'

'Oop...sorry, laddie.' Ness nods to acknowledge the weird moment, backing off to a less invasive position. 'Eye sight's not what it used to be.'

'The Swamp...what do you think?' asks Chico, taking another peek.

'Aye, well just a hunch mind, but I'm fairly sure these are blueprints. Construction diagrams of some kind. Me brother John's an architect, and I've laid me eyes on plenty down the years, so I have. Soonds like plans were afoot to build in the wee Barro Forest.'

'Construction plans, right. Any idea what for?'

'Afraid not, laddie, hard to tell with such wee fragments of paper, and moost of them are frazzled. Whatever it was, those wee beavers were none too pleased. How would you like it if someone planned to knock down *your* home? Aye I'd not be a happy chappy, I'll tell ya that for nothing.'

'And then they burnt them?'

'Aye but of course, *burn the evidence*. I very much doot these were plans meant for their attention. Argh I'm no detective sonny but soonds like Lucas, bless him, felt inclined to share these wee prints with the brothers. Now doont ask me why, doont ask me what they mean, doont ask me how a wee detective comes by such plans...but I'll bet ya ma months wages right now that the fate of The Swamp is key to all this doom and gloom.'

'You could be right. Maybe the county planning department can shed some light on things. I'll keep ya posted. And hey, pop upstairs sometime...must go crazy stuck in a cave all day.' Chico shakes hands with Ness for the second time and turns to walk away.

'Oh...I forgot...before you go sonny, one other thing.' Ness spins around, rushes over to another table and swipes something off it. He toddles back and opens his hands to reveal the single tuft of white fur found at the Red

Valley Motel. Nearly butting heads, they both look down. After a second, they raise their eyes, and each looks directly upon the other – their faces now inches apart.

'Honestly, you are way too close again, Ness, but please, what is it?' asks Chico in a hushed tone.

'This, laddie, I'm afraid, belongs to a wee... *white* gorilla.' Ness is almost apologetic knowing full well the daunting task that lays ahead, for those who would try and catch such a fearsome beast. Chico looks once more at the fur, resting on the sticky palm of his wacky new friend - and he looks with dread.

****

Everyone assembles in the ground floor briefing room. The space is packed; mainly detectives but a handful of gum-chewing officers linger at the back. Even Mayor Leopard is present with an entourage of chameleons and anteaters. Frank is parked up front; the chief might ask him to provide further details. Chico is comfortable hiding on the back row, peeking over Jake's bulky shoulder. Hudson casually takes up three seats slap bang in the middle; he checks his watch and groans – it's lunch time.

'Where is she already? I swear, I'll swallow Ruben if she ain't here in five minutes,' bellows the hungry rhinoceros as his bubbling belly rumbles.

'Yeah real funny ya chunky unicorn,' replies Ruben, cupping his hands around the mouth while at the same time hoping that Hudson was kidding. Yuriko pats him on the shoulder to let him know she always has his back. She knows all too well his habit of taking even the emptiest of threats a notch too seriously.

'Somebody get the rat a box, it's hard to see back there.' Hudson slaps the koala beside him, followed by a booming laugh.

Ruben thinks about trading another blow then stops himself. 'Actually, he has a point...could you fetch me a box? All I can see is the back of a monkeys head.'

Yuriko rolls her eyes.

'LeRoy Beaver have much to say?' asks Chico, twisting his head to quiz Yuriko.

She smiles, happy to provide an update. 'Frank ask him about argument he had with beavers. He say it's nothing, just unhappy they do business with bulldog. Said they always arguing, bicker like children, said it was normal. He very angry that Frank question him though, punch wall many times. But alibi look strong, so maybe he innocent.'

'He did seem genuinely upset that they were missing. But, with a temper like that, best we don't rule him out just yet. Maybe stick the eagle on his tail for a few days, see if he's acting strangely.'

'Good idea, I'll speak with Thelma.'

Jake is about to fall asleep when Chief Vulture finally makes an appearance. Everyone immediately sits up, wakes up, and tries to focus. Jake snaps out of his impulse to nap. The vulture swoops into the room followed by her trusty assistant - the ever helpful but new and slightly jittery, Miss Vera Llama. The chief takes her place on a high stool behind a wooden lectern. Vera drops a couple of important documents but quickly recovers them, places them in order, and hands them to her stern looking boss. Slightly flustered, the young llama takes the last remaining seat at the front. The vulture briefly stares at the notes whilst the audience wait in silence. Hudson looks at his watch again and shakes with disbelief; at this rate he's sure to miss the lunch time deal at Barneys Deli across the road.

'John, Benjamin, and Charles Beaver,' says the chief, now addressing the crowd. 'Also known as Johnny, Benny, and Chuck Beaver. Were kidnapped from the Red Valley Motel early Saturday morning. Keaton Mule, son of the establishment's owner, reported them missing. We estimate they were removed from the premises no longer than ten hours before our arrival. That means they were kidnapped on the evening of Friday, Hudson...before you get all muddled.'

Hudson smiles and waves at the room, taking the sly jab on the chin.

The chief turns to a fresh page of notes. 'We have one witness, who is adamant he saw a blue van parked outside his motel room on the evening in question. Please be on the look-out for this particular vehicle, but approach with caution. Blood *was* found at the scene, and all traces were that of the beavers, but we proceed under the assumption they're still alive, until proven otherwise. White fur was also retrieved from the bedroom floor of the motel room, and we can now confirm this belongs to…a *white* gorilla.'

The chief pauses for a moment as the sound of whispering fills the air and a slight look of panic contorts every face between the four blue walls. '*Settle down,*' demands the chief, banging the lectern like an irritated judge. 'We have good reason to believe the disappearance of Detective Lucas Panda was also linked to this case, unless you know of any other creature with a taste for bamboo who shared a meal with three beavers just last week. Remnants of construction plans for The Swamp area were also found at the beaver's residence, but we have no further information on these at this moment in time. In fact, at this stage I'm afraid to say we have *very* little to go on…so we need to work as a team, we need witnesses, we need evidence, *and* we need swift results. The city demands we find the culprits and bring them to justice. This is one we really need to win. Ok, enough from me, lunchtimes over boys and girls, hit the streets.…and find these *wretched* criminals.'

Chief Vulture doesn't hang around for questions or response; she's extremely busy and under pressure from the powers above. Within seconds she's vanished. Vera grabs all the papers from the lectern and promptly follows suit.

As the room clears, Frank pulls together all the main animals involved to discuss next steps. Jake, Chico, Hudson, Ruben and Yuriko all huddle round.

'Seriously, how hard can it be to find a white gorilla in this city…they hardly breed like rabbits. Surely one of you clowns has a lead on this?' says Frank to the group surrounding him.

'I know gorilla family down in San Shem. Me and Ruben check today,' says Yuriko.

Hudson dips forward. 'There's a gorilla community center round that way too. Might wanna swing by.'

'I'll ask around, Frank, but I ain't heard of no albino gorilla from Kingdom,' adds big Jake Bear, leaning in. 'Surely we'd have it on record?'

Now Ruben pipes up. 'Yeah they tend to stand out. I mean we all know

Pete the Pink Elephant, right?'

'What about this Fat Chinchilla guy, maybe he knows something?' Chico looks around at the gang for agreement.

'Nice thinking, kid. I'll shake down chunky…if I can find him.'

'Me and Hudson can sweep Luc's apartment again. Maybe there's something we missed…some link to those crispy plans,' says Jake.

Frank whacks himself on the head as punishment for his own stupidity. '*Of course*, we're forgetting the damn blueprints. Chico, do some digging around. Find out some more about these plans, or whatever they are, will ya? I wanna know why my old partner was knocking back bamboo shoots with three scumbag beavers.'

Backs are slapped before the troops disperse to acquire some much-needed answers. But first - lunchtime. Jake and Hudson grab tuna to-go and gobble their meals in the car. Frank introduces Chico to the wonders of Kingdom Crab Shack, despite its continuous failure to comply with health and safety regulations. While Ruben takes Yuriko to a joint around the corner owned by world famous chef, the great Jean Paul Giraffe (it's not cheap but pay day's also around the corner, and rats love to spoil their friends).

9

Hell Hath No Fury Like A Spotted Panther

'**M**onkey!!' screams Madam Porcupine, marching down the hallway armed with a rolling pin. She appears to be in an extra foul mood today. Chico was hoping to enter his apartment without another ear bashing from his militant landlady, but alas that dream is crushed. He raises his arms to create a shield and takes a few steps back – as it's entirely possible a whack to the head is imminent.

'Madam Porcupine, I was about to come and see you…I promise,' grovels Chico, lying through his teeth. 'I hope you're not planning on swinging that thing. I'd really hate to arrest the lady of the house.'

'*Rent. Now*,' demands the porcupine, prodding the anxious monkey in the chest with her wooden utensil. She's a raging ball of spiky quills and equally prickly by nature. Her bland brown dress is littered with flour following hours of manic baking.

'Alright…just…put the weapon down,' says Chico, hurriedly ransacking his pockets for a bundle of coins.

'If it's late again, sir, you can kiss goodbye to those pretty lil kneecaps, *and* you'll be finding yourself a new roof.'

'Are you always this joyful?' replies Chico, handing over a wedge of money.

'Any more sarcasm, Mr Chimpanzee, and I'll double the rent. Now I'll bid you good night.'

'Good night, Madam Porcupine. Sweet dreams,' says Chico, resisting the urge to explain once again that he is a monkey and not a chimpanzee (chimps are bigger than monkeys, and missing a tail).

'Oh, and I warned you about guests. She was tired and shivering, so I let her stay but there shan't be a second occasion. Tell your friends to meet you elsewhere. This *isn't* a cafe.'

'*Guest*...wait, what guest?' asks Chico, staring at the door in bewilderment.

Madam Porcupine is half-way down the hall but stops to respond. 'She said you're expecting her. An old friend, she said?'

'Right...say, it wasn't a white gorilla by any chance?' asks Chico quietly, with a sudden shudder of panic.

'Oh no, quite the contrary...*quite* the contrary.'

Chico pulls out his key and slides it in the lock. He takes a deep breath before carefully opening the door. Another deep breath and a peek down the hallway, then he flings himself inside and rolls along the floor. He jumps to a crouch with his guard held high, ready to tackle any mysterious intruders. A glamorous panther is sat up straight on his couch, *tutting*, as she looks him up and down with nothing but sheer disappointment.

'This really won't do. I was praying for someone far braver. If you're frightened of little old me...then...oh this really won't do,' says the panther, shaking her head as she scrambles to her feet, ready to leave. She's young but knows how to dress like a lady: red polka dot dress, ruby heels, and a matching cloche hat with fresh white roses pinned on the side. The head wear resembles a big red bell, nesting at an angle and slightly hiding her poker face.

Chico instantly realizes how foolish he must appear and adjusts his posture to a less degrading stance. 'Wait, *hey* wait a second, I'm sorry ma'am, you startled me is all,' he explains, blocking the panther's exit with a firm arm.

'I'm mixed up in some pretty unpleasant business at the moment, right. And I thought you might be a dog or a white gorilla.'

The panther delays her escape and stares at the monkey again, but now with a confused expression. 'Do I look like a dog? Or what did you say...*white* gorilla? I doubt that such a creature even exists. How awfully absurd.'

'Lady, believe me, I hope it doesn't exist. Now, please, can you explain why you're sat in my apartment without an invitation?'

The panther returns to her spot on the couch, ready to share her tale. She talks like a queen, dresses like a star, but behaves like the strictest nanny. It's not hard to imagine her slapping your palm with a cain, all for a slip of the tongue.

'I need your help, or I thought I did, though I'm not so sure now I've laid eyes on you, and this ghastly apartment.'

'You're not related to a porcupine by any chance, are you?' asks cheeky Chico, pouring two glasses of orange juice. He passes one to the fiery panther and eagerly knocks back the other. She nods to hint at 'thank you' and takes the smallest sip.

'I'm Charlie, but they call me Chico.'

'Yes, I know who you are. I'm Eliana, and you *will* call me Eliana.'

'Nice to meet you, Eliana. Now please...why are you sat on my couch?'

'Truth be told, I don't know who else I can turn to. My friend said you were new in town so there's a tiny chance you're trustworthy, unlike all the others.'

'Friend, what friend? And what do you mean *unlike* the others? What's going on?'

She takes another sip. 'You don't know him, he's a journalist for the Kingdom Echo, *but* he knows of you...and he knows you've just arrived. Oh, please tell me you're a good one, not another bent swindler losing sight of his oath, all for a handful of coins from a hoard of filthy crooks.'

'Hey lady, *relax*, I'm a good cop...or at least I try anyway. Are you in some kind of trouble?'

'I was the mayor's secretary. Until he fired me that is.'

'Mayor of Noah's Kingdom? Mayor Leopard?'

'That's right, Mayor Leopard. I've been his secretary for six months. Always had a fascination with politics, and this seemed like a marvelous way to learn the ropes. Anyway, it was all going splendidly up until a few weeks ago. The mayor was fine to begin with, you could say a perfect gentleman, and then, suddenly everything changed.'

'Everything changed. What changed?'

'It all started the day those weasley beavers paid him a visit.'

Chico's ears prick up and his head nearly springs off his neck. He grabs a wooden chair and straddles it so he can listen carefully to the rest of the story.

'Beavers? You said beavers, right? Three of them...brothers?'

'That's right, brothers, the ones in the newspaper. They came to the office a few weeks back. I couldn't hear the conversation clearly, but I know the tone of an argument and I assure you it was just that...they were clearly unwelcome. George, or should I say *the mayor*, wasn't the same from that day on-.'

'Eliana, do you know what the argument was about? This could be crucial to our investigation.'

'I asked the mayor if he was ok and he said it was nothing, to mind my own business. So, I knew something was wrong, as he'd never snapped at me before. I'm not one to take a ticking off lightly, so I sought to find out *what* exactly was troubling him. As soon as the coast was clear, I sneaked into his private office, and would you believe it, I stumbled across a collection of plans in his desk drawer...construction plans...blueprints-.'

'Wait, *whoah* hold on, tell me about the blueprints. We found some remains at the beaver's home and we think it's some sort of plans. *Not* that I should really be discussing evidence with a panther that broke into my home-'

'Oh, do stop over reacting Mr Monkey, I'm here for help and *to* help. Anyway, look, I only cast my eye over the prints briefly, but I knew they were important. Everything of importance finds its way into that drawer. They were plans for various structures due to be built in The Swamp. I don't recall all of them, but I remember one was a casino, another a hotel, there were all sorts of grand designs. And he'd managed to get them *all* agreed and signed off.'

'For *who*, Eliana? This is important. For who?'

Eliana finishes her orange juice, thumbs the lipstick stain off the glass out of habit, and gently places it on the floor beside her feet. 'Well, those that I picked up, were all for a Mr Salvatore– .'

'Bulldog!!' shouts the monkey, punching the air. He bounces out of his chair with a warm feeling of satisfaction and a smidgen of progress. Both hands slip behind his head and the brain starts working overtime. 'I knew it, I knew it!! Who is this crazy dog? I mean, he's got his paws in everything.' Yet Chico's cheer is short lived; he's struck by a puzzling thought. Hands slump back to the waist, stumped by the peculiarities of the case. 'Wait, hang on, hang on…what's wrong with buying up land in The Swamp?'

'Only the fact that hundreds of animals live there, Mr Monkey. How is it that a dangerous crime boss is granted numerous building permits by a respectable mayor? When all before him who tried to build something other than homes on that land, were immediately rejected. If there isn't blackmail at play here, I'll eat my finest shoes.'

'OK, we need to speak to my partner about all this. And get some kinda statement.'

'*No*, absolutely not. I don't trust the Kingdom Police. The whole force is riddled with corruption and greed. None of them can know of my whereabouts…please.'

'Corruption? What do you mean, corruption?'

'Don't be so naive monkey. I know for absolute certain there's a mole.'

'What…*Squinty*? Not a chance.'

'No, you buffoon…a rat.'

'*Ruben?*'

Eliana looks ready to strangle Detective Chico. 'No, I am trying to tell you that a number of your colleagues accept bribes from criminals to provide assistance or information. I know this for a fact. I know that Lucas Panda was betrayed by one of his own, betrayed by a cop.'

Chico runs a hand through the fur just above his forehead; he wasn't expecting this many bombshells from one conversation. He takes a second consider to his options and wishes he'd stocked up on lime juice.

'Lucas was friends with my father, I knew I could trust him, he was almost family. I told him about the construction plans, about the beavers, and he agreed to take a look. If I'd known what would happen…oh, how I wish I'd never told him.'

Despite the sad truth of the story she isn't one to shed a tear; this is clearly a creature of incredible resolve and sturdiness. 'He phoned me the night before they found him on that riverbank. *Eliana I'm bringing him in*, he said. The mayor that is. He said he was en route to the racetrack to bring him in. Said I shouldn't be worried, as a friend was going with him…*a cop*. And that's the last I heard from him.'

'A cop? Wow my day gets better and better. Ten minutes ago, my only worry was a giant killer white ape. Now I gotta watch my back while I'm sat at my desk. Great.'

'I could have run you know…moved towns and settled somewhere else. But guilt won't allow that. You need to help me, for Lucas, *please*. You must confront the mayor.'

'I had a horrible feeling that was coming. But what if I do? The last guy that tried got attacked and kidnapped. I'd rather the same didn't happen to me.'

'He's a good man, I know it, he can't be behind this. They must have bribed him or threatened him. Trust me. If you can get him to talk…it's the only way.'

'I sure hope you're right, cause if I grill a city mayor and it goes sour…well, I'll be handing over my badge that's for sure, if not my measly life.'

'Thank you, oh thank you, Mr Monkey. And apologies for hiding in your apartment. I had nowhere else to go.'

'Ahh it's not a problem ma'am, you can stay here till we sort out this mess. Beds all yours, couch suits me fine. Would offer you a hot meal too, but I'm out of ingredients.'

'Could I treat you then? I know a quaint little restaurant not far from here?'

'That really a good idea? I mean, whoever attacked Lucas might be looking for you too?'

86

'Oh, nonsense we'll be fine. It's not far, and it's whereabouts are only known by a lucky few.'

What the lady wants, the lady gets. Chico smiles and concedes defeat despite his concern for the panther's wellbeing. 'After you, ma'am,' he says, holding the door open for his new guest. Eliana responds with a thankful curtsy, before heading into the hallway.

Chico takes another deep breath.

The unlikely pair make their way outside and onto the busy streets of Central Kingdom. Almost immediately, Eliana abandons discretion; she storms across the road ignoring speeding traffic and the chorus of fuming horns that inevitably follow. Chico treads with a touch more caution, keen not to lose his life for the sake of an early dinner. As Miss Panther promised the destination was merely a stone's throw away and following a brisk walk they arrive at The Boar's Theatre. The name of the venue is printed boldly in black gothic font against a long white background, all surrounded by rows of shiny bulbs.

'Theatre? I thought we were going for a meal. Didn't know I was getting a show too?' says Chico, with a look of surprise.

'Just follow me,' replies Eliana, charging up the steps like a child outside a toyshop.

The reception is nothing exciting: a simple room, head to toe in burgundy. Even the pig parked inside the ticket office is clothed in an identical color. He's a grey pot belly with a round snout and incredibly squidgy face; you could store a week's supply of food within his droopy chins. Beside the office is a drawn curtain which presumably leads to the theatre, and slapped right opposite is a dusty old payphone. The pig looks up from a novel as Eliana and Chico rock through the door; he reluctantly puts down his read and prepares for business.

'Two tickets for The Pigs Belly please,' shouts Eliana through the thin window of glass that separates them. The portly grey book-worm nods and steps out of his office; he heaves himself across to the payphone and spins the dial.

'Pigs Belly? What's that?' whispers Chico, still confused by the whole situation.

'You'll see,' replies Eliana with a sly grin.

'Two more,' grunts the pig into the receiver before hanging up and returning to his cozy quarters. He picks up his book and resumes his chapter. A secret door slides open beside the phone and another pot belly emerges, but a black one this time and clad in smarter attire; he appears to be the security, for whoever, or whatever hides within these walls.

'Sir, madam, welcome to The Pigs Belly, follow me please,' says the stocky black pig. Chico, Eliana, and the bruiser step into a hidden section of the theatre while the secret door slides shut behind them. The grey pig in the office doesn't bat a single eye lid - he just turns to a new page, and thanks his lucky stars there's no more guests.

The Pig's Belly is particularly quiet tonight, though not that many clandestine restaurants are ever really crammed. A handful of candlelit couples are enjoying peaceful meals to the crackly sound of mellow hits from jazz supremo Chuck Mongoose. A square bar takes center stage; there's a bearded pig trapped in the middle, knocking up a lemon with soda (ice and a slice of lime, but no straw). Surrounding the square is a whole load of booths with comfortable padded seats – the perfect spot for reasonable privacy.

Eliana and Chico opt for comfort over feeble stools at the bar. Both grab a menu and flick through with haste, desperate for something to fill their hollow bellies. It's not long before a waiter looms over the table: one ginger pig with a huge head, pointy long ears, and crumpled notepad at the ready.

'Evening sir. Evening madam. Can I take your order?' Or would you like more time?'

'I'm ready,' announces Eliana boldly. 'I'll have *you* please.'

'I'm…I'm sorry…did you say me, madam?' The waiter looks positively perplexed.

'That's correct, I'd like a big juicy pig please, on a silver platter if possible. Thank you.'

The waiter glances at Chico who is equally surprised by the request; his porky limbs begin to shake while a burst of nervous laughter can't help but escapes his lips, as he discreetly looks out for the manager.

'It's a joke…it's a joke. Calm down,' announces the panther with a smile. 'I'll take the fish tuna sprinkled with crickets and soaked in lemon sauce. Oh, and mango on the rocks to wash it all down.'

The waiter lets out a huge sigh of a relief. 'Oh, oh right yes of course…sorry madam. Very good, very good.' The color returns to his cheeks, he wipes away the sweat seeping from his brow, and he jots down the panther's order.

'And for you, sir?'

'Mango on the rocks, I like your style,' admits Chico, peering across the table at Eliana. 'I'll have one of those too. And a pile of your finest banana pancakes.'

The waiter finishes his jotting, takes the menus, and heads off to the kitchen - safe in the knowledge that he shan't be served as a main (at least not tonight anyway).

Eliana removes her hat and places it by her side. 'It's rude to eat with your hat on don't you know?' she says, looking up at the monkey's trilby.

He smirks and yanks it off.

'So, tell me, Charlie Chico Monkey, what do you think of Noah's Kingdom? Is it everything you expected?'

'Well, my aunt used to bring me up to the city all the time, so I'm not quite a fish out of water, or monkey out of water, whatever the expression is. Swung by Emzara's Palace for the first time though. Won't forget that in a hurry.'

'I met her once you know, the Lioness Annabella. She came to the office one afternoon for tea with the mayor. Never seen him so frightened.'

'How come? Just a rich lion, right?' says Chico naively, prompting Eliana's eyes to bulge like small inflating balloons.

'Do you know anything, Chico Monkey? I get the feeling you've lived quite the sheltered life, foolish thing. She's not *just* a rich lion, far from it. Nothing happens in this city without her say so, and anyone who's anyone is so because she allows it.'

'Assumed she was just some wealthy kitty cat, hiding in the penthouse of her flashy hotel. What about the tiger, Omar? What's his story?'

'Oh, he's just her errand boy, or so I'm led to believe. Looks like muscle but I doubt he ever flexes. Far too busy frittering away his earnings on jewels and pretty outfits.'

The ginger pig eventually returns to the booth with two plate-loads of sumptuous food balancing on his arm: a healthy serving of lip-smacking golden pancakes and mouth-watering seared tuna chunks. He then grabs two glasses of cold mango from the barman and drops them off at the table.

'Enjoy your meal,' he says, before taking a well-earned break.

Eliana smiles at the waiter then returns to her story. 'My father was a journalist for the Echo, that's how he met Lucas. I still have a few contacts there which comes in handy when you're searching for helpful monkeys. Anyway, my father used to hound Lucas for stories or a bit of inside gossip. They didn't get along at first but eventually became close friends. Sadly, my father passed a few years back, yet I never lost touch with sweet Lucas and he was always good to me. I remember as a child he'd always slip a coin or two into my paw whenever he saw me...'*don't tell your father*' he'd say. I miss him, dearly.'

'Sounds like a good bear. I know my partner misses him too.'

'Maybe we should focus on more cheerful topics tonight, leave the harsh realities of life for morning, what do you say?'

'I'll drink to that, lady,' says Chico raising his glass. 'Let's talk about jazz or favorite movies, please. I'm all outta lines on beavers, pandas, and misery.'

10

One Thief. Eighty Teeth

R ise and shine - it's a warm and pleasant morning in the suburbs. Sunlight bounces off the roof of Jake's beloved emerald sports car, while he scrubs his way to spotless perfection with a sponge and soapy water. He's finally ditched the trademark shirt in favor of a vest and shorts. This is one of the nicer neighborhoods in Noah's Kingdom; a queue of charming properties jammed with happy families. Jake's perfectly content with his bone white bungalow and stretch of tidy lawn - what more could a polar bear ask for?

As he dunks the sponge in his bucket for the hundredth time, he hears the unpleasant sound of a gas guzzling banger struggling to shift along the street. He looks up knowing full well that he's heard these sounds numerous times before. Frank's clunky wreck is chugging towards him and doing a handsome job of waking all the neighbors. It stops just shy of the driveway. Frank sheepishly hops out, aware that it's frowned upon to pester polar bears during their downtime.

'Morning, big guy,' says Frank, waddling over to admire the sports car. 'Nice shorts.'

'Bit hot for a mac, Frank?' replies the giant bear. He drops the sponge in the foamy water and faces his fellow detective.

'You're right, I'm more of a rainy day kinda bird. All this sunshine...*meh*...not for me.'

'What do you want? It's my day off. Taking Michael fishing,' says Jake, waiting for Frank to unveil the real reason behind his early morning visit. Before either of them can say another word, Jake's son sprints out of the family home, armed with a happy face and a fishing rod.

'Frank!!' he shouts with joy, dropping the rod to hug a penguin. He's only a young polar pup but still stands taller than Frank and nearly knocks him over with the crushing embrace. Frank laughs and pats him on the chest as he takes a step back to avoid being smothered again.

'Sheesh, Mikey, growing up fast there, kid. Gonna be bigger than old pop in no time.'

'Sure am, Frank. Gonna be big as a mountain, just like pa.'

Jake ruffles his boy's head. 'I need a bank loan just to pay for all the fish he inhales. Guzzles nearly as much mackerel as you do.'

Frank smiles and clears his throat. 'Say, Jake...mind if we have a quick word?'

'Like I said, Frank, day off. Fishing with my son,' says Jake firmly.

'I really need your help on this one, Jake, please...it's gotta be you.'

Jake kneels so Frank can hear a little clearer. 'I took an oath and kiss the badge with pride. I promise to serve and protect. But you know what, Frank? That ain't nothing like a promise to a son.'

'Are we still going fishing, dad?' asks Michael, picking up the rod.

'Wait a minute, son. The grown-ups need to talk.'

Frank looks at Michael and the rod - fond memories of days with his daughter flash through the mind like a flicker book.

'Ok, ok look, I promise we'll be back by lunch, we're an hour tops, I promise. If we're late, Mikey can scoff me for supper.'

'If we're late *I'll* scoff you for supper, Frank,' says Jake, as far from joking as one could be.

'I'm sorry, Jake. I know you got your boy and you're coming up to retirement… but it's Mason Gator. I need you talk to him. If I walk in, I don't walk out. But you know him, he respects you. So, there's a chance he'll open up and it's a chance we need to take.'

'What has Mason got to do with all this?'

'Last night I caught up with Fat Chinchilla, over at Lover's Rock. He said that Mason Gator mentioned a white gorilla to him, on more than one occasion. So, he might know something. Come on, buddy, this is all we got to go on right now. What I'd give for a few damn leads and a witness.'

'Alright…I'll try, but this ain't my Aunty Betty we're talking about here…this is a crazy alligator. I want you outside with twenty pigs, cause there's no guarantee he'll be in a welcoming mood.'

'Don't worry, Frankie the mac's got ya back like always, big guy.'

Jake now approaches Frank and points a very sharp claw towards his neck.

'Don't *ever* swing by on my day off again. And quit mentioning retirement, there's still a few rounds in the tank.'

Frank backs away again with wings held high. 'I gotcha, Jake, I gotcha, won't happen again. Promise.'

'Are we still going fishing?' asks young Michael again, fearful of a day without dad.

'You're fishing, kid, don't you worry. And you're gonna catch a biggun, I can feel it.' Frank wades in before Jake can say a word.

'I'll be back in a flash, son, just need to go with Uncle Frank for a while. You be a good boy now and wait inside. I won't be long.'

Michael rolls his eyes and huffs as he wanders back to his bedroom, with the fishing rod drooped over sloping shoulders.

'Want me to drive?' asks Frank, still tingling with guilt at having delayed a family fishing trip.

'I'll drive,' replies Jake, flashing his keys. 'We'll never make an hour tops in that clunky death trap of yours.'

****

Sunset Grill House sits on Maple Avenue where only the richest can afford to reside; you need to book at least two months in advance if you wish to acquire a table and it's a popular choice for guest's at Emzara's Palace. Many a celebrity can be spotted of an evening chomping their way through the fine selection of dishes. Last week the world-famous actor Jimbo Fox popped in to sample their lobster and a few fruity juices, while schmoozing his latest sweetheart. Rumor has it that even Lioness Annabella frequents the premises from time to time - but insists on private quarters.

From a distance it resembles any other mansion. The only clue to this being more than a grand attractive house is the dinky gold sign posted beside the doorway, but you'd be hard pushed to find a creature who wasn't aware of this distinguished eatery. It's head to toe in white painted bricks and looks upon a car park of sandy colored pebbles. A vast garden lies at the back with grass so fine it could easily be jade tinted carpet, and rarely does an evening pass without it hosting a stylish party. The surrounding residents are rarely afforded a comfy night's sleep.

The decor, as you step inside and drift across the dark oak floor, is a glimpse of an era long forgotten. Take your eyes off the high painted ceilings and you'll find a gallery of intricate portraits, exquisite antique furniture, and three giant windows providing beautiful natural light. Even the shiny cutlery is worth a small fortune - so clumsy beasts like elephants and hippos are frequently turned away.

Maybe the most puzzling site of all, within this dazzling dining room, is the creature who greets the arriving guests - for at front of house is an impatient 'naked mole rat'. Short and thin in size with tiny grease black eyes, two long teeth that hang past his chin, and a wrinkly pinkish body completely stripped of fur. This is certainly not a species you'd like to encounter in a dark alley, or truth be told - any alley, at any time night or day. The black waistcoat and matching bow tie can't disguise the fact that it's an odd sight to behold upon entering a classy establishment. Jake the Bear like so many guests before him, fails to conceal a look of both shock and horror as he barges through the doors and spots the peculiar host.

'*Whoah*, what the heck??' yelps Jake, clocking the pasty rat. He nearly leaps out of his freshly polished shoes.

'Hey, I got feelings ya know,' responds the rat, shaking his head with disbelief - though it's doubtful this is the first time his features have caused a stir.

'I'm sorry, hey I'm sorry, I didn't mean to leap. It's just that...*what* are you?' Jake is clearly embarrassed by his rude reaction but it's rare you'll witness a polar bear blushing.

The rat stares at the fuzzy intruder for a few seconds, clearly not amused.

'Despite my best efforts to prevent it, they call me *Frosty*. And for the record, you ain't no oil painting yourself ya big dumb bear. I happen to thrive better underground *if you must know.*'

'Like I said, I'm sorry...didn't mean to cause offense, little guy. It's just, I've never met a hairless rat before.'

'Look, what do you want? We're extremely busy...*wait*...are you the new window cleaner? Cause you're an hour late.'

'Window cleaner? No. I'm a detective, and I'm here to speak with the boss.'

Frosty frowns and waves towards the exit. 'The boss don't want no visitors, so take a hike, or do me a favor and clean the windows.'

Jake puts his thumbs under his braces and stretches them while he tries to remain polite. 'I don't think you quite heard me, I *said* I'm a detective.'

'I heard exactly what you said wiseguy and it changes nothing. The boss made it quite clear he was *not* to be disturbed. Now if you don't mind, I have plenty of starving customers waiting for my assistance.'

'Frosty, I'm trying extremely hard to stay calm here, given that I insulted you when I walked in. But you have ten seconds to escort me to the alligator before you become another painting on that ceiling.'

'Gee take it easy, no need for threats, mister,' says the rat, glancing at the artwork above his cold bald head. 'This is a classy joint. And dead rats are bad for business.' He looks at his watch and tuts, but caves into the mountain's request. 'Ok, look, come this way but quickly cause I'm real busy ...and don't blame me if you end up a rug.' He hurriedly leads Jake towards the back of the restaurant, passed plenty of pompous diners, to a door clearly marked: 'No Entry'.

Omar Tiger spots the detective and watches his movements with interest;

he's in the midst of lunch with glamorous friends.

After a maze of corridors Jake finally finds himself in the lavish personal office of Mr Mason Gator (this is generally where the alligator tends to reside and snooze most mornings). The room looks more like a library, each wall laden with recipe books from *'The Joy of Oysters'* to *'Baking Made Simple' by Luigi Cockerel.* Curtains are drawn but there's ample light to make out the expensive golden carpet and the impressive desk it carries. Waiting behind the glossy workspace on a towering navy leather chair, we have the chunky lizard himself - comfortably the most feared chef in town.

Mason Gator -also known as 'El Caiman'- has his greedy green claws in plenty of pies and not just those of an edible kind. He owns the Sunset Grill, numerous blossoming restaurants, and a whole host of stores around the Kingdom - but there's also steady income through his partnership with various criminals. His specialty is stealing antiques and selling abroad, but that's not the extent of his dabbling's with unlawful activity. In 1947 the DPC (Department for Population Control) found a network of 'factories' in a valley, two hours south of Kingdom. Mason had been paying off rabbits to breed in an effort to create a larger workforce and cheaper labor. When cops finally kicked down the doors, they found close to three thousand 'cottontails' living in appalling cramped conditions. The laws of the land forbid any creature from bearing more than two offspring, due to the risk of over population and lack of resources - but each of Mason's rabbits had at least a dozen kids, if not more. Most of them worked at his restaurants but some were used for lucrative building projects. It's easy to win big contracts with a buck toothed army at your disposal. However, Gator's brash use of the workers and his naive attempt to muscle in on control of the dam, was inevitably his undoing (arresting officer: a younger and slightly more upbeat, Frank Penguin). Among other things he was found guilty of employing illegal staff and breach of the strict breeding rules, but he escaped with a measly three-year sentence. Only someone with a lion on their contact list escapes with such startling leniency.

'I'm sorry, boss, forgive me...claims he's a detective. Gimme me the word and I'll chuck him out,' says Frosty nervously and barely confident enough to make any eye contact.

A lavender suit topped with a white cravat - typical Mason. He's half-way through a bulky cigar. Clouds of smoke escape the giant juicy jaws of the chic beast as he stares at the bear on his priceless rug. Frosty gulps but Jake barely flickers as the huge gator stubs out his cigar and stomps around the desk for a closer inspection. The rat slides backwards till he's pinned against the books, keen not be involved in a scuffle. Gator and Bear are eye to eye, chest to chest. Mason suddenly unleashes a beaming smile and flings his short arms around the detective. Frosty is so shocked by the cuddle that his tongue nearly thumps the ground.

'Jake the bear. It's been too long,' bellows Mason in his slow husky voice, patting his old buddy on the cheeks. 'Heck, let me get you a drink. Frosty, a drink for my old pal Jake. Grew up in the same neighborhood. Our mamas were thick as thieves.'

Frosty still looks slightly bemused as he peels himself away from ten rows of classics.

'I'm good, I'm good,' says Jake, waving away the offer of a beverage while he takes a seat. Mason returns to the comfort of his leather throne.

'Will that be all, boss?' asks Frosty.

'Yes, thank you,' replies the alligator, toying with the idea of lighting up a fresh cigar, despite having only just finished the previous one.

'I'd hate to be your lungs,' utters Jake, staring at the mound of ash upon the desk.

'You're right, I should quit, I know. But you know me, Jake, old habits die hard.'

'I'd rather not discuss those old habits.'

'Here to arrest me, Jake?' replies the gator sarcastically, followed by another smile as he caves on his craving and lights up a smoke. 'I prefer it when the cops knock after lunch. Unpleasant to wait in a cell on an empty stomach.'

'Not this time, Gator. Although I'm sure there's laws against that outfit. You're spending too much time with chinchillas.'

Mason begins to laugh but finishes with an unpleasant phlegmy cough -

he can't be in the best of health. 'So, what can I do for my buddy? Assume you're not here for my fine shrimp salad?'

'Ok look, rumor has it that you might know something about a white gorilla,' says Jake hesitantly and fully aware of how ludicrous his line of enquiry might sound.

Mason doesn't laugh this time, nor splutter - in fact he suddenly appears quite serious. Another puff of foul smoke wafts through the air in the shape of a doughnut.

'*Rumor* has it? Heck boy, you mean that ol' meatball with the motor mouth. Wait till I get my claws on that blabbering buffoon,' scoffs Mason jokingly.

'All I care about is the gorilla, I swear.'

'I seen me a white gorilla, sure, but only once. I'd had a little disagreement with a pest over some money. He felt I'd been *less* than generous with his cut. I'll spare you the details, cause we just two old pals talkin' now right?' says Mason with a wink and a puff.

'Right. Anyway, we met right here, this very restaurant. Soon as the head chef quit his cooking and the closed sign dropped in the window, we have our lil meeting. We gotta come to some kinda arrangement. I have my usual posse keeping me company for a bit of protection. But the pest ain't alone either and rolls into town with his own little band o' brothers. In he walks, heck, with the meanest mob I ever did see, and I sure as hell seen plenty. Now I got twin bison behind me, both shakin' – and heck they're meant to be my damn bodyguards. Be honest with ya Jake, I'm a beefy old gator with eighty teeth and even I felt mighty darn queasy. First time I ever laid eyes on such a beast. Pure mountain o' muscle, with fists the size o' watermelons, face like thunder, and these crazy blood red eyes. No doubt about it...this was one *scary* lookin' ape. You kinda think that'd suffice, but heck there's two more, jackal and a hog. Not one of them said a word, not a peep or whisper. Hell, they didn't need to.' He shakes his head and splats the cigar on an ashtray.

Mason scratches his chinny-chin-chin with a claw. 'You still play cards, Jake? Well I do, and I know when I'm dealt a bad hand. The pest walked in with three aces. I had to pay up. Paid double to prevent any trouble. Heck, I don't like losing money you know that, but what could I do? And that was that, not had the pleasure of their company since, thank the lord.'

The suave gator stands and looks out the window, his stare lingering on freshly trimmed lawns. 'You really wanna chase monsters, Jake? At our giddy age?' he says, turning back to face his boyhood chum. 'I know we don't always see eye to eye, different sides of the fence and all that, but from one friend to another, these boys are dangerous... seriously dangerous. Maybe best to walk away from this one, while you still can, cause even old king o' the ring, Honeypaws, is no match for this thing.'

'Appreciate the warning, Gator, but polar bears ain't so great at walking away from danger. Just tell me one last thing...who was the pest?'

'Why, heck, *Johnny Beaver* of course.'

The plot thickens – but why would an associate of Johnny Beaver want to kidnap him and both his brothers? Was the gorilla even guilty? Maybe he'd paid an innocent trip to the motel and happened to leave some fur? Jake doesn't bother with notes - he stores it all his head, but he knows it's crucial knowledge.

The alligator escorts him off the premises, via a tour of the impressive grounds; thankfully, he never spots the police cars, waiting patiently in his pebbly car park – ready to assist the bear should chaos erupt. But fortune also favors the gator, in that Jake never inspects his kitchen. Had the detective demanded a view of the chefs, he would have met thirty bunnies and counting.

A leopard never changes its spots. Alligators never shake old habits.

11

A Parting Gift

'The racetrack please,' demands Eliana, sliding into the taxi.

Chico joins her in the back. 'Racetrack? What about the mayor and City Hall? We need the lowdown on those plans.'

'All in good time dear monkey. Look, the tracks on the way so I thought we could snoop around a little? Ask a few questions? Seeing as Lucas *was* there the night he was attacked...*detective*.'

The whistling wolf in the front seat was trying to mind his own business but can't help nudging his flat-cap and smiling in the mirror; Chico pretends not to notice.

'Ok, I suppose. But let's get one thing straight, this is *my* case, I make the calls. I'm letting you tag along, purely to keep you safe till this all blows over.'

'Well let *me* get one thing straight,' snaps Eliana, with a pointed finger. 'I crave the answers *just* as much as you do, so if I can help I will. I'm not a journalist, copper or private eye, but what I am, is an incredibly determined panther. So, you needn't fret or huff at my every suggestion. I'm simply providing assistance, free of charge, while I *tag* along.'

Chico is put in his place. He peers out the window and narrows his eyes while he juggles potential responses. 'As long as we're clear.'

'Crystal, Mr Monkey...crystal,' says the panther, peering out her own window.

The wolf correctly senses tension and tweaks the volume on the radio. They cruise the remainder of their journey to the soulful harmonies of 'Louis Llama and the Bears.'

Chico waves to the taxi. Eliana blows a kiss. The wolf dropped them off outside the San Shem Racetrack: one of the most popular sporting venues in town. They're just in time for the day's first race.

A bored hedgehog stuffed in a booth takes their money in exchange for standard tickets.

'Ever seen this guy at the track?' enquires Chico, splatting a picture of Lucas on the booth. The hedgehog takes a look but shakes his head.

'First time?' asks Chico, as they enter the arena and wander through crowds of punters. He flashes the picture of Lucas at all the passing faces, but it's only met with a shrug or frown.

'Sadly not, my father would often drag me along to these ghastly events. I'm not one for gambling, sport, or boisterous crowds...so I do hope our time here is brief.'

'Eyes peeled for a puffin. Used to work the beat back in West Bay. Great guy. Could be our ticket to a quick getaway.' The couple march along the railings that separate the swarm of fans from the track.

A line of horses approach the starting line. Roars of excitement pour from the bustling masses as six competitors await the sound of a gunshot that will send them hurtling towards the finish. Each is draped in their chosen colors: the heavy white stallion with blue and white stripes will surely go close. The lean grey in the middle looks mighty confident; his front left hoof drags along the ground scuffing up puffs of sandy dust. On the end is a horse which looks closer to timid pony; she's half the size of the grey, coated in chestnut brown, and a bag of sweaty nerves.

A fluffy grey cat in a green visor is sat upon a stool right beside the starting point. She raises her pistol into the air. As the deafening bang rings out around the track, each horse is up and away on only their two back feet, sprinting as quickly as possibly - to victory or crushing defeat. Bedlam ensues as hordes of wild animal's cheer on their pick of the bunch through screaming, jumping, waving, and prayer. But - would you believe it - a plucky 'pony' storms home first, much to the surprise of the others; her heart's twice the size of her legs. The tiny party of backers rejoice and scamper away to collect their considerable winnings.

The detective and nosy panther wriggle their way free of the mob, and onto the pleasant pastures of a crowd-less stable yard. A puffin armed with a rake is shifting bundles of hay, determined to make it tidy before all the new horses arrive. He also needs to dust down the sofas and check the televisions (horses love to relax before hitting the track). Like most puffins he's stocky with black and white plumage, and a multi-colored beak. His movement is incredibly slow due to a bad limp but he's content with his simple duties; the cheerful grin and constant hums are all the proof you need. Yet the humming stops, as does the raking, when he spots the shadow of two snoopers standing inside his doorway.

'You're not meant to be back here,' says Buddy angrily as he takes a break from staring at piles of hay to look at a pair of intruders.

'Wait a second...*Chico*...Chico Monkey, is that you?' His outraged expression vanishes in an instant and steps aside for joy. He drops the rake and shakes the hand of his favorite monkey.

'Long time, Buddy. Was worried you'd be retired by now.'

'Well, if I could afford retirement I most certainly would be. But coins for cleaning a stable and washing down horses ain't so bad. Plus, I get to watch a few races for free.'

'Buddy, this is Eliana Panther, she's a friend of mine. Eliana, this is the great Buddy Puffin, one of the finest cops to tread the streets of West Bay.'

'Lovely to meet you, Eliana. Ain't she a pretty thing.'

'I'm glad you're still here, Buddy. We could really use your help.'

'Help if I can. Course, memory ain't what it used to be though. Lucky if I remember what took place this morning in all honesty.'

'We think Lucas Panda, the detective attacked by the riverbank-'

'Yep seen the papers, poor thing.' Buddy scratches his chin, dusting off the cobwebs within his mind. He tries his best to think of anything helpful.

'Well, we think he may have come here, the night he got into trouble,' says Eliana, jumping in. 'He was coming to confront the mayor...possibly arrest him?'

'We thought that...I mean, Eliana suggested that we swing by here and take a look around. That's when I thought of you. If anyone at the track can help it's old Bud Puffin.'

Buddy's face suddenly comes alive as if a light bulb pinged above his head. He waggles his finger and looks once more at the ground, desperately trying to recall all the facts.

'That's right, why missy I think you're right, there *was* an incident. Must've been last week. Didn't see it mind, but folks round here kept hollering about it.'

'Anything you can tell us would be dreadfully helpful, Mr Puffin,' says Eliana. She pulls out a pad and pen, which wins her a sigh from Chico. 'Oh, do unscrew you're face monkey, it's a few harmless notes. I have no desire to steal your job...well, not yet anyway.'

'Way I heard it, missy, some detective approached the mayor in the *VIP* area up there in them stands, during the big race. Nobody mentioned a panda, but I suppose it must've been. I'm sure they said *two* detectives though, not one...or maybe I've got that wrong.'

'Two detectives, you're sure they said *two*? Did they mention a penguin?'

'Sorry, Chico, like I said, things are hazy upstairs these days. Pretty sure they said two...don't remember no talk of penguins though.'

'And, what happened?' Eliana cradles the puffin's cheeks in her hands, trying to force his concentration.

'Pretty *and* feisty ain't she, boy.'

'Tell me about it!'

'Well, I do believe there was some sorta scuffle, mayor didn't go quietly. But eventually he was cuffed and driven away.'

'Was the mayor alone? Who was he with?' asks Chico, scrawling notes on his trusty notepad - though half as many as Eliana.

'Well now, that I *do* know. Black Thunder won again that night, ten on the spin and his owner ain't missed a race. Same owner that *decides* if you're a V…I…P.'

Chico sighs with fear that he already knows the answer to his next question. His head presses firmly against the roof. 'This owner wouldn't be a mix of *bull* and *dog* would it by any chance,' he asks, kicking a small tuft of hay.

'Sure is. He a suspect or something?'

Chico drops his notepad and snaps his pencil with frustration. 'Everything leads to the dog. We need to kick his door down, right now.'

'Well, snapping pencils and tossing aside vital notes is hardly going to help now is it, Chico Monkey. And, neither is *kicking down doors,*' blasts Eliana.

'Right again there, missy. Best ya listen to reason, Chico, not rage.'

Chico mulls over his options for a moment. He picks up his notepad, dusts it off, and nods at the panther. 'Either of you got a spare pencil?'

Time to visit the mayor.

****

Police HQ. Everyone's hard at work, and the clock's a few ticks from lunchtime. *Ping* - the lift doors slide open, followed by a long-wet parcel slumping out onto the ground. A heavy slab of post reluctantly slides across the floor, kicked by a panting baboon; he's layered in sweat and struggling to catch his breath. Like all good 'chacma baboons' he's coated in grey fur with a long muzzle shaped nose, and close-set eyes below his impressive bushy eyebrows. Mucky brown overalls are his outfit of choice; it's been years since he put on a shirt.

'*Penguin*…I'm looking for a Frank Penguin,' he shouts, puffing between every word and clutching his lungs out of fear that he might collapse. 'Anyone seen a penguin?'

'What the hell…is that?' yells Jake, leaving his desk to investigate the mysterious package. 'Please tell me it's not a beaver?'

'No sir, but probably weighs the same mind you. Busting my back carrying this darn thing around,' replies the baboon, leaning backwards and stretching his spine.

'Frank,' says Squinty, tapping his desk. 'You got company.'

Frank looks up from his typewriter, unhappy that he's been disturbed. 'Yeah, what is it? I'm busy. Mail room's second floor ya schmuck.'

'Afternoon buddy, I'm Vincent, Vinnie's deliveries.' The baboon whips out a sheet of pink paper from his back pocket and taps it with a nibbled pen that had been resting above his ear. 'And it says here, *look*, to be personally delivered to the desk of Mr Frank Penguin. Signed by errr Mr Panda...a *Mr Lucas Panda.*'

Frank stops typing.

'You say Lucas Panda?' asks Yuriko, unable to resist the urge to join the peculiar scene. 'When was it sent?'

'Mmm let me see.' The baboon skims over the paper and flips it over. 'Ah yeah here we go, Friday morning, nine am.'

'We reckon he was attacked late Friday night, or early Saturday morning. So, he sends this just before he bumps into trouble,' says Frank, waddling towards the baboon while he scratches his beak.

Jake rubs his paws and can't stand still. 'Open it up, Frank. He was retiring remember, so it's probably a little farewell present. Ten coins says it's nothing but a stack of bamboo shoots.'

'Somebody fetch me a blade, and not you, Squinty.'

Yuriko grabs a reasonably sharp knife from a desk drawer and hands it to Frank. He wastes no time and plunges it through the brown paper wrapping, and slices along the side. 'I know that smell. Know it all too well,' he mumbles, ripping the paper away to reveal a humongous blackfin tuna.

Jake can't hold back a smile. '*Tuna.* That it? Just a big old tuna? I told you Frank. Just the perfect gift for his greedy partner.'

'Jeeze,' sighs Frank. 'Well somebody fetch some salad. Looks like lunch is on me.'

'No, *but look,*' says Yuriko, pointing a claw at the belly of the tuna. A short patch of black leather stitching lines the fish's gut.

'What the...?' Jake leans in close and peers at the tuna, sniffing while he handles confusion.

Frank slashes the stitches without a second's thought. He stuffs a wing in the tuna's belly and steadily has a rummage. 'Jackpot.' Out pops a sealed bag stuffed with a bundle of photos. 'My farewell gift.'

'Well, you don't see that every day,' remarks the surprised baboon, sliding his pen back behind his ear. 'Tuna with a taste for photography.'

Frank uses his teeth to rip open the bag, then lays three photos down on the floor. Picture number one shows a smartly dressed leopard outside a bar with a beautiful poodle. The second shows the same leopard with the same poodle sharing a candle lit dinner, *and* they are kissing. The final picture captures the leopard and poodle outside Emzara's Palace, arm in arm for a midnight stroll.

'Sheesh, that looks like Mayor Leopard. Who's the poodle?'

Jake crouches and stares at the piccies. 'That's the mayor alright. Don't recognize the dog.'

Yuriko is down on her paws and knees. 'You think Lucas blackmail mayor? Make no sense.'

'What about the beavers, Frank? We know he met them for supper. They must have had a role in all of this.'

'Why put the photos in a fish and send it here?'

'Well,' says Yuriko, chipping in. 'He probably knew life was under threat. *And* he knew that sending in tuna, big chance hungry Frank discover them. Bold, unique and genius idea if you ask me.'

Frank strokes his beak. 'Three photos stuffed in a bag. Stuffs them in the tuna before he gets in a scrape and arranges the delivery to me. He was taking precautions, a backup plan. Must've clocked someone was onto him.'

'Knew he was playing with fire. So hides the pics in case he gets burnt,' adds Jake. 'But why not leave them at his apartment?'

'In case the goon that attacked him got there before we did.'

'Now you need who and why?' says Yuriko, placing the photos carefully into a new, cleaner evidence bag. She hands them to Jake.

'I bet my left wing that damn mayors got some answers. Let's take a little trip to city hall.'

12

Trouble At The Top

George C Leopard was elected Mayor of Noah's Kingdom in 1948, but up until now there'd been no reason for cops to knock at his door. The vast majority of citizens saw him as a decent, hardworking cat, who was true to his word. Since his appointment, the tram had finally been put into action, employment rates had begun to rise, and four new schools arrived. Pockets of the city remain rife with crime and poverty, but he was making efforts to address these issues swiftly. Therefore, any involvement with the disappearance of Lucas Panda or three beavers would come as a complete surprise to his flock of devoted supporters.

Whispers of corruption were a common occurrence of course – but aren't they always where elections and mayors are concerned? Listen carefully to rumors exchanged in shadowy corners of local bars and you'll be enlightened on various conspiracies. Some of the more cynical creatures of Kingdom are *convinced* that Lioness Annabella runs the show and this leopard is merely a puppet. Unfortunately, proving such wild accusations and producing concrete evidence has thus far escaped the ability of all who would dare suggest it.

As you would expect, the mayor has a spacious office down at City Hall, slap bang in the beating heart of Noah's Kingdom. A towering white building shaped like a rocket and sat beside the river - yet prepare for thirty steps before you finally touch the entrance. Its neighbors are smaller structures (smaller rockets): mainly council offices and headquarters for major businesses such as The Mane Corporation which is a precious metal firm owned by the prosperous lion.

The mayor is currently chairing a meeting with two shady camels; both are wearing long brown tunics, unnecessary sunglasses, and red fez hats. A tailor-made pin stripe suit for the mayor which perfectly fits his slender figure - though spots would be more appropriate given his patterned fur. Also, in attendance are a serious looking anteater and an *even* more serious looking chameleon; both are wrapped in swish charcoal suits and acting deputy mayors. Everyone has the luxury of a brown leather swivel chair and a fabulous view of the city. The camels have travelled from overseas to discuss a new trade agreement, but the matter is struggling to reach conclusion.

****

Chico and Eliana slip into the City Hall reception and try their best to discreetly reach the elevator; they were hoping to avoid unwanted attention from the raccoon in charge of security.

No such luck.

'Hey, hey, where do you think you're going in such a hurry?' shouts the critter, leaning over his desk. 'Get back here!!!'

The monkey on tip toes and crouching panther both stop dead in their tracks. They lock eyes, and instantly regret not conceiving a more cunning plan. Reluctantly they march to the front desk like naughty school children caught by a canny teacher.

'Sorry, buddy, you looked busy. Thought we'd save you the hassle and head on up. Mayor's expecting us,' says Chico casually, trying his best to look important. The raccoon's unconvinced and not the type to cut corners when it comes to standard procedure. You can tell from his crisply ironed

108

light blue uniform, and rigorously buffed shoes that he takes his role very seriously.

'Can I see your passes please? You're meant to wear them at all times,' says the raccoon slowly and clearly. Chico slaps his police badge on the desk.

'Will that do?' replies Chico. He treats Eliana to a quick shrug of the eyebrows and a confident smile.

The strict security guard picks up the badge and examines it closely. 'Hmm alright detective, but the mayor's currently in the middle of an important meeting. If you take a seat, I'll let you know when he's available.'

The eyebrows slump. 'Yeah we kinda need to speak with him right now. How about you just turn a blind eye, while we mooch on upstairs and have a quick word with the boss?'

'I never turn a blind eye, detective, I'm professional at all times. And that's why I've won employee of the month three times.' The raccoon taps a glistening gold badge pinned to the chest of his uniform: *Employee of the Month*.

'Impressive. Maybe a few coins would help change your mind?' Chico winks and pushes shiny pieces of gold across the desk.

The raccoon tuts and looks at Chico with genuine disappointment. 'Keep your dirty money, monkey. Employees of the month don't accept cheap bribes.' All coins are nudged back into the monkey's furry hand.

Eliana barges in front of Chico and takes charge of the situation. 'Now look here, Mr Raccoon, we need to speak with the mayor *right* now. It's a matter of the utmost importance. There's a panda and three beavers missing, and the mayor might know why. So, we *shall* begetting in that elevator and so help me lord if I hear another peep or quarrel come from that tiny little mouth of yours. Is that understood?'

Security staff at City Hall don't get paid enough to justify riling panthers. Despite being frozen with fear he stutters a short response. 'Yes ma'am,' he whimpers, before quietly watching Chico and Eliana dash to the elevator. He removes his gold badge and tosses it over his shoulder.

****

'This is a reasonable offer, Mayor Leopard. We won't drop the price any further,' declares the shorter of the two camels in rather animated fashion. He's hunched over the desk, bidding to resolve the day's dueling.

The extremely serious chameleon leans across and shares his opinion via a quiet word in the leopard's ear. Mayor Leopard nods, mumbles a few sounds to make it clear he's listening, then nods a couple more times, before eventually standing and offering a handshake.

'Agreed,' announces Mayor Leopard with a suave smile. The camels accept the handshake followed by numerous bows to everyone present.

'Marvelous, you won't be sorry, Mayor Leopard. You won't regret your decision I promise you that. Let us celebrate tonight with a feast, I insist,' says the excited camel. His taller colleague seems quite content not to voice his own thoughts on the matter and is yet to share a word.

Before the mayor can reply to the camels offer, Chico and Eliana arrive to spoil the party.

'Eliana, what are you doing here? What's the meaning of this!?' yells the leopard.

'Shall I fetch security, sir?' The chameleon slithers off his seat in such a state of shock that his skin switches from fluorescent green to raging red.

Chico wastes no time in flashing his badge again. Everyone enjoys a clear look at the Kingdom Police Force logo while he clarifies his position. 'Detective Chico Monkey, Kingdom PD. Mayor Leopard, we need to ask you a few questions. Can you step outside please? Or ask your little buddies here to take a walk?'

'This is absurd, I demand to see a warrant. You'll be on traffic duties by morning, boy,' huffs the hot-headed ant eater. His long snout swings in the direction of the unwelcome duo.

The leopard seems more concerned with trade agreements and the maintenance of healthy relations with important foreign guests. 'I'm sorry gentleman, there's clearly been a misunderstanding. It's nothing, I promise. Maybe Mr Chameleon, Mr Anteater, you could escort our guests to the rooftop bar. I'll join you shortly,' says Mayor Leopard apologetically, trying to regain his composure, keep the peace, and remain civil. Both camels are slightly confused and not best pleased as the deputy mayors shepherd them out of the office.

Chico calmly helps himself to a comfy leather chair.

'You better have a good reason for barging into my office detective, *and* you Eliana. Mark my words, one phone call to Chief Vulture and you'll both be sorry.'

'I know about the plans, George,' says Eliana, reaching her point straight away.

'I found them in your drawer. You're under the bulldog's thumb, George, aren't you? Granting all his wishes, his grand designs for The Swamp...I just pray it's bribery and not your own greed.'

If the mayor was a tortoise he would've slipped back into his shell. The elected leopard is clearly hurt by the words ringing out from the panther's lips and at a loss on how to respond. But like all good politicians, he knows if all else fails - deny deny deny.

'I'm sorry, Eliana, that's just not true, not true. Lies I tell you, all of it lies,' he cries as his usual calm demeanor begins to implode. Eliana isn't stirred by the backlash and before the mayor can stop her, she drags out the bottom drawer of his desk. Pretty piles of blueprints still sit tightly inside; not of all them had found their way onto a beaver's fireplace.

'That's my private drawer, you can't just rummage through my office. Where's your warrant? I demand to see a warrant!!' continues the furious leopard, but his whining only falls on deaf ears. The blueprints have already found their way on to Chico's lap.

'My oh my, you have been a busy mayor,' says Chico, with a touch of delight. 'A casino, we got a hotel.....and what's this one, oh a nightclub. All signed off for construction in The Swamp. Amazing. I bet Salvatore just couldn't believe his luck when you *happily* agreed to build all these horrific ideas on top of our lovely forests and rivers.'

'Don't take that tone with me, detective. I'm friends with powerful people in this city. I signed off a few plans, *so what*, I'm the mayor. It's my job.'

'I know you, George. You're a good leopard and a good mayor. The George I know would never destroy The Swamp. It's home to hundreds of creatures…they'd be ruined, and for what? An ugly casino and another tacky hotel. Just tell him the truth, George, I'm begging you. He can help. He can protect you.'

Mayor Leopard stares out the window looking for his next move. He stares at his city, he stares at his dam, and he stares at inevitable defeat. 'I'm sorry, Eliana, I'm sorry detective. I can't help you I'm afraid…I'd be ruined too,' he mutters quietly. 'Unless you can prove any wrongful behavior has taken place, I'll have to insist you take your leave now…and hope we'll speak no more on the matter.'

No sooner had he finished his sentence when Frank and Jake explode into the office. Ruben and Yuriko wait outside and hold off the raging raccoon, who's failed miserably today to protect his mayor from interruptions.

'Kid? What are you doing here?' says Frank, with genuine surprise.

'Little chat with the mayor. Found his secret stash of blueprints.'

'Who are you?' I've had enough of this madness. Leave before I call Chief Vulture.'

Frank and Jake take a quick glance over the blueprints. The frustrated mayor now takes a seat and tries to make a phone call for some urgent assistance. Before he can beg the voice on the end of the line for help, three black and white photos slide before his eyes. He drops the phone.

Eliana also peers at the snapshots and suddenly it all makes sense.

'Bribery,' she says, almost with a sense of relief. 'It *was* bribery!'

Mayor Leopard almost manages a smile as he looks, not for the first time, at photos that had cost him everything. One last look at the poodle as he imagines what could have been. 'I was in love with a dog. A leopard that pined for a dog, that was my only crime. Taloolah Poodle, what a wonderful name, a wonderful soul, but I'm a happily married mayor right? And elections are coming. Three beavers show up with these photos, say I gotta play ball, sign off these plans for The Swamp. What could I do? What could I do? I *had* to do what they asked. It was the only way I could keep my job, the only way…they'd let me see her again.' He shakes his head and strokes the photo softly.

'They bribed the town planning chief and a number of other councilors too, so it wasn't hard to get the building permits granted. But, as for the beavers vanishing, well that's where I am innocent. I may be guilty of corruption gentlemen, may be a rotten mayor, but I can assure you there's no blood on these paws-.'

'What about Lucas?' asks Chico, taking a spin in his new favorite chair. 'He told Eliana that he was coming to take you down, the night he was attacked. Witnesses can testify they saw you scuffling at the racetrack. Say you were driven away in a vehicle.'

Frank has a million questions to ask but Jake leaps in first. 'Wait...who's Eliana? And why was Lucas after the mayor?'

'Vehicle? We never found a vehicle near the riverbank. Who was driving?' adds Frank.

'I'm Eliana,' says the panther, waving her hand regally. 'I used to be the mayor's secretary before he sacked me for questioning his behavior. And it was me who, regretfully, dragged poor Lucas into this mess and asked him to investigate. That night at the races, he must have uncovered the truth and tried to arrest the mayor. I dread to think what happened after that.'

The mayor holds his hands up, bubbling with anxiety. 'Ok ok, look...I did see Lucas that night, I was at the track. Salvatore wanted to speak with me and promised Taloolah would be there too, so I went along. We'd met there on previous occasions to discuss certain matters. I preferred it to meeting in his sleazy bar. Anyway, next thing I know, this panda barges in and arrests me. A few of Salvatore's pooches step in and there's a bit of pushing and shoving but nothing more than that. I called them off and agreed to go with the panda. I'm the mayor, I'm not going to resist arrest in front of a crowd.'

'And then what, how come you're standing here and not in a cell?' asks Frank, twitching slightly and clearly looking for reasons to launch a leopard out of a tenth-floor window. Jake lays a paw on Frank's shoulder - a silent suggestion that the penguin should keep his calm and listen to the all facts first.

Mayor Leopard takes a sip of water then continues. 'I'm cuffed and stuffed in the trunk of a car with a gag around my mouth, sack over my head, don't ask me why. Plenty of space on the back seat but he insists. He seemed nervous…like he was expecting trouble and wanted to hide me. I was jammed in there, pitch black and I'm next to a bag of golf clubs. Then we begin moving, except there's someone else in the car as well…I can hear another voice.'

'Another voice? What they say?' probes Jake, shuffling a step closer.

'Did it sound like a gorilla?'

'Would you know if you heard it again?'

'I'm not sure, they didn't say much, it was muffled. But not long after we left, the car came to a sudden halt…a nine-iron struck me right on the head. Then I hear both voices, sounded like they were arguing. I'm sure they get out of the car, doors slammed shut and I hear lots of voices and lots more shouting. Then nothing…silence.'

Everyone looks at everyone else. Nobody quite knows what to make of the story.

'Are you sure, George? Oh, please be truthful, George. You must recall something else, some clue to what happened?' begs Eliana, taking the mayor's hand. The leopard shakes off the contact and steps away, angry at the lack of faith in his statement.

'It's the truth. I know you all think I'm some good for nothing crook, but it's the truth. If I knew who was in the car, I'd tell you. If I knew what happened when they left the car, I'd tell you. All I know is, someone drove the car back to city hall and dumped me by the steps. Mr Raccoon found me when he arrived for his morning shift.'

Frank helps himself to one of the colorful treats on the table and drops a couple in his deep dark pockets. 'Ok I've heard about enough. You're coming downtown mister mayor and trust me, question time is *far* from over. Jake cuff him, no need to toss him in the trunk…unless he starts getting wise. We'll continue these discussions back at the station. Get Ruben and Yuriko to check out Lucas's car for clues and prints again. It's still parked outside his apartment. Chico, get these blueprints and photos back to HQ and I wanna statement from your lady friend here too.'

Eliana steps towards Frank and towers over him with both sets of sharpened claws placed firmly on her hips. 'I shall do no such thing. I demand to remain anonymous throughout this terrible affair. It's quite clear to me that someone from your law enforcement agency was involved with the kidnapping of poor Lucas. He told me as much the night he was attacked. Maybe it was this big polar bear oaf? Maybe it was you, mister impertinent penguin? How do I know? So, I mean to walk out this door *right* now and slip back into hiding, until you've done your job and brought the culprits to justice. I most certainly won't be strutting around your offices and interrogation chambers waiting to be permanently muted.'

Frank is stunned into silence himself, for the first time ever. It's usually just his wife who puts him in his place.

'It's ok, Frank, she's like this with everyone. You get used to it,' says Chico, grabbing the photos and blueprints.

'Good day gentlemen,' says Eliana, marching out of the office with her head held high, followed by Chico.

'Think we may have found the *new* mayor. I'd sure vote for her,' jokes Jake, cuffing the old mayor. The leopard is far too crushed to acknowledge the slight.

'Sheesh. You know what? She gets my vote too.' Frank stuffs one more treat in his pocket.

13

Rotten Apples

C hico and Eliana bid farewell to the halls of power. They're met by a strong gust of wind as they tackle the endless steps leading them down to the road.

Hudson Rhino waits at the bottom, slouched against his car with a chunky cigar to keep him company. As the monkey and panther finally complete their descent, he drops his roll of tobacco and squishes it with one of his feet (rhinos have rather dainty feet given the huge size of their bodies, so it's odd they never collapse in a heap).

'Chico, what you doing here? Thought it was Frank and Jake takin' down the mayor?' asks Hudson, before attention quickly shifts to Eliana. 'And who's the lovely lady? Hudson Rhino...pleasure to meet you.'

Eliana refrains from shrieking or striking a detective, as the rhino plants a slobbery unwelcome kiss right on the palm of her paw.

'Big mistake,' mutters Chico immediately, before madam panther can share another piece of her mind.

Too late.

'I'm Miss Eliana Panther, and if you ever touch me again with that hideous tongue, I *shall* remove it.'

Hudson typically responds with a big smile and complete oblivion to the hornet's nest he was poking. 'Easy lady, just being friendly. You must be new on the force?'

'She's just a friend, and she's had a tough day. What brings you here? Frank and Jake are bringing him in,' says Chico, balancing numerous blueprints over his shoulder.

'Jake mentioned a bust on the mayor. Said I'd swing by in case the old timer needed some backup. What's with all the paperwork?'

'These, oh just blueprints. Turns out the mayor was granting stacks of building work for Salvatore Bulldog. They blackmailed him with this pile of black and whites.' Chico gives the rhino a flash of the photos. 'Caught red handed with a poodle that wasn't his wife. You believe that? All this chaos for a pretty dog.'

'Always said that spotty sleazebag looked suspicious.'

'Anyway, if you wanna help out, I wouldn't say no to a ride. Need to drop this off at the station pronto.'

'Sure, hop in. Sweet cheeks joining us too?'

'I'm perfectly alright thank you.'

Chico turns to Eliana with eyebrows in fully raised mode. 'Come on, Eliana. He can drop you off at mine on the way.'

Eliana wastes no time in firing back a firm confirmation of her preferred method of transport. 'Chico, I think I made myself *quite* clear in there with your colleagues.'

Hudson shrugs with confusion and climbs into his car. 'Suit yourself, pussycat.'

'I'll see you later then.' Chico nods and hands Eliana the key to his apartment, before joining Hudson in a cozy little police car. Due to the extreme weight on the driver's seat, their departure from the scene isn't particularly speedy. As they plod off down the road, a taxi appears in the distance; Eliana waves and waves like a panther possessed until it eventually arrives at her side. A friendly looking squirrel in a sky-blue sports jacket leans out the window. She smiles but opts for a seat in the back - small talk with taxi drivers really isn't her style, no matter how friendly.

Half-finished pastries and empty bottles of soda jostle around on the back seats as the rhino's messy ride chugs along its course. A tree shaped air freshener dangles from the rear-view mirror and faces a futile battle. The car begs for a wash and a whole new interior, though it might be easier if Hudson is introduced to the benefits of Kingdom's tram network. That said, the rhinoceros doesn't appear in the least bit concerned, and even sparks up his next cigar to puff on throughout the journey. It's extremely likely that the lungs and major organs buried inside this rhino are in just as sparkling condition as his transport.

Chico was hoping to catch some winks, but he's kept awake by the rhino's incessant chatter. Each anecdote is louder, lewder and longer than the last. Hudson occasionally slaps his knee or ruffles the monkey's reddish fur- a reminder to chuckle and pay attention. It's fair to say, that for Chico, the first twenty minutes of the journey feels like an excruciating lifetime.

The deal was a free trip back to the station, but the car takes a wrong turn and Chico is swift to realize. 'Thought we were heading back to HQ?' he says, looking over his shoulder at the route they should have taken.

'Need to swing by a buddy of mine, won't take long. What's the rush anyway? You and that crazy lady got plans?' Hudson executes his trademark smile again - the one that signals when he's being annoying.

'No, it's just...well, Frank wanted me to get all this stuff back. That's all,' replies Chico sheepishly. He realizes he's been sitting on a festering doughnut and tosses it on the pile behind him.

'The panther, she a journo or somethin'? Seems like the type,' asks Hudson before another long puff.

'She's a former secretary, a scary force of nature, and she helped us catch the mayor. Might be in danger as well given what she knows, so I promised to look after her till we solve the cases,' replies Chico, trying his best not to touch anything for fear of catching disease.

'So, the mayor fessed up to all this corruption business then? Say anything about Lucas, or them beavers?'

'He's involved for sure, but I don't think he arranged any kidnapping...doesn't seem the type. Way I see it, he was bribed by the beavers into signing off these plans for the dog. Agreed to everything just to see his cute poodle friend again. Then Lucas finds out about it and arrests him, so Salvatore sends a posse on a rescue mission. They catch up further down the road and attack him.'

'Must have been this *white gorilla* though, right? Who pinched ol' Luc and snagged the beavers I mean? All makes sense now. That's who we need to find. Big damn gorilla.' Hudson slaps Chico on the shoulder as if he's single-handedly solved the case. Chico isn't so sure and pulls out his notebook. His head shakes as fingers flick through pages of jumbled messages and various ludicrous doodles.

'Eliana is certain that Lucas took a friend the night he made the arrest. She thinks it could be a cop.'

'*A cop*? What like Frank? How's the panther know that?'

'She doesn't know who it was but she's sure he wasn't alone because he phoned her that evening and mentioned taking a buddy. *And* the mayor said the same thing. *Two* people in the car he said. Surely Frank wouldn't turn on Lucas, would he? He didn't flinch when the mayor mentioned it, plus he loved the guy and despises Salvatore.' Chico's head is close to exploding with confusion. He kicks a box of decaying shrimps to vent the irritation.

'You know what, monkey, between me and you, I seen a lot of good cops cross the street. One second they're kissing the badge, next thing, too many unpaid bills, they need the money, bingo bongo, they join the bad guys. Sad, I know, and it's never the ones you suspect neither. Lot of good apples turn out rotten.'

Hudson slams the breaks as they hit the traffic lights. The car behind toots it's horn, so a fuming rhino leans out the window and waves a stocky arm. While he trades insults with gridlocked drivers, Chico notices a slip of paper resting by his foot. Previously it was hidden by shrimps but now it catches the eye. Chico thinks he can read what it says but picks it up to be completely certain. He was correct.

'Stupid traffic, busiest time of the day. Should have taken a short cut. Don't worry, monkey, not far now.'

'Black Thunder,' whispers Chico, his eyes glued to the single slip of white paper.

'What you say, monkey? Speak up. What's that your holding?' Hudson loosens his collar. 'Is it me or is it getting hot in here?'

'Black…Thunder,' repeats Chico again, though louder this time, more confidently and with eyes fixed on Hudson.

The rhino appears confused. There's that smile again but this time it looks more forced. 'Black Thunder? What are you talking about, chimp? What is that?' he says trying to remain playful but snatches the slip away and takes a look himself.

'That's a betting slip for Black Thunder, Salvatore's horse. He won that night…the night Lucas was attacked. You were there weren't you? The other cop, it's you. *You* were there at the track with him. And no, it's not hot in here Hudson…it's ice cold.'

Hudson dismisses the slip and lets it fall out his hand. Another puff on the cigar while he looks straight ahead, waiting for the green light. 'I was there watching the race yeah. I like the horses, so what, that a crime? Maybe Lucas was there too, I dunno, didn't see him. I was just there with a few buddies of mine. Sue me.'

'You're the rotten apple, Hudson. *Why?*'

Hudson slams his horn, clears his throat loudly, and tries once more to loosen the collar. A twitching wreckage of nerves now sits in the driver's seat. He flicks his cigar out the window before finally facing the monkey.

'Betting slip,' he says, chuckling to himself. 'Caught out by a damn betting slip.'

'Hand yourself in, Hudson, you're finished. Don't do something stupid,' says Chico, suddenly realizing the difficulty of arresting a rhino who may choose to resist.

'You know what, monkey, my mother was right…gambling *is* a suckers game.'

'Hudson, step out of the vehicle, you're under arrest.'

The rhino sighs, holds up his hands, and steps out of the car. Plenty of horns from the traffic jam explode into full swing as Chico slides out too. His heart pounds like a drum solo, his tummy twists as much as it tightens, and sweat begins to seep from every inch of his slender shaking body. He whips out his cuffs.

'You know the drill,' says Chico nervously. Traffic lights switch to green but the rhino's 'junkyard on wheels' remains a blockade for all the parade of cars that trail it. Tooting and yells of despair get louder and louder.

Hudson places his hooves on the roof of the car and doesn't say a word.

Chico approaches slowly and carefully, fully aware that if things turn sour, he could potentially be in danger. The raging noise of the cars seems to reach near deafening levels, as the anxious monkey side steps his way behind Hudson and prepares to slap on the shackles. 'Hands behind your back please,' he says firmly, trying to convince himself he's in control of the situation.

'Sure thing, monkey,' huffs Hudson before slamming a left elbow backwards into Chico's stomach, instantly winding him. The helpless monkey drops the handcuffs, slumping in pain to the ground. He clutches his gut and desperately fights to breathe. Horns and yells from the traffic jam fade away, replaced by looks of shock and horror. Drivers and passengers step out to improve their view, but none are willing or daring to intervene.

Unfortunately for poor Chico this happens to be a quiet part of the city, hosting only derelict towers; the streets are bare, and you could count on one hand the number of faces at windows. Chico drags himself off the ground, but Hudson hammers his jaw with a fist, sending him flying backwards into a puddle by the side of the road. Face down and motionless he lays in muddy water, while Hudson turns on the mob behind him. A rowdy crowd of animals has gradually formed, all booing and jeering this despicable behavior. The rhino pulls out his badge and holds it aloft.

'Police business, police business…get back in your vehicles right now. Anyone else wanna take a nap in the mud? Yeah, so back in your vehicles right now!!'

Suddenly Hudson spots a creature climbing on top of a car, fifth in the queue. The mysterious figure leaps to the car in front, then the next, then the next. The crowd watch in amazement as Eliana Panther skips from car to car, before throwing herself at the rhino. She growls, sinking each of her bladed teeth into his thick-skinned throat, before furiously flinging her claws across his face. Streams of blood pour down Hudson's cheeks, gushing around his neck like a ruby red necklace - but a cat's no match for a warrior such as this and the best she can do is stall him.

Enraged, the riled rhino charges at Eliana and butts her with his long pointy horn. She slides across the road with a scream and into the hands of the rabble. Hudson senses the crowd's fury and jumps back into his car, as several creatures finally find courage and start to charge towards him. Not the ideal set of wheels for a getaway but he manages to escape all the same – *with* the blueprints and photos.

'Are you ok?' asks a concerned zebra, helping Eliana back to her feet.

'Of course not, madam. Look what he's done to my favorite dress, not to mention my pride. I truly utterly detest the taste of defeat,' snaps Eliana, dusting herself down and assessing the damage to her polka dotted frock. Suddenly she remembers Chico. How could she forget? The small group tending to his wounds stand aside as she runs to his aid. He's out of the puddle but not out of slumber and far from over the pain. Eliana strokes his head and holds his hand.

'I'm so sorry, Chico. I shouldn't have let you get in that car. I had my suspicions the second I smelt his breath.'

Chico stirs to the sound of her voice, like someone enjoying the comfort of perfect dreams.

She smiles and strokes his head once more.

'Miss...*there* you are, I thought you were skipping the fare. I'm parked down the street if you need a helping hand?'

Eliana looks up to see the friendly squirrel, and his sports jacket, looking back at her. Not quite a knight in shining armor, but a welcome sight all the same.

'Perfect timing, Mr Squirrel,' she says. 'Now could somebody help me carry this poor detective.'

The pack of onlookers duly oblige.

14

Supper With Flightless Birds

His eyes peel open slowly. A thumping migraine and spells of dreadful dizziness make it tricky to know where he is. It's a cozy bedroom with low ceilings and ugly lime green walls. Plenty of traffic makes plenty of noise outside an open window. Stars beam brightly across a moonlit sky, suggesting that hours have passed since he was last awake - unless Hudson had a left-hook which knocked you out for days, but that was unlikely (an uppercut from Jake however, and it's la la land for a week).

'Where am I?' he mumbles, trying his best to sit up. The injured monkey is wrapped up tight with fresh linen sheets, his head sunken deep into a puffy feather pillow. Certainly not the last place he remembers - this is notably comfier and lacking a treacherous rhino.

Chico spots a small picture frame on the bedside table, a faded sepia photo of a young female penguin: she's smiling and dressed for a wedding. Somehow, he finds himself at the residence of Frank Penguin, resting beside a picture of his beloved daughter, Maria. He gently holds the picture with both hands and makes a brief inspection. 'Much prettier than your father.

Happier too,' he remarks, before placing it back on the table. 'Must take after the mother.' Chico cringes with discomfort and rubs his head; the healing process is evidently far from complete. The jaded chimp considers returning to sleep when the door creaks open an inch. Frank's ever frowning head peers delicately around the corner, fearful of waking his guest - except that guest has already risen and is staring at the bird with bewilderment. Frank drops his efforts to enter the room on tip toes, sighs, and saunters in to check on his partner's condition.

'Damn it, he's alive. I bet twenty coins with Yuriko you wouldn't make it,' chirps Frank, slapping his friend on the back. Chico winces again, his aching body is not yet ready for slaps, pats or even friendly jabs. 'Sorry, kid, how you feeling? Sounds like you took one hell of a whack.'

'Well, I can see *four* Frank Penguins standing in front of me right now. So yeah, it's pretty bad.'

'Four Frank Penguins? Hmmm maybe this is heaven, kid?'

Chico rustles up a smile oozing with sarcasm. 'How did I wind up at your home anyway?'

'How d'you know it's *my* home?'

'Picture of a penguin on the table and the bed sheets smell of shrimp.'

'My daughter, this was her old room, before she got married and shacked up with some lousy two-bit lawyer.'

'But how did *I* end up here? I should be down at Kingdom hospital with some gorgeous monkey nurse looking after me and feeding me grapes.'

'You fancy another slap? My wife's been working her wings off to keep you tickin', kid. Her and the wolf. Your little lady friend, the panther with the anger issues, she brought you to the station in a taxi. And she told us what happened with that scumbag rhino,' rants Frank, forgetting to breathe from time to time.

'Jeeze, kid, we got every pig in the force working shifts all night. We're searchin' every corner of the city, lookin' for that no-good piece o' work. Jake, Ruben, and Thelma all out lookin' too, but we'll find him don't you worry. Dumb rhino's never get far. Anyways we brought you back here, just to be safe.'

'Thanks, Frank, and thank your wife, I mean it. Thought it was the end of the road when I saw that big old fist flying towards me.'

'Glad you're alright, kid, glad you're alright.'

'I need to thank Eliana too. Sure, there's a bit of a short temper, but she's a good egg, Frank.'

'Sounds like she's the one protecting you, kiddo. Look do what you gotta do…wanna look after her, fine… but remember she ain't got a badge. She says she knew Luc, but for all we know she's involved, so just be careful what you tell her.'

'Sure thing partner,' says Chico, wading through the pain barrier to attempt a climb out of bed.

Frank lends him a helping hand. 'Sure you wanna do this? Yuriko and the wife said plenty of rest. I tend not to argue with either.'

Chico looks at Frank and plants a firm hand on his shoulder. 'I will rest once we find out who snatched Lucas Panda and the Beaver Brothers. Until then, Frank…I shall not rest.'

Frank smiles. 'Alright, that's the spirit,' he says, slapping his back once again.

Chico winces and bites his tongue. 'Ok maybe I better rest…little bit longer, gimme an hour, tops…actually make that two. Cause now I'm seeing six frank penguins…not good.'

Frank sighs and swaggers his way out the room.

Chico falls back onto the bed to catch more precious winks.

'The Chuck Rabbit Quartet' is playing quietly on the radio, though the sound is somewhat scratchy. Detective Chico Monkey finally finds the strength to join his friends in the living room. Frank is busy flicking through the evening edition of the Chronicle, happily swaying back and forth on a rocking chair. Yuriko and Eliana are squidged on a miniature couch playing cards. But the rocking stops and Yuriko spills her aces, the second they all spot Chico.

'Oh, Chico,' bellows Eliana, leaping off the couch - much to the delight of Yuriko. She throws her arms in the air, wraps them around the flustered chimp, and hugs him as tight as she can. 'I'm so happy you're ok, really I am.

Promise me there'll be no more scuffles with horned beasts twice your size?'

Chico smirks, escaping the firm grasp of Eliana's embrace. 'Trust me, I'm done with fighting bulky lumps. He nearly whipped my head off.'

'You're very lucky monkey,' says Yuriko, patting the penguin's shoulder. 'Another blow from Hudson and we'd be fitting you up for coffin.'

'Thanks for taking care of me, wolf. Owe you one.'

The hypnotizing smell of cooked fish fills the air. Chico's nostrils flare as they pick up the scent and he's curious to know where it hails from. His busy nose drifts towards a door in the corner. Suddenly that door crashes open, nearly knocking out Chico again, and a hefty penguin storms in the room with haste, carrying boiled squid. She lays the tray of feasts on the table and removes her grotty apron. Calamari drizzled with lemon, garlic, and oil. Supper is served.

'Honey, this is Chico. And Chico, I'd like you to meet the empress and love of my life, Mrs Dolores Penguin,' says Frank proudly, whilst swapping a chair that rocks for a sturdy one tucked beside the dinner table. Dolores is taller and rounder than her husband with tufts of yellow fur along her chest: she's also more courteous, approachable, and positive than grouchy Frank.

Mrs Penguin scoops a dollop of steamy squid onto five patterned plates, already laid at the table. Frank opts out of a knife and fork, ploughing in with his beak instead, but a nifty whack to the back of his head soon puts an end to that (Dolores is a strong advocate for impeccable manners under her roof).

'Francis' favorite dish. Isn't that right dear?'

'I told you honey, don't call me Francis around the guys,' moans Francis James Penguin knowing an inevitable ribbing was forthcoming.

Chico's face beams with delight upon hearing his partner's cute little name. 'Yeah tell us about your favorite dish...*Francis*.'

'One more peep from you *Charlie* and you'll be seeing stars again,' snaps Frank. Inevitably, this earns him his second whack of the evening.

A particularly unhealthy chocolate dessert and numerous fruity drinks follow the main meal. Time flies. As the sun sets on Noah's Kingdom this merry little group arrive once again at the hot topic of Hudson Rhino and four missing animals.

'So, this Salvatore guy pays off Hudson to help him kidnap Lucas,' says Chico while Mrs Penguin clears the table around him. He kindly passes his dirty dish, before a glug from his mug of 'Mango Heaven'.

Yuriko shakes her head. 'Slashes on Lucas's coat not made by rhino though. Definitely some form of canine. Hudson involved but he didn't attack Luc, and I doubt he kidnap beavers either.'

Frank is deep in thought and back in full swing on the rocking chair. 'Luc arrests the mayor at the racetrack. Then something happens on the journey back, probably an ambush. Luc thinks the rhino's got his back but yada yada we know the rest. Winds up in a tussle on the riverbank. Rhino drives the mayor to city hall, ditches him right outside.'

'Then you arrested George, sorry...*the mayor*, and that rhino *thing* has to try and gets hold of the evidence which might incriminate Salvatore, so he agrees to give Chico a ride,' adds Eliana, licking drops of chocolate off her claws.

'Who's the white gorilla then? Where's he fit into all this? And why pinch the beavers? I thought they were working for Salvatore as well,' blasts Chico. 'We're missing something, Frank, and it's giving me another crazy headache.'

Frank nods and rocks in agreement. 'You're right, kid, something don't smell right, and not just my breath. Let's hope that rhino's as dumb as I think he is...cause he's got some explaining to do.'

15

Confessions Of A Rhino

The crown of the sun rises over the deep blue sea and a glorious new morning arrives. A vulgar white van parks up outside police HQ; the engine sounds close to death and the exhaust splutters tar colored smoke. Two doors at the back *ping* open and Hudson rolls out with a suitcase full of evidence – assisted by two hooded figures suspiciously shaped like bison. Feet tied, hands tied, and a gag around his mouth - the rhino crumbles concrete as he crashes down on to the ground. As soon as he lands, the poorly disguised twins yank the doors shut and kickstart a hasty getaway. Hudson tries to shout and scream but his efforts are muffled by the hankie wedged in his cakehole. He can only watch as his captors race into the distance, leaving a fog of dirty fumes.

A bewildered officer pig approaches the angry delivery. His eyes dart around, convinced this must be some sort of prank. Hudson has abandoned any attempt to escape and lays in silence while he awaits arrest – staring up at the clouds while he deals with utter embarrassment. The pig carefully grabs the suitcase, and a rolled-up note poking from the rhino's pocket: *For the attention of Jake Bear. Care of Mason Gator and Fat Chinchilla.*

Not before long, Hudson is hoisted away for questioning. Jake is kind enough to drag him through the office by his horn and toss him in a vacant room. Unlike many visitors he's awarded no coffee, no call, and no seat (corrupt cops tend to be denied standard privileges). Instead he's stashed against a chilly wall and yet to shake the handkerchief. He isn't graced with the presence of a regular interrogator either, but rather Chief Vulture, who suddenly enters the room and enters alone. Wrapped in black as per usual, you'd be forgiven for thinking the grim reaper had paid a visit; either way it wasn't good news for Hudson. She leans in slightly with her talons behind her back, so that her crooked beak can touch his funnel shaped ear.

'Listen to me *very* carefully, rhino. I will not tolerate treason within this force, I will not see our spotless reputation dragged through the dirt, and I will not sit back while you jeopardize my rightful position to lead this force. Is that clear?'

'Police corruption never makes for pretty headlines and none of us wish to see it, certainly not the powers that be. You have betrayed your colleagues, betrayed your kingdom, and you have betrayed yourself. It cannot and will not go unpunished. If you wish to see the light of day again, then I strongly suggest you tell the truth, the whole truth, and nothing but the absolute truth. Though I might add…even that may fail to save you now.'

The vulture finishes her veiled threat and departs the room, leaving Hudson alone to mull over his situation - but his mulling is quickly quashed by the arrival of Jake. The bear hooks away the handkerchief, then leans against the back wall with those big old arms folded across his chest.

'It's all over, Hudson,' growls the bear. 'So, spill the beans. What happened to Lucas?' He stands and stares. The rhinoceros matches his stare with stubborn determination not to crack so freely.

'I ain't frightened of you, Jake. Or that old hag. I'm saying nothing.'

'Oh, you'll talk,' says Jake coolly. 'The judge is gonna put you away for a long old time, and the last thing Hudson Rhino needs is a *cozy* little reunion with all them nasty mammals rotting away behind bars cause he stuck 'em there.'

Hudson snorts and gawks at his twiddling fingers, trying to blank out the threats and focus on hiding the truth – but the cracks are starting to show.

'Maybe we could hook you up with Scarface Armadillo again. Be like old times,' says Jake sarcastically, with his deep gravelly tone. 'Hey, isn't Deontay Dragon banged up down at South-Central slammer as well? I'm sure he'd just be *itching* to meet a fine detective like you.'

Hudson closes his eyes, rolls both hands into fists, and looks above to the ceiling; maybe he prays for a God to come and save him, but on this occasion none of them do. Instead he's left to wrestle with the uncomfortable prospect of prison and potentially fatal reunions.

'Maybe you could share a six by eight with that charming maniac...what was his name? Ah yes...Rocky Cheetah.' Jake delivers his quip with enough glee and gusto to send the rhino toppling over the edge. The horned villain hammers his elbow against the wall with absolute rage and frustration, before slamming a clenched fist down on the ground. His unprovoked attack on a freshly painted wall and green linoleum floor leads him no closer to freedom - but it does leave him with a rather sore arm.

'Alright!! alright, I was at the track with Lucas...I needed the money. Like I told the monkey, we all got bills to pay. The dog throws me bones for favors once in a while, that's all. And I didn't do no kidnapping before you think about jumping me. Salvatore said the panda was sniffing around the mayor and it was bad for business. The dog's got all these construction deals in place and Luc was gonna ruin all that, no pay day for anyone. So, yeah, I warned Luc, said let it go, don't touch the mayor, but would he listen? Course not. Stubborn as his pesky penguin partner.'

Jake unfolds the arms and takes a step closer, his tired old face lit up by the lonely bulb hanging directly above.

'What happened down at the track, Hudson?'

'Nothing...to begin with. We watched a couple of races, I bet on a few of the losers. It was just, you know, like a regular night...bottles of soda, I bought some crab, he picked the oysters, usual kinda thing. Everything was fine, then the big one, the big race...and that's when it all got crazy. The second Black Thunder crosses the line, he spots the mayor and Salvatore schmoozing up in the stand. I try and warn him again, *not a smart move panda,* but the moron arrests the leopard and drags him back to my car.'

'And then what?'

'He's spooked that someone's been following him, so we gotta gag the stinkin' cat and drop a sack on his head. Straight after that we hit the road, head for the bright lights. Suddenly this blue van appears out of nowhere, blocks our way. Luc steps out, walks towards it, bold as brass!! I'm thinking it's a pack of dogs come for an ambush. Well, I don't need to see that, so I put my foot down, got the hell out and didn't look back. Ditched the mayor at city hall, then home sweet home. Next time I see Luc...he's splashed across the front of the Chronicle.'

'See anyone get outta the blue van?' asks Jake, stroking his furry chin.

'Not a thing, could have been a dog, gorilla, something else, I got no idea. Didn't hang around to find out.'

'Sounds like the van from the motel,' remarks Jake.

'What I gotta do for a coffee and a doughnut? I'm dying here,' moans the hungry rhino clutching his enormous belly (he's used to consuming vast quantities of food at regular intervals).

The polar bear happily ignores the plea.

'You'll be lucky if you get a jug of swamp water after what you did. Now tell me about the beavers,' snaps Jake, returning to more pressing matters than lunch time.

'Listen ya dopey bear, I ain't never even met those dirty beavers. Got nothing to do with me...I swear. Maybe I heard Salvatore mention them once or twice but that's all. They did favors for money same as me. I know as much as you do...Salvatore got them to bribe the mayor with photos. Next thing they been grabbed by some ape in need of a suntan.'

'Maybe Salvatore wanted to teach 'em a lesson? Maybe he wants you hushed up too?' suggests Jake, tapping the table with claws while he considers the possibilities.

'*Maybe* I'm tired of answering all your stupid questions, Jake. I didn't touch the beavers and frankly, I don't care who did. And you know what, until I see a box of six doughnuts and a fresh cuppa coffee, I ain't saying another word.' Hudson returns to twiddling fingers, like a stroppy child who can't have it all his own way.

Jake nods and decides to take a break from questioning, for now. 'Let's find you a cell, fit for a snake. Preferably chilly with zero windows.'

Hudson confessed to collusion with Salvatore – confirmation that the dogs were involved. That morning also provided a breakthrough with sneaky Old Badger – who, on the promise of witness protection, came clean about the *unsavory* savory goods produced beneath his bookstore – and made a point of implicating the bulldog. Evidence galore and enough to obtain an arrest warrant. Finally, and much to his delight, Frank was authorized to take down the doggies. He rallies the troops and sets off to bag his nemesis.

16

Has Its Day

Most species within the city are quite content to mingle and live among the others. It's not uncommon to find a family of elephants who invite the neighboring mice around for tea (and dunkable chocolate biscuits). Nor is it unheard of for a cougar to escort an elderly pigeon across the street. Or find a penguin who works with a monkey, despite contrasting tastes and temperaments. The majority of animals live together in harmony, embracing the variety of creatures they call a friend. But there are some communities, such as that of the dogs, who would much prefer to simply stick with their own. It's seldom you find a pooch who strays too far from New Carnival. They tend to stay close to home - in a run-down patch of scummy land, more commonly known as 'The Dog District'. Though from time to time you find the odd exception, such as Taloolah Poodle, who fell in love with a mayor and yearned to be a leopard, free of her miserable life in a ramshackle bar.

The lunchtime crowd at The Hound Lounge aren't a particularly impressive bunch. A handful of lonely dogs coming to drown away their sorrows – yet

Taloolah always tries her best to raise their spirits. They sit out of sight and hide in the shadows, cursing a pointless existence, while she lights up the stage with only the help of a fragile stool. Even the moodiest pups, hugging their half empty glass of doom and gloom, can't help but be moved by her abundance of magical melodies. And like all great poodles she certainly isn't lacking in hair; the slender face and sweet button nose are engulfed by a big ball of fluff - all of it white and carefully groomed.

She composes herself for the next of her ditties. A tail sneaks out of her slinky black dress and wags like a feathery duster.

An over eager golden retriever stumbles towards the stage but he's greeted by a couple of Dobermans; they're modelling black suits, sharp white ties, and extremely sour faces. They immediately drag the pest away and ditch him out back in the alley - with a clear message not to return. Nobody moves an inch the second that singing begins; even Sid Dachshund behind the bar ceases cleaning glasses to relax and enjoy the performance.

Bathed in red smoky light Taloolah delivers a note perfect rendition of 'Dream A Little Dream', bringing a tingle to each spine in the room. The poodle chuckles to herself with embarrassment, struck by the sea of slackened jaws.

Sid's so engrossed that he barely notices his tongue flop over his chin, nor the parade of new punters quietly entering right behind him. Half the Kingdom Police Force are now witness to the fine vocals on display, steadily piling into the lounge and waiting at the back for the song's conclusion. Frank, Chico, and Jake huddle tightly beside the entrance – each of them bewitched by the poodle's spell. Even Yuriko and Ruben join the crowd in time to catch the last few verses; they were due a day off but didn't want to miss the occasion, for it's not each day you see a crime boss delivered comeuppance.

The show eventually draws to a close. All the lonesome dogs, representatives from the local police force, and unpleasant Dobermans, applaud wholeheartedly. A couple of beagles are even brought close to tears. Taloolah acknowledges the warm reception by way of numerous bows and a shake of the wiggly tail.

The cops pounce.

'Where's the bulldog ya mangy pooch?' yells Frank to one of the Dobermans, who's now surrounded by pigs and a polar bear. The other Doberman's already in cuffs and heading for a glowing mauve 'exit' sign, courtesy of Yuriko Wolf.

'Out the back, first left,' mumbles the Doberman reluctantly with paws held high.

'Pigs. Cuff him. Take him away,' hollers Frank, looking for the door that leads out back. Two of the pigs grab the Doberman and escort him outside so he can join his touchy colleague. 'Kid, you're with me. Jake, Peggy, find that poodle. See if she talks as good as she sings.'

Ruben leads a group of pigs through a set of double doors, right into the middle of a tension packed pool match between a greyhound and hustling husky.

'Game's over folks,' announces Ruben, confidently for once and secretly proud of his cheesy line. His troop of piglets round up the doggies for a nice little trip in a police car.

Another team of officers with snouts descend upon the kitchen. Pots are bubbling and something smells delightful, but conditions are overwhelmingly filthy. Hygiene is clearly not high on the priority list for this particular catering team. The canine chef and his puppy assistants are far from amused with the surprise invasion, yet efforts to resist are short and futile. Meals are left to simmer and burn as one by one they're marched out into the daylight, guided by regular prods in the back from an efficient Kingdom pig force.

First door on the left. Frank looks at Chico, winks, and swings the handle anti– clockwise. Penguin enters first like always, while Chico glances over his partner's shoulder and crouches forward in a hesitant manner. His spine resumes its usual position when he lays eyes on the bullish gangster.

Sat behind a modest desk laden with stacks of coins and various medication, is an elderly bulldog half-way through a plate of healthy lunch. However, it's the red velvet dressing gown with quilted silk collar that first catches the monkey's eye; you usually find such obscure gowns wrapped around fat chinchillas. His drooping bloodshot eyes are magnified by thick brown glasses; he presses them gently as he looks up from his meal to see who dares interrupt him. Salvatore takes a napkin from off the table and dabs his slobbery lips, followed by an unexpected smile which reveals an impressive set of gnashers. He's relaxed and unshaken, but that might be explained by the hulk of a rottweiler standing guard in the shadowy corner: a black and gold mountain of fur with eyes like dark brown marbles. A jagged scar runs down the rottweiler's face, following a dispute with a couple of felines which quickly got out of hand. It's common knowledge that a prison cell is much like a second home to the infamous Leonard Weiler and his criminal record speaks for itself (it comes in volumes – so in this case the bite is without doubt, far far worse than the bark). The arrival of detectives is met with a fearsome snarl. All his frightening fangs are laid out bare, as he awaits a signal from Salvatore to chase them out of this lair.

'Knew I smelt something fishy. Thought it was just my lunch,' remarks Salvatore with a twinkle in his eye. His voice echoes the sound of someone battling soreness of throat, tinged with a hint of growl. 'Should have told me you were coming, Frank. Could've had the chef knock you up a little something.'

'Salvatore Bulldog, you're under arrest in connection with the disappearance of Detective Lucas Panda. You're under arrest for bribing government officials, for paying off lowlife cops, and I won't even start on the bakery beneath the bookstore. You're under arrest because we have reason to believe you kidnapped Johnny, Benny and Chuck Beaver. And I'm a semi–aquatic bird, not a fish.' Frank straightens his tie, folds both wings into his pockets, and waits for the dog to make his move.

'Want me to break 'em in two, boss?' asks the rottweiler, desperate to be unleashed. 'Hear penguin tastes *real* sweet.'

'Who are you? The maid?' quips Chico, bringing the pumped-up pooch down a couple of rungs. His sarcasm wins him one more peek at the furious henchmen's saliva covered incisors, as the beast step forward and flashes them for all to see. Chico flinches slightly and leans back to avoid being covered in drool.

The bulldog gestures for his loyal servant to calm down and appears to find the fury amusing. 'Thank you, Leonard, but that won't be necessary. Just pass me the pepper, would you?' he says, before puffing on his inhaler (any breed of dog with a smooshed face tends to have severe difficulty breathing and Salvatore is no exception. He's also crippled with poor eyesight and dangerously allergic to chocolate, cheese, and cats).

Leonard reluctantly retreats and grabs the pot of pepper from a shelf packed with condiments. He stands over his boss much like a professional waiter and sprinkles it all over the meal. The bulldog licks his lips and consumes another mouthful before washing it down with a sip from his hot steamy mug.

Chico, almost stunned, can't contain a snigger. '*This*....is the scary gangster you keep chirping about?' he says, directing his confusion towards Frank. 'Seriously? *This*...wheezing old timer. I swear my grandmother wears those exact same glasses. He's wearing slippers for crying out loud.'

Salvatore puts down his knife and fork. 'Piece of advice, chimp. Never leave your manners at the door when you step in my office. You're a click away from a seat in a rottweilers belly and do well to remember that.' He nudges his glasses again, picks up his silver tools, and returns to eating.

Leonard cracks his furry knuckles.

Frank's patience is wearing thin and the clock's ticking. 'Hurry up and finish the meal, Salvatore. Cause you got about one minute before I click, and a polar bear joins the party.'

'Prawn salad and honey tea. Doctor's orders,' replies Salvatore, clearly in no rush to sit in a cell.

'A crime lord on a strict diet? Now I've seen it all,' mumbles Chico as he starts to poke his nose in a few of the drawers (he doesn't have a particularly great attention span for a detective. It rarely takes long before he's overcome with a need to fidget or move around).

Salvatore's last meal at The Hound Lounge finally reaches its end. Another dab on the lips with a napkin, before tossing it over to Leonard. Slowly and not without creaks he just about manages to stand. He shuffles towards the detectives using the aid of a cane; it's short but sturdy and sculpted from chestnut wood, with an ivory bone for a head. After only a couple of steps, he pauses to clear his throat.

'Time beats us all in the end. And as you draw close to that final breath you start to reflect on your legacy. How will I be remembered? Sure, I own this joint and a few crumby stores, but then I'm presented with a golden opportunity for *so* much more. Chance to make my mark on the Kingdom. I could build a maze of hotels, restaurants, and entertainment...enough to rival the lions and all the bright lights of Paradise Valley. Ok, I ruffled a few feathers down at City Hall. Took pity on a rhino desperate for cash. But gentlemen, you'd be surprised what one is capable of in the pursuit of a dream.'

Frank is not in the mood for excuses or sympathy. 'Capable of abducting a panda?' he responds bluntly.

Salvatore nods, accepting the assumption that he would order the silence of Lucas *and* the beavers. He knows his words mean little or nothing to enforcers of the law but shares it all the same. 'Lucas Panda was meddling in my affairs, and if he'd locked up the mayor then my plans would be left in tatters. And I assume Lucas shared my blueprints with the beavers...which rattled them, cause they realized I'd build on their home...so they handed over the photos.' Another deep puff on his blessed inhaler.

'Anyway, to discover the panda and beavers had vanished...was music to my ears. Problem solved. *But*, detectives, it was *not* me who undertook this unsavory task. Nor any of the dogs under my command.'

'Tell it to the judge. Now you comin' quietly, or I gotta roll up my sleeves?' Frank has faith in Jake assisting should the situation rapidly deteriorate - but he sincerely hopes there'll be no requirement to fend off a hot headed rottweiler, for any length of time. He tries his hardest to disguise the touch of sudden nerves.

'A younger bulldog might have tried his luck, Frank...fought his way out in a blaze of glory. But I'm tired, partially blind and I'm wearing loungewear. If it's alright with you, I'll just come peacefully.'

'What about your nurse?' says Chico, already looking Leonard right in the eyes. Frank gives him a shove, determined to avoid any carnage. Leonard growls; it sounds like a motorbike revving and raring to go. But deep down he knows he can't save Salvi. Even a tower of power like Leonard can't fend off the boys in blue.

'Go back to your homes, there's nothing to see here!! Police business. I repeat, please go back to your homes!!' shouts officer Thelma Eagle into the megaphone. Word has spread like wildfire; Salvatore has been arrested and every dog in town has gathered to find out why. Crowds of pedigree and crossbreed pups descend upon the streets outside the lounge, determined to catch a glimpse of their hero being dragged away from his fortress. A line of pigs assist the bird-of-prey, holding back the horde of bitter canines.

A shaggy sheepdog stuck at the back of the crowd lets off a powerful howl in support of his fallen idol, instantly sparking the others to follow his lead. Local reporters from the Kingdom Chronicle arrive at the scene, hauling heavy cameras and desperate for juicy headlines.

Ruben and Yuriko wait patiently in one of the police vans. It's stuffed with dogs in chains and ready to roll –but they're reluctant to depart while there's a good chance of ending up lynched. Ruben slumps low in his seat before locking the door. Yuriko gives him the look.

'You such coward,' she says, vigorously chewing some gum while she follows the events boiling over outside.

'Hey, I'm a rat, we don't do crowd control,' replies Ruben. He raises his head to take a quick peek before slinking back out of sight. Yuriko watches as a pig is pushed to the floor by a couple of fiery terriers. She retrieves the ball of gum from her mouth and flicks it out of the window.

Leonard swaggers out of 'The Lounge' but he's cuffed and pushed along by a frowning Frank. The rottweiler barks at the top of his lungs, knowing fully well it will send the crowd into a frenzy. Struggling pigs are barged back at least five or so paces; the courageous police shield looks ready to fold and crumble. Taloolah then exits The Lounge, and as she does so, Jake charges passed and runs towards the crowd. He stands tall, beats his chest, and roars with each ounce of his might. Even the officer's shudder to their core with fright. Leonard is thrust in the back of a car, watching in disbelief as his efforts are thwarted by a courageous bear. The whole crowd freezes and nobody dares move a muscle - like a rabble of worried statues.

Then they fall silent.

The only howl that can be heard right now is that from a bustling wind. A dog in a velvet dressing gown stumbles out of his bar. Paws cover jaws, heads slump and shake. He's paraded in front of his tribe wearing nowt but his favorite fancy jim-jams. Slowly and without any fuss, he makes his way towards a carriage. Chico guides him all the way.

'One last question,' says Chico, helping the elderly boss climb into the back of a van. 'Why did you choose The Swamp?'

'What do you mean?' utters Salvatore, trying his best to get comfortable in an extremely uncomfortable police vehicle. He has the pleasure of a grouchy looking Leonard to keep him company; Mr Rottweiler is perched on the opposite bench, particularly miffed, and unable to contain a bout of huffing.

Chico refrains from closing doors till he's scratched the nagging question tickling his mind. 'I'm from West Bay, and between here and there is heaps of good land to build as many casinos and hotels that you could possibly dream of. There'd be zero push back from the mayor, he'd give the green light, no questions asked. None of this dirty work, black mail, and kidnapping would be necessary. So, why take The Swamp? Doesn't make sense.' Not expecting a response Chico sighs and goes to push the door...but Salvatore isn't finished.

'It wasn't my idea. Didn't he tell you?' says Salvatore, trying to nudge his glasses despite being cuffed.

Chico reaches the conclusion that his ears must have deceived him.

'He? Who's *he*? You mean the mayor?'

'The *goat*...it was all the goat's idea,' grumbles Leonard, not bothering to look up while he drops the bombshell.

Chico eases his grip on the door and his hands flop to his waist. He doesn't make a sound while he tries to piece it all together.

Salvatore is struggling to breathe without his trusty inhaler but digs deep and musters a few more lines. 'Swamp's *church* land, didn't you know? Thought you boys were detectives. Father Goat asked, *begged*, for me to buy the land off him at a cut price. How could I say no?'

141

Chico rattles his brain, unable to process the possibility that this might in fact be true. 'You want me to believe that this was *all* masterminded by an old goat? Are you kidding me? I might be young, but I'm not stupid.'

'He needed the money for some project, a new orphanage or something he said. Couldn't believe my luck. All my dreams, handed to me on a plate.' There was nothing in Salvatore's manner which suggested he was spurting lies, even with all his wheezing. His statements appeared sincere, and anyhow, surely if one were seeking to lay the blame at another creature's feet – Father Goat would not be the name you would pick out of the air. But the monkey refuses to believe it for now, until he has further proof, and closes the doors on Salvatore. He straightens his hat and heads on back to his ride.

The fleet of vans and kingdom police cars finally commence their procession, awkwardly trundling slowly through an angry and sullen crowd. The howls resume, pups arching their necks to wail towards the stars. And so ends the reign of Salvatore Bulldog, as leader of the dogs.

17

Vulture Wants, Vulture Gets

'*Salvatore 'Babyface' Bulldog Arrested'*. Yuriko's eyes skim the front page of the Echo, while her feet take a rest on the desk. Today's edition - bar a few adverts - is predominately pictures of Salvatore and the details of his tense arrest. The curious wolf, however, is far more interested in celebrity gossip and snaps of famous couples.

'Hey, Frank, you know Louis Dodo is coming to town? One night only at the palace, maybe you take Dolores?'

Frank finishes bashing a sentence into his typewriter; he's been tackling paperwork all morning. 'Louis Dodo? You kiddin' me. I'd rather eat my wings than listen to that heap o' garbage. But hey if I pay, could you take Mrs Penguin? What I'd give for an evening of peace.'

Squinty the Mole, longest serving officer in the force, delicately approaches Franks desk with a strong cup of coffee. The penguin fears for the worst as the mole trips along the way, nearly drenching the team in steaming hot liquid. Thankfully, she regains her composure and everyone's spared the third-degree burns.

'There you go, Mr Penguin, black coffee. Two lumps of sugar as requested.'

The mole's shaky little claws gently lay the saucer and cup on the table. Only half the contents have spilt during the journey so it's a better job than usual.

'Did you stir it clockwise?' probes Frank, half-jokingly.

'Of course, Frank.'

'Good work, mole, good work.'

Squinty smiles and walks away to crack on with more pressing duties. Impressively she only bumps into three desks before finally reaching her own.

'For the record…if you ask me for clockwise coffee, I pour over your head,' says Yuriko, peeping over her desk at Frank.

She receives no witty response.

Grumpy-chops gulps down his brew. He dabbles over which letter to strike next on his office piano, as he races to complete his report. Out of the corner of his eye he notices Yuriko sliding her legs off the desk and attempt to look extra busy. She coughs and shoots him a look, but he's slow to catch the drift. *Sniff* - he catches a whiff of familiar lavender perfume, a smell which can only mean one dreaded thing. He turns around, and low and behold, the vulture stands before him.

'Oh, chief…wasn't expecting you,' says Frank, trying his best to avoid looking alarmed by the sight of her withered face.

'Congratulations on the dog, a job well done. Nothing I enjoy more than seeing scoundrels in handcuffs, sprawled across the front page.'

'Me too, chief, me too. Knew we'd snag him in the end.'

The vulture moves in close till their beak to beak. 'And yet, we have no *actual* evidence to connect Salvatore with the kidnappings…do we? We've only linked him with a construction scandal at The Swamp.'

'*Ahem*, well not yet, chief, but we're working on it. Jake's been putting the squeeze on mutts around the clock. One's bound to crack, ma'am.'

'We have rhino confession and statement from old badger, so he go to jail,' says Yuriko, standing up and stepping in.

'I'm not talking about bookstores and rhinos, Officer Wolf. I'm talking about pandas and beavers. *Missing* animals. And they shall *all* be found animals if you wish to keep your jobs.'

'Yes, chief.' The wolf rolls her eyes, but only when the vulture looks away.

'Gorilla's the key,' adds Frank, flashing a 'wanted' poster: it's stamped with a handsome reward but a feeble artists impression of the great white beast haunting the penguin's dreams. 'If we find the gorilla, or anyone else from his little wrecking crew, and link them back to the dog, then we've nailed it. Case closed.'

'Any how many phantom white gorillas have you discovered on your travels thus far?'

'Well zero, ma'am, but we're close, I know it. He can't hide forever.'

'*If* he's still in the country.'

Yuriko had whipped a pocket mirror out of her purse to briefly inspect her fangs, but all being fine she pops it back and continues the conversation. 'We believe he is. An officer was attacked yesterday in Cain's Garden. Shape of wounds match the cuts on Lucas's coat and motel room curtains. Officer also say she find blue van. Then she attacked from behind by crazy jackal with wild amber eyes. Left for dead, but family of hawks spot her and come to rescue.'

None of them had noticed Chico make an appearance, despite the ping of the lift - especially the vulture who was stewing on potential ideas. Without saying a word, he whacks a stack of blueprints onto the penguin's desk. The *bang* catches the attention of the entire office, who quit what they're doing to check out all the fuss. Chico looks at Frank, but every other eyeball is fixed on the monkey - so this better be good.

'It was the goat, *not* the dog,' says Chico bravely, with his terrifying boss practically breathing down his neck. 'I'm sure of it.'

Frank's reaction suggests he's convinced the monkey's lost his marbles; his forehead crinkles and his face contorts like he's swallowed a bitter pill.

'What are you talkin' about, kid?' enquires the puzzled penguin.

'Are you feeling ok, Chico?' Yuriko's muddled too.

The vulture's a touch more supportive and intrigued by the strange accusation. 'Carry on, Charlie Monkey...do explain,' she says with an air of authority.

'The Swamp, the *whole* swamp area, was owned by the North Beach Church. Eliana Panther made a call to a friend from the planning department, and they confirmed it,' explains Chico, one hand in a pocket, the other waving above his head, delivering all his gestures - like a pro preacher hitting his stride, passionately submitting his theory.

'I believe that Father Goat approached Salvatore and urged him to buy The Swamp, for a reasonable price. A *golden opportunity* the dog just couldn't ignore. But *why* you ask? *Why,* sell the land? To pay for a project. To pay for *this*.' He holds up a blueprint for all to see.

'All these plans were signed off for the dog, all except *one*, this one. The biggest one, the crucial one. The permit for the grandest design, was signed off for a Mr Victor Goat, aka *Father* Victor Goat. Why would Babyface Bulldog, the city's biggest crook, sneak, and creep, snatch up *all* the church land only to hand them back the best spot? Unless, the whole deal was proposed by the goat, which I bet my bottom coin it was.'

'Have you totally lost your mind?' shouts Frank, leaving his chair to stand at the monkey's side. 'You think that creaky ancient goat is droppin' cops and robbers? *Come on*, snap out of it, you sound like a freakin' idiot.'

'Does sound pretty far-fetched,' squeals one of the officers, trying to join in. Plenty of faces agree.

'What about crazy bulldog? It must be him. He arranged the photos and blackmail the mayor. Why he do that, if he was innocent?' says Yuriko, joining the list of doubters.

Chico hesitates slightly given the wave of heckles firing in his direction, but he's not done fighting his corner. 'This is the building permit for the goat, for his new orphanage. Note the measurements. Unless he's building the *biggest* orphanage that the world has ever seen, then this plan is incorrect. Who lies about building an orphanage?'

Frank sweeps his typewriter off the desk, his self-control flying out the window.

'*Stop*, stop talking, chimp, I mean it. This is Kingdom. We lock up scumbags. We ain't shakin' down nuns and orphans.'

'Look, don't ask me about motive, don't ask me what they're building, don't ask why a goat of the cloth's involved. But trust me. *Please*. North Beach has something to hide. The least we could do is look.'

Frank shoves the monkey. 'I won't tell you again, kid-.'

'He's right, Frank,' says the vulture, examining the blueprint now clamped by her claw. She frowns at the simple diagram; it depicts a lengthy block shaped structure, and the peculiar measurements highlighted by the passionate monkey.

'What? Oh please, come on, chief' Frank is stunned and backs away from his partner.

'*I said*, penguin, that he is right.'

'But, chief...what about the dogs? It's the dogs what done this, for sure.'

'Frank, I think your passion for catching dogs is clouding your judgement. I have a sneaking suspicion the monkey is onto something. And seeing as all the dogs are locked away in cages, I see no reason not to explore this further. No stone left unturned, as they say-.'

'But, chief-.'

'Frank. You *will* visit the goat. Is that understood?'

'Yes, ma'am,' mutters Mr Grumpy Wings under his breath.

'Jake can speak with the injured officer and see what else she remembers. And you, Detective Monkey, shall find us the treasure.' The vulture passes the mysterious blueprint back to Chico. 'The public won't stand for this. Criminals on the loose. I want answers, I want suspects, I want results. And I want them *now*,' she harps, strutting back to her private office.

Frank addresses the room, swatting the unbearable tension. 'Alright...you heard the bird. Get to work.'

Rat-a-tat-tat, all the typewriters swing into action. Phones are off the hook. Officers dash between desks. Detectives share a stare. The brooding penguin begrudgingly parks his rage and pokes the monkey's chest.

'Damn it, you better be right, kid. Cause if this all leads to nothing, the vulture will have us for breakfast.'

Without a word, Squinty the Mole calmly picks up Frank's busted typing machine and places it back on his desk.

18

Flight Of The Silver Rocket

Mayor Leopard makes for a sorry sight - alone in a rotten cell and driven close to madness by the drips that drop from the ceiling. His head has been sunk between paws for hours but surely it feels like days; he only props it up and against the wall due to the sound of footsteps approaching.

Chief Vulture appears beyond the bars, flanked by heavy pigs. She appears to be bubbling with fury, but then it's a look she's flaunted often.

'Took your time, chief,' moans Mayor Leopard, now covered with only rags. 'Was starting to think you might just leave me to rot.'

She snatches a key from one of the piggy's and unlocks the cage. 'This way please, Mayor Leopard.'

'You need to work on the menu here as well. That gruel they served me for lunch was truly dreadful.'

'This way please, Mayor Leopard,' repeats the vulture, firmly glaring at the wall as opposed to the eyes of her spotty prisoner.

The leopard drags himself away from his dusty bed, sarcastically waving goodbye to the cell. 'Lead the way, ma'am. My chariot awaits,' he says, suddenly dropping a smile.

'Cuff him.'

'Will that *really* be necessary, chief? And where's my suit? This horrible cloth is unbearably itchy.'

'*Cuff him*,' blasts the bird. She may be haggard and gaunt, but there's still fire to be found in her belly.

The pigs push the leopard against the bars and slap some cuffs around his wrists. He's marched through empty corridors until they reach a deserted car park – which lurks beneath headquarters. A black police van awaits their arrival, the back doors slightly ajar.

'Wait, what's the meaning of this!? Where's my taxi? You need to set me free!!' screams the mayor, aiming every drop of his rage at the cold-hearted chief.

'In you get please, Mayor Leopard,' she says politely, refusing to address his concerns.

The leopard tries in vain to wriggle free. 'I want my lawyer, *right* now. Right now!!'

'You can speak to your lawyer when you arrive at your destination.'

'Where are you taking me!?' snarls the leopard, dragging himself towards the vulture till he's a whisker away from her beak. He lashes out with all his teeth but only catches a bite of the air.

Chief Vulture doesn't move a muscle, nor consider a step of retreat – she remains calm and undeterred. 'You're being transferred to South Central Prison, while you await trial.'

'Oh, oh I see, it's like that is it. Think you can cut me loose now. After everything I've done for you...and your little party of friends.'

'Take him away,' says the vulture, pointing a wing at the daunting van.

'I've got a whole team of lawyers you know. I'll be on a beach swigging jugs of Raspberry Surprise before sunset, and you *vulture*, are doomed beyond belief. Oh, the things I know, *the things I know*. Wait till the Chronicle hears the truth about you, about them, about *her*. Then you'll be sorry.'

'*I said* take him away!!' snaps the chief, stomping the floor with her twisted talons.

The pigs grab the leopard by his arms and yank him towards the van, his heels scraping along the ground. There's a last-ditch attempt to slip free, but this breed of pig has the strength of an ox and they toss him inside with ease.

Doors slam shut. *Screech.* The van wastes no time in hitting full speed.

Chief Vulture retrieves a cockroach from the deepest dark depths of her pocket, stares at it long and hard, then flings it in her mouth and crunches.

Two hours pass, but the leopard can't be sure having spent most of the journey sleeping (well, trying his best to nap whilst bumping along inside a prison on wheels). He checks his watch for the time and *huffs* when he remembers it was confiscated with his other possessions.

A blinding ray of light occupies the back of van as the doors are slowly prized open. The mayor throws his hands across his eyes and cowers in the corner as he tries to make out what's happening. There appears to be two bulky shadows climbing in to join him.

One of the shadowy figures takes the mayor by his tail and pulls him out with complete disregard for his feelings. They grant him a short drop to the ground and watch him land with a thud. He still can't see thanks to all the harsh sunlight and now he's chewing a mouthful of sand.

'What…what is this? What's going on?' shouts the mayor, spitting and spewing the gunk now stuffed in his cheeks. 'I demand to see my lawyers.'

'Pick him up, darlings. Some of us have other pressing matters to contend with today.'

'Heck, what you waitin' for boys, pick him up.'

The mayor recognizes the voices but struggles to place a face. A firm hand wraps around his throat, rising him off the ground. His eyes finally adapt to the radiant weather and he's face to face with a bison. Impulsively he shoves the beefcake aside and stumbles away, before tripping over a rock and collapsing rather awkwardly.

'The Bison Brothers, what are you doing here? Where am I?' The mayor regains his footing and tries to assess where he is. Nothing but desert and deserted roads for miles, except for two black limos and the empty police van. Omar Tiger has taken the opportunity to do some sunbathing on one of the limousines, sprawling himself across the roof in shorts, shirt, and shades. Mason Gator isn't one to bathe in the sun but looks like he's come from the golf course given his cap and checkered attire. Then there's the bison brothers: heads shaped like anvils and matching brown leather jackets. They're building up quite a sweat with all this blistering heat.

'What's going on? I demand an answer. I thought I was going to jail.'

'Change of plan I'm afraid, Mr Leopard,' replies Mason Gator, oozing with charm even when he's delivering gloomy news.

Mayor Leopard - already stricken with panic- considers his options to the north, south, east, and west; it doesn't look promising. 'What do you want? Money? I've got money...take it, it's all yours. I don't need it.'

'We're doing just fine on the money front, but thank you all the same,' sneers Omar, sliding himself off the car.

'Silence, you want silence. I'll keep quiet, I promise. What you guys get up to is your own business. I won't tell a soul, I swear.'

Mason sniggers. 'Think we're a bit far down the road for apologies, partner, wouldn't you say? Seems to me like you made your bed, and now you sure as hell gotta sleep in it. Heck, we trusted you leopard, but you're up to those pretty little eye-balls o' yours in dirt, and it's bad for business. Mighty shame, but only one thing for it.'

'I was blackmailed, what else could I do? They threatened to take her away from me, my sweet Taloolah. What else could I do?'

Mason looks at the Bison Brothers and clicks his fingers - like he's ordering two of his waiters back at the restaurant. The gesture needs no explanation; the beefy brothers grunt and tackle the leopard, stripping away all his rags.

'Are you out of your minds? I'm the mayor of Noah's Kingdom.' The leopard, aghast, crosses both arms and legs in a frantic effort to restore some much-needed dignity.

'*Were* the mayor,' quips the tiger. 'You helped that dastardly bulldog and stabbed us in the back. And you just know she detests a backstabber.'

A white horse - chauffeur for the day - exits one of the limousines and opens the rear passenger door. A female lion emerges in a full-length black satin dress, a long black cloak, and a hood. She strolls through the harsh afternoon sun towards the nervous mayor, who scrambles backwards determined to keep his distance. Her outfit reveals very little; all the leopard can see is a fluffy white chin peppered with dozens of whiskers, but that's enough to gauge who it is.

'Anna...*Annabella*,' announces the shocked leopard, squirming with fear. He feels his paws instinctively pressing together, not for prayer, but to beg for mercy.

Omar checks his watch, eager for a swift resolution.

She removes the hood. Short golden fur, small rounded ears on top of the head, hypnotic eyes, and teeth like daggers (lions can turn their ears from side to side and catch sounds from any direction, so be careful when you curse them). Underneath the layers of satin hides a nimble hunting machine - a stealthy mass of powerful lean muscle. She ignores the opportunity to engage in conversation with the leopard, preferring instead to stare in silence.

'What are you going to do? Just leave me here, like this, it's preposterous. Bury me alive maybe? What's the plan? You won't get away with it...whatever it is.' The leopard's manner dances closer to manic with each passing word, and his entire body now rattles with desperation.

Another click of the fingers. The matching bison snap into action, now relieving the lioness of all her clothing - extremely carefully. Naked, the lioness slumps onto all fours – a sharp leap backwards in evolution.

'You might want to think about running somewhere, Mr Mayor,' shouts Mason, lighting up his latest cigar.

'Why, why should I run?' His legs decide to pick up a jog and head towards the sun.

Mason grins and puffs out a cloud. 'Because it's *lunchtime*.'

'Savages, damn it, you're nothing but savages!!' The desperate cat tries his best at a sprint but only scampers away on two feet. He's slow and runs like a clown - not like the wind as would the leopards of old.

'Run!!' bellows Omar, giddy with a burst of excitement.

Annabella watches each stride of her prey, with narrowed eyes, sparing no time for blinking or glances elsewhere. Her chest puffs out, her head stands high. She strokes the ground with a paw, each razor-sharp claw cutting through sand and grit. The tail - all black fur at its tip - sways from side to side like the pendulum in a grandfather's clock. Her face scrunches tight, phlegm leaps off the fangs, and finally she unleashes a roar (boy oh boy, can she roar). Both bison shudder. Mason's palms go sweaty with fright. The pale horse looks away. Even gods likely tremble at such a menacing sound.

And then, she gives chase.

****

Frank didn't anticipate a requirement to wander through the Barro Forest again. Yet here he is, approaching the Church of North Beach for a second time this week. There's no sunshine to greet him this time around - only rows of grey clouds and a brewing storm. He buttons the mac to keep himself warm and clutches his hat with a wing (you never know when a cheeky gust of wind might relieve you of favored possessions).

An apple tree still blocks a clear view of the church, yet the blustery weather did a splendid job of shaking out most of the fruit. Resting against the trunk is none other than Enoch the blinded ferret; he's busy sorting ripe from rotten. Perfect apples are placed in a mouth-watering pile beside him while those plagued with worms have simply been tossed away.

'What color are these apples, detective?' asks Enoch, sensing the presence of an exhausted penguin.

'They're green, bright green,' answers Frank, helping himself to a fallen juicy orb. *Ewww maggots* - he flings it over his shoulder and tries again.

Enoch smiles. 'Green, perfect. But really, they're any color of my choosing...I suppose.'

'Where's Father Goat? Need to speak with him. Is he there in the church?'

'Master forbid me to eat these you know. Said they were *strictly* for orphans. Yet what harm can it do now? I shall spend what time remains with oh such sticky claws, consuming the treats that drop off the branches. Will you join me, detective?'

'What do you mean by *time that remains*? Where's your master now? This is serious ferret. I need to speak with him.'

'I am not welcome on the journey. What use is an old ferret without the blessing of sight. They take no organ, no garden, no need for a broom.'

Frank grabs the ferret and shakes him from side to side. He doesn't drop apples, but he might spit the truth. 'Listen ya greedy weasel, if that goat's up to something, I need to know what it is *right* now.'

'Master insisted my lips remain as sealed as my eyes.'

'No more apples till I get some answers. In fact, you got five seconds before I chop down the whole damn tree.'

The ferret sighs like a child forced to eat their greens. 'I believe he means to bring about an end to Noah's Kingdom. I can't be sure of all the facts, but I know for certain...he's lost his mind. There's a private office up in the orphanage, which may provide more answers.'

Frank shivers at the very thought of climbing. 'Not that blasted hill again.'

'I can take you there. Plans are afoot and it was all conceived in that office. My eyes let me down but never my ears. I could hear his ramblings, even through the walls.'

'Is there a private lift or a private elevator by any chance?'

'Only a charming stroll towards the stars I'm afraid. Could I take an apple or two for the journey? Would you pick them out for me?'

With ample supply of fresh fruit stuffed in pockets, the penguin and ferret make their way up the hill. Unfortunately, the wind is on its way down, which further delays their appearance at the summit. But after plenty of crawling and wheezing, Detective Penguin eventually arrives at the peak - closely followed by a rodent with cramp in his belly, due to over-indulging on snacks throughout the journey. They carry each other the last few steps, before collapsing through the door in a heap.

A deserted orphanage. The patter of tiny feet and high-pitched laughter noticeably absent. Walls remain dotted with photos, floors remain paved with childish mess, but zero sign of life.

'Hello, anybody home!?' yells Frank, picking himself and Enoch off the ground.

'Like I told you before, sir, they've all departed,' says Enoch, rubbing his rumbling tummy full of apples. 'There should be an office, dead ahead. The key's on a hook under a painting of Noah, so I've heard.'

'Gee thanks, there's about thirty paintings of Noah on this stinkin' wall,' huffs Frank.

Enoch begins a frantic game of 'find the hidden key'. He slides along the wall ruthlessly tearing away the artwork. Half-way along he lands on a small framed painting of animals leaving the ark ; a much more professional effort than all the surrounding pictures. He flings it across the room with disregard for the remarkable quality.

'I've found it!' he announces with glee, snatching the dinky key off a hook on the wall. 'I found it, sir!!'

Thud. Crash. Smash. Too late. Frank has put his foot through the door and entered the private office - he's not one for waiting around. 'Me too,' he sniffs, flicking on the light switch. It's only a tiny office but there's plenty of treasure. Enoch is happy to linger around the doorway while Frank does all his snooping.

'What's with all the colors?' asks Frank, confused by the walls all laden with paintings of rainbows.

Enoch smiles. 'I have set my rainbow in the clouds, and it will be the sign of the covenant between me and the earth, said God. Whenever I bring clouds over the earth and the rainbow appears in the clouds, I will remember my covenant between me and you, and all living creatures of every kind. Never again will the waters become a flood to destroy all life.'

Frank just frowns, still bemused by the rainbow's relevance. He's drawn to a short dusty bookshelf standing beside the door; it's an odd mix of religious and military texts. The penguin's thumb glides along the title's as he searches for a piece of the puzzle.

'*Antonia the Turtle, ...The Story of Noah,...Noah's Tale*, Noah, Noah, *Military Tactics*, classic military strategy...*The Craft of War*...jeeze, strange bedtime reading for a vicar wouldn't you say?'

'Oh...he wasn't always a vicar, sir. No, he was a soldier in his youth and a highly respected one at that.'

Resting on top of the bookshelf is a black and white snap of a dashing young goat in uniform - all smiles and a full set of medals. 'Now what's he fighting for?' replies Frank, staring a war hero right in the eyes. His focus adjusts for another photo hanging on the wall above the mini library: a group of chirpy orphans huddled together outside the orphanage, accompanied by Father Goat and Sister Turkey. All the other photos of previous tenants are displayed in the living room, yet this shot is hidden away within the private office. Given that the goat looks rather sprightly and the turkey far less wicked, one can only assume this was one of the earliest groups of orphans to live in the home on the hill. Three rows of cheerful animals – tallest at the back, shortest at the front. Frank scans the front row: a cheeky hedgehog pulling a face and a bored badger with thick black specs catch the eye.

A brief glimpse at the middle and top rows before turning away - then he freezes - and slowly looks again, but more closely this time. Third from the left, top row - *jackpot*. 'A white gorilla…that's…a white gorilla,' says Frank, stunned with surprise, confusion, and joy.

'Augustus, oh yes sir, *my* that's going back a long way. He was one of the first.'

There he is indeed - an intimidating giant even in youth, either side of a skinny orphan jackal and podgy orphan hog. He looks happy here and even presents a grin, as do his brothers in arms. The troublesome trio are each wearing flat-caps and matching blue sweaters. It's hard to comprehend how three adorable faces could evolve into monsters, or how a master who appears so full of love and kindness could eventually be wrecked by madness.

'The beavers, probably Lucas too…they were attacked by these three orphans. Attacked on the orders of Father Goat,' rambles Frank, sharing his thoughts aloud. 'They were his henchmen all along, carrying out his dirty work. Poor damn orphans groomed into nothing but goons. Jeeze, the kid was right all along. But why? I still don't get why?'

The detective turns his attention away from the past and forward to a messy desk, slap bang at the heart of the secret room. In the corner of the desk was a melted candle to provide a glimmer of light during late night plotting. Sprawled across the surface of the desk was yet another blueprint, most likely a gift from the mayor, but this time it wasn't a plan designed by

Salvatore or Father Goat. This blueprint was in fact the layout of Shepherd's Dam, and right at the top of the diagram, in white chalk, was clearly scrawled an 'X.'

'Shepherd's' Dam...why does he care about the dam? Weasel, he mention the dam to you?'

'Ahem, did I mention I'm a ferret, not a weasel? And no, sir...never heard the dam mentioned I'm afraid.'

Frank knows some evil deed is at play here, but can't put a fishy finger on it. Ramping up his internal panic stations, he aimlessly twirls around the office in sheer desperation to decipher the goat's intentions - but all he finds are spare candles, further religious texts, and numerous empty drawers. Infuriated he concedes defeat and is seconds from walking away when he spots the slightest square shaped lump protruding through the blueprint. He peels away the dam's design to reveal a slender book: *The Improvised Munitions Handbook.*

Frank's clenched wing thumps the desk. 'Blow it up, the damn crazy goat thinks he can blow it up!'

'Blow up Shepherd's Dam?' replies the confused ferret.

'Ah jeeze, today's the parade...he's gonna blow the dam...the *damn* dam...*the God damn dam.* He'll wipe out half the Kingdom, the maniac. Please tell me there's a quicker way to the bottom of this hill. I gotta stop him.'

'Oh, there's a quicker way, sir, a much quicker way...not sure you'll like it though.'

Enoch leads Frank outside before disappearing around the side of the building for merely a matter of moments. The ferret returns pushing a silver wooden race cart, usually driven by the bravest of children.

'Here you go, sir, this'll have us down the bottom in no time at all. Master made it for the children, they loved it. Mind you he banned it after the incident with Malcolm Ostrich. Still walks funny even now, poor Malcom.'

'What do you mean *us*?'

'Well sir, if it's all the same, I'd quite like to reach the bottom soon as possible much like yourself. Feeling rather peckish again. Apple pie if I can find my way around the kitchen. But maybe it's safer if you drive? I tried once…with dear Malcolm Ostrich. Never again.'

Frank mutters something to himself and looks down the hill. 'Maybe I could just run down there?'

'I may be somewhat lacking in the ability to see, but all my other senses are telling me…that would not be a wise idea, sir.'

Reluctantly the crabby detective lowers himself into the driver's seat of the race car, while a rather excited passenger cuddles up beside him. *Silver Rocket* has been carved on the side in wobbly red crayon letters. Frank finds a pair of goggles beside his seat, gives them a quick wipe, then slaps them on just to be safe (the last thing you want when you're flying down a hill is pebbles striking your eyeballs).

Frank braces himself and takes a deep breath. 'The things I do to keep the peace.'

'Good luck, sir. Godspeed,' says Enoch.

Frank begins to pedal, cautiously at first, as the silver rocket gradually springs to life and trundles towards the slope. But as soon as the rickety little car gets a sniff of downward motion the pedals take on a life of their own. All Frank can do is steer best he can while gravity does the rest and fires them towards the apple tree. Enoch savors the ride, the cool waves of air gushing through his fur. Frank prays for the first time in years.

Somehow, they reach the bottom without a scratch or a cardiac arrest. Enoch even discovers a brake pedal in time to prevent a tragic collision with the side of a church.

Frank Penguin forgets any well-wishing or kiss goodbye; he pedals the box on wheels towards his police vehicle, still parked beyond the forest. But to be brutally honest, he'd probably have reached Shepherd's Dam a damn sight quicker, had he continued his journey in the Silver Rocket.

19

Pairs

Following a multitude of wrong turns and dead ends, the coppers exploring The Swamp for a mysterious new orphanage finally strike gold: a deserted blue van book-ended by bundles of long wooden planks. *'Keep Out'* – a wonky sign lays hidden behind the van, hammered half-heartedly into the ground, and guarding a twisting thorny path. They must be close.

'Hog Construction?' mumbles Ruben to himself, noting the writing on the side of the van. The rodent scratches his head with a tiny paw, then turns to grab Chico's attention. 'You know, my cousin Levi used to work for Hog Construction, back in the day,' he says, pinching the monkey's elbow. 'They closed down about ten years back, but I remember he had a van...*just* like this one.'

'Where were they based? Could be the hideout we've been looking for?'

'The old shipyard, top of Cain's Garden. Deserted and real spooky, but it's the perfect spot if you really don't wanna be found.'

'Alright, well let's tick off the orphanage, then we'll hit the shipyard.'

Chico draws the blueprint out of his pocket like a knight revealing his sword. Eliana peeks over his shoulder while he takes another look. There's a rough location on a small map of The Swamp plus some basic measurements for the proposed development, and a very basic diagram of how it should look. Chico's still confused by the magnitude; if the plans are precise then it must be more than an orphanage - and even if your intent *was* indeed to create a lavish new home for unfortunate youngsters, then surely you wouldn't construct it on boggy land?

Nobody was quite sure what to expect or confident of what lay ahead, but they were eager to find out. As quietly as possible, Chico wades his way through a soggy narrow track. Without question or doubt - nor a hint of hesitation - the rest of the party follow. They battle their way through a haze of muck and brambles. The monkey is so relieved to reach the end of the trail and untangle himself from spiky branches, that it takes a moment to realize he's discovered 'the orphanage'. *Perplexed* would be an apt word to describe Chico's expression as he absorbs the shocking truth. The diagram on the blueprint was indeed considerably different to the astonishing reality.

One by one the officers drag themselves free of the treacherous slushy path and one by one they're rocked by the sight that greets them. Ruben is so taken aback that he trips and falls in the arms of Yuriko. The wolf is surprised by what she finds but remains calm and keeps her footing (it's unlikely her heart rate skipped a beat either).

The Swamp is a massive region littered with trees, rivers, and bumpy roads - yet here at the heart was a stretch of clearing. Any colossal oak tree that had once stood proud upon this patch of earth was now removed. Any plant desperate to grow and blossom now ripped away. Parked in the middle of this wide-open space was indeed a new orphanage in the form of a magnificent ark, towering as tall as a three-story house and the length of a typical football field. Chico and friends are nothing but tiny specks in the shadow of a gargantuan boat - a monstrous wooden structure built from scratch here in the depths of The Swamp.

'What...the heck....is that?' yelps Ruben, breaking the stunned silence.

'Good gracious me, what on earth is a ship doing in the middle of a forest?' asks Eliana, pressing a paw to her lips.

'Smells like pine wood,' says Yuriko, pointing her nose to the sky.

Chico is battling the sound of alarm bells ringing uncontrollably inside his head, as everyone circles the vessel with extra heaps of caution. The sneaky pack of animals tip toe around to the other side until they arrive at an entrance; a broad door attached to a couple of chains lays open like a drawbridge. They whip flashlights out from the hip, flick a switch, and light up the hole inside the doorway.

Sounds ring out from deep inside the boat - hisses, squawks and quacks all leak from the darkness. Cautiously, the group step inside and head towards the noises, spraying every nook and cranny with hectic lights. They find their way across the lower deck, a seemingly endless stretch of cold damp wood in a pitch-black cavern, as the hissing, squawking and quacking gets increasingly louder.

Not before long, Ruben's caught by surprise and damn nearly leaps out his skin; the bewildered face of an elephant child is captured by his wandering torch. Then the shriek of an infant hippo struck by illumination. A startled lion cub in the arms of a kangaroo. A pair of tiger toddlers trying to shun the rays. A short grey bear cowering from unwanted attention.

'What's going on here? Why are they all sat in the dark?' bawls Chico, zipping his torch between all the fearful faces. 'You don't need to be afraid. We're police officers. We're here to help.'

And then there was light.

A string of dim light bulbs lining the ceiling snap into life, brightening the front of the ark. Sister Aurelia Turkey stands by a switch accompanied by silent rabbits in robes, and as far as can be from amused.

'You are not welcome here,' says the tetchy turkey. 'I must insist you leave immediately.'

'Oh, good lord, what have you done? What on earth is this place?' asks Eliana, glaring at the twisted bird.

Sister Aurelia clucks and fans her feathers. 'The ship sits, waiting for a fallen dam and floods to carry her forth. She prays for a Kingdom beneath the waves. She prepares for a voyage across the seven seas, under sun and moonlit sky, to seek out and conquers new shores. She dreams of new beginnings.'

Chico hardly catches a word the sister says - he's fixated by all the young creatures sat in silence. Then it hits him. '*Two*...that's it. Two monkeys, two horses, *look*, two parrots, two alligators,' he says, skipping around the crowd while he points his torch. A pair of each creature is sat in the boat, brainwashed by Father Goat into believing a flood is essential. Most were orphans from North Beach, collected over a period of years for one specific purpose. The others were kidnapped by his trio of henchmen; a jackal, a hog, and white gorilla. They would roam Noah's Kingdom at night and load their van with all of those required. Even Keaton Mule is present, a loyal servant to the cause, who was only more than happy to make a call from his mother's motel and reveal where the beavers were hiding.

'*Two by two*,' announces Eliana. She finally cottons on.

'The time is nearly upon us. I *demand* that you leave the ark,' screams Sister Aurelia, ditching her composed demeanor for a burst of fiery fury.

'We're going nowhere saggy neck till I get some answers,' says Chico, marching towards Sister Turkey and the herd of creepy assistants.

'You're too late, detective. Noah's Kingdom will perish. These creatures are the future, a brighter future.'

'What do you mean Kingdom will perish? Where's Father Goat?'

'The *time*...is nearly upon us.'

A loud scraping sound interrupts the stand-off as three beavers emerge from the shadows, each shackled with a ball and chain. 'Help...us,' they quietly beg in unison, too meek to say anymore.

'The beavers,' harps Ruben. 'They're alive!'

'What have you done to them?' snaps Yuriko.

Sister Aurelia responds with a chilling smile. '*Traitors*. A servant to servants shall they be to their brethren. That is their punishment.' She clicks her wing and the rabbits immediately react, slapping the beaver slaves till they fall to their knees.

Yuriko snarls and officers oink with rage. Ruben takes cover behind a flustered pair of flamingos.

'The time is upon us to lock you up. And your little bunny buddies,' says Chico. 'So, kiss goodbye to your boat lady. We're taking you in and setting these creatures free.'

'Then we're all damned detective…we're all *damned*,' declares Sister Aurelia.

Something smashes out of sight, towards the very end of the ship - an area yet to be explored by the police force. It sounded like a tower of crates crashing apart on the ground, and an echo bounces around the walls.

Chico spins the turkey around and wraps her wrists in cuffs; the mute rabbits get similar treatment from Ruben and one of the pigs. Fearless Yuriko fires a light towards the back of the ark and edges her way towards it. *Sniff sniff* - her nose picks up a scent that would make even the sturdiest of stomachs turn, the scent of a creature not devoted to regular cleansing (or quite possibly bathes in a sewer). Then a *grunting* sound. And an *oink*. The wolf's glow pans along the back till it lands on a wild black hog. Chunky tusks poke out from his slimy lips. A long hairy face and rounded snout, which is dotted with two snotty nostrils. There are two eyes somewhere but it's incredibly hard to spot them. His ears prick up as he grunts again, and a trotter drags across the dirt. It's safe to assume he's set for a daring charge.

'This not good, boss. Not good at all,' shouts Yuriko, preparing to roll out the way. She drops the light and dives to safety as Clayton Hog commences his plucky getaway. A woolly black turtleneck and brown suede trousers do little to hinder his movements, as he rampages his way through the ark – knocking down all on his path, like a hog shaped bowling ball slamming through piggy skittles. The officers are much smaller pigs and helpless against a juggernaut.

Ruben knows if he attempts to block the hog then he'll be crushed like a flimsy can – so he sensibly steps aside.

Chico on the other hand, does try and tackle the speeding swine but he's brushed aside and skids along the deck on his back. Not for the first time Eliana comes to his aid and slaps the dazed look from his eyes. She helps him back to his feet and allows him to wriggle free – for he's desperate to try and give chase.

Despite a wobbly start, Chico soon regains focus and manages to catch up with Clayton who is tiring as he scrambles through brambles. The chimp fights his way through the prickles and sludge, but not quite in time to detain him. He arrives by the road as the hog takes his place on a bike. Mud sprays in every direction as it hits full throttle and flies away through the trees (Clayton reached a swift decision that his blue van couldn't cope with an inevitable high-speed chase). Chico slides onto his own wheels, slams the accelerator, and so begins the hunt.

The Swamp really isn't the best area to drive at excessive speeds due to the constant ups and downs of poorly constructed roads.

Chico narrowly avoids ploughing into a fallen oak and hitting some unwelcome roots, niftily swerving the traps laying set in his way. The hog is still in his sights, and likewise, struggling to prevent a calamity. One after the other they hit a small hill and glide for a lifetime through the air, before hitting the ground with an uncomfortable bump and instantly steering right.

Eventually they reach a smooth path that runs alongside the river, a lengthy trail where there's a chance to pick up some speed. The hog thrusts as much as he can but Chico's not going away. Sensing his opponent is bridging the gap, the hog slips off the road to thick forest. He darts between the trees, skips between the streams, and thrashes through clusters of vines - desperate to shake the tail.

Clayton looks back to check for a monkey – big mistake. His front wheel strikes a log, flipping him into the air. He rolls and rolls along the ground, till he's halted by a thick solid stump. Bleeding and bruised he looks for his bike but it's no longer there to be seen. He does spot Chico though - revving and staring across the marsh that now divides them.

Chico steps off his bike and heads for the hog but his footing sinks in the squelchy ground. He pulls himself free, shakes off the blocks of mud, and scans for an alternative route.

The hog wipes blood from his snout and grunts. His vision's blurry, energy sapped, but it's not in his nature to ever surrender. He runs a trotter along sodden mud. One final charge…for the hell of it.

Chico decides to stand his ground and let Clayton Hog come to him. The hog oinks like he's never oinked before - then a bolt through the boggiest of bogs. But charging across such unforgiving ground is only a fools-errand and he finds himself snared in a trap.

The crazed hog is sinking, swallowed by mud brimming with lost souls, and desperately search as he might, no branch is close enough or strong enough to offer a helping hand. He gasps and grunts. Another grunt. A squeal. He's up to his chest and thrashing around, trying his best to move forward - but the more you thrash the faster you slip away. Further oinks, till only tusks remain. The murky water bubbles and gargles. And then, he's gone.

Chico sits on the ground, brushes some muck off his cheeks - and sighs.

Miraculously the monkey finds his way back to the ark unscathed, though he took some wrong turns and twice stopped a toad for help along the way. By the time he shows his face again, Sister Aurelia and the herd of rabbits have all been taken away. Two by two, young prisoners march off the ark, some back to families and others to a far nicer orphanage.

'The hog?' enquires Ruben.

'The Swamp,' replies Chico quietly. An unpleasant way for any creature to leave the world. Ruben nods and looks to the floor, pondering whether the hog got just desserts.

'*What ever* will you do with this ark?' wonders Eliana, looking again at the grand new ship waiting patiently before them. 'Seems rather a shame if it was simply left to rot.'

'Who knows. Maybe a day will come when we *do* need it again,' says Chico.

Eliana tuts and shakes her head. 'I was thinking more of a fancy restaurant, rather than a haven from the wrath of God.'

'Maybe new police force headquarters,' adds Yuriko with a smile.

'Well let's decide the future of this big old hunk of wood later. First, we have an appointment with the old shipyard,' says Chico, conscious of the fact that culprits are still on the loose.

With no time to waste the group saddle up for another long journey. Eliana insists on holding the map. They kiss goodbye to the ark and swampy marshlands, then head for the mountains of Cain's Garden, and the home of Hogs Construction.

20

Of Mice And Monsters

Yuriko drives gently through veils of mist, past wide-open gates, and a sign for the old creepy shipyard (though the sign *actually* says 'Cain's Shipyard' as opposed to 'Old Creepy Shipyard').

Ruben's face presses firmly against the window, peering up at numerous cranes dotted around the site, like a dazzled child in awe of mechanical giants. Yuriko notices a collection of blue trucks, each stamped on the side with the same two words: *Hoggs Construction*.

Twenty years ago, this area would've been bustling with activity and busy laborers, but now it's reduced to a ghost town – an eerie graveyard for derelict ships and a refuge for wanted criminals. A vast deserted tanker sits proudly in the middle surrounded by festering fishing boats; the yard closed before completion of the tanker's construction, but the crew coated it with red and black paint before their departure. Towards the back of the yard are crumbling red brick buildings, one of which comes with a towering chimney. Only a handful of the buildings have a window that isn't smashed or missing, but the majority are riddled with holes. The area looks out to the roaring Scarlet Ocean, yet no fence in sight to stop you from falling in. Ruben steps out of the car and carefully peeks over the edge; frantic waves are tormenting an island of rocks way down below. He shudders at the thought of being caught in such swirling chaos and decides to stand further in land.

Rain and fog are not perfect ingredients when searching for dangerous animals, particularly if it's a spine-chilling shipyard. Yuriko knows this all too well and holds back Ruben till backup arrives, but waterfalls leak from the clouds and the double-act face a drenching. Thankfully, it's not long before three more cars emerge from the mist, each one stuffed with pigs - closely followed by Eliana and Chico who roll through the gates on their bikes. In a flash the entrance is blocked with vehicles and swarming with determined piggies. If there was a criminal lurking within the yard, then they're now a trapped criminal – unless that is, they can reverse a partially built red and black tanker.

'Stay here and don't move a muscle. It might not be safe,' says Chico to Eliana, staying true to his word that he'd always protect her from danger.

'It's *you* I'm worried about, Chico Monkey. What if there's another barking mad rhino on the loose in here? I'm not carrying you into that ghastly police station again!'

Chico cringes and holds a finger up to his lips, concerned that Eliana just alerted every crook in the vicinity of their unexpected arrival (whispering is an art the panther has yet to truly master). Before Chico can fire off another one of his famous sarcastic remarks, he spots a dull yellow item resting beside Eliana's latest pair of expensive shoes. A banana skin - fresh. He drops to his feet and scoops it up.

'*Whatever* are you doing?' scoffs Eliana, already forgetting the instruction to keep her voice down.

'We got company,' says Chico, quietly gathering the troops. They huddle around the monkey praying he's sharp like Frank or Jake; they're not used to taking orders from monkeys out of West Bay, nor anyone so young of age. Chico certainly feels the pressure and knows it's time to step up and prove he's competent. 'Alright let's move out but everyone stay close, this place gives me the creeps. And keep your eyes peeled. If it ain't wearing a

OF MICE AND MONSTERS

badge...take it down. *Oh*, unless it's Eliana, the panther, *do not* take down the panther.' The pigs look at Chico and then each other; confidence in their leader is already evaporating rapidly but they follow his orders all the same.

Chico charges to the front, eager to lead the hunt and win back respect from his team. The group sneaks forward at sluggish pace, delayed by the thick sooty smog, like hesitant soldiers wading through fields towards an inevitable clash.

Eliana watches nervously from the bonnet of Yuriko's car whilst chewing on brightly colored claws. She's so hooked by events that the possibility of a creature rising from a puddle behind her, never really crosses the mind. In the panther's defense, nobody else spotted the jackal's nose poking out of the muddy pool.

Carla the Jackal remains seated and soaked in muck while she wipes all the grub from her eyes, before silently climbing out and onto her feet. The cops move further away from the panther and on towards the tanker, as the wet filthy jackal slowly staggers closer and closer. Heaven empties another bucket of rain across the land, lightning crackles across the sky, and a set of knife-like teeth sink themselves into the shoulder of Miss Eliana. A piercing scream echoes around the yard. The band of cops instantly twist and sprint towards pleas for help. Again, Chico leads the charge - a determined monkey is quicker than any pig.

Eliana lays crumpled in agony beside the front left wheel, one hand plugging her wound while the other tries desperately to save her dress.

The rescue party surround the mangy menace, but she's not in the mood for capture. She bursts through the circle and heads for a maze of machinery, before climbing to the top of a crane. After a long howl, the jackal crawls along the top in the hope that she can leap off the end to another – but the next crane is so far away that any jump would surely be madness.

Yuriko gives chase and is about to make the climb – when Chico arrives and confidently moves her aside.

'I got this,' cracks a winking Chico. He grasps the opportunity to demonstrate his monkey talents, flying up the crane with incredible speed and agility.

'Maybe we should get ready to catch him?' remarks Ruben, lacking confidence in Chico's chances. Yuriko gives him the stare - a gentle reminder of which side he's backing.

Biting storms are even less enjoyable when you're balancing at the top of a crane. Chico hangs on tightly, trying to avoid being blown away as he crawls towards his enemy. The jackal has reached the end and weighs up ambitious options: stay on the crane and tackle the police force...or jump and hope that jackals can fly. She stares at the floor of the tanker waiting a long way down below. She stares at the detective creeping towards her. She stares at the opposite crane, a leap of faith away.

'Don't do it, jackal. You'll never make it!!' shouts Chico through wind and rain, pleading with his suspect to give up and hand herself in. Carla looks at Chico and smiles, pumped with over-confidence. She stands and howls, then takes a step back and prepares for lift off. 'Don't do it!!' begs Chico one last time but his words fall on nothing but deaf pointy ears. The jackal launches through the air, howling all the way.

She was never going to make it, and she's not even close. Half-way between two cranes the jackal begins her rapid descent towards the tanker. Suddenly - out of nowhere - an eagle swoops down like a rocket, clutching the vermin with talons. Chico looks shocked but not half as much as those watching from down below. Officer Thelma Eagle summons all her strength to try and keep Carla from falling; she drags her through the air, aiming for a monkey detective. But just as she reaches the crane, Carla bites the eagle's leg. Thelma yelps and reels from the blow. One claw now holds the jackal. One claw is not enough.

Chico stands at the tip of the crane, but as was the case with poor Clayton Hog, he's unable to offer assistance. The rabid predator slips from the grasp of the eagle and falls to the ground in silence. Chico thumps the crane with his fist, then he thumps it again, and again.

A thunderous roar now rattles the bones of every creature stuck in the yard. It came from a red brick house, the one crowned with a sleeping chimney. Then a second roar, even louder than the first, and this time worryingly closer. Something was coming, and that something sounded enormous.

Chico tries to deduce the source of such horrifying sounds, but mist and fog blight his view. 'Thelma, take a look but don't get too close!!' he yells to the injured eagle, before scampering back down the crane as sharply as possible.

Ruben, Yuriko, and most of the pigs have reached a unanimous decision to head towards their cars – freakin' quickly!

'What the hell was that? It sounded like a dragon!!' shouts Ruben, now catching a ride on the back of Yuriko to save some precious time.

'Sound like trouble,' says the wolf, struggling for breath as she dashes back to a safe position. Eliana is still waiting beside the car when they eventually arrive; she's slightly dizzy from loss of blood but full of beans as always. Yuriko makes certain the bleeding has stopped.

Ruben keeps watch with a crowd of nervy pigs.

A grateful Eliana takes Yuriko by the arm. 'It's not my place to say anything, you're all officers of the law, and I know I'm merely a secretary cursed with a giant mouth, who tends to rub people up the wrong way. *But* whatever that is, whatever it is, no matter how loud it roars, no matter how scary it *may* seem. Know this. You are a team, and if you work as a team, you can overcome even the most frightening of adversaries. He's one. You're a dozen. Work together and he'll surely be undone.'

'Amen,' mutters Ruben, keen for a taste of bravery, yet hindered by his tendency to always side with fear. Then he spots something. His heart nearly pounds its way out of his chest. There's movement beside the tanker. 'Guys, twelve o'clock.'

The pigs brace themselves for action. Deep breaths all round. Teeth chatter. Bodies shake. Everyone wishes they were home with loved ones, not facing impending doom in a rainy shipyard.

Relax. Sighs of relief all round. It's only Chico with Thelma Eagle flapping along beside him. They're travelling with haste and keen to join their colleagues. As Chico reaches the group he trips and falls beside their feet, gasping and fighting for air. He rolls over and manages to whisper a single word.

'Gorilla.'

The last word Ruben wanted to hear; the rat feels himself shifting backwards uncontrollably. Temptation to flee the scene overcomes him, but he hits a wall in the form of Yuriko, who tries to nudge him forward.

'Rats don't fight gorillas,' says Ruben, his eyes filled with genuine panic.

'You such coward, Ruben.'

'Yes, ok yes, I am, I'm scared of giant apes. Sue me. We need to leave *right* now.'

Then they see the red eyes for the first time. Bright bloodshot eyes. Out of the mist stomps Augustus the humongous albino gorilla, sporting nothing but a grey flat-cap and denim dungarees despite the brutal weather. There's a wooden pennant in the shape of an ark, strapped to his hulking neck. A frowning pink face, squidged in the middle of a furry white head - which must be the size of a watermelon. His arms are the size of thick steel pipes and at first glance his legs are tree trunks. In one hand he firmly grasps a chain, which leads to the neck of a panda. Lucas is dragged along the ground by the ruthless brute, stumbling across the land on all fours in a wire muzzle. Tired and far from healed, the bear is close to broken – reduced to a pet for a brutal henchman.

'Lucas!! Oh, good lord, poor Lucas,' cries Eliana. 'Those *beastly* beasts. How could they?'

'*Servant to the servants,*' whispers Chico recalling the words of Sister Turkey, as he wipes his clammy palms across his jacket. 'The price of betrayal.'

After a few yards Augustus stops and yanks the chain. Lucas can't help but fall flat on his face, and onto the awful mask of mesh now wrapped around it. The gorilla picks up the hostage using his extremely sore neck as a handle and flings him aside like tossing away the trash. Lucas is still breathing - just about - but he's badly concussed and understandably dares not move.

'It's all over, snowball. You're surrounded,' shouts Chico, in a feeble attempt to resolve the matter without breaking sweat. The gorilla grunts, beating the plate of armor that is his chest. His fingers wrap around a heavy block of wet timber and he holds it above his head, before skimming it through the air like a frisbee down the park. Everyone ducks or dives for cover. The flying wood slices through the front window of Yuriko's car and crashes into the seats, which fortunately aren't currently occupied. Eliana can only cover her ears, scream, and hope for the best, as her head is sprinkled with glass from shattered windows.

'Something tells me he ain't carrying a white flag,' says Ruben from his hiding spot behind the back wheel of a piggy's car. 'Come on, Chico, this is madness. We gotta get outta here...that thing'll kill us.' He's got one eye on his boss and the other on gates to freedom.

Augustus marches onwards like a tank, convinced that he can't be hurt.

Thelma Eagle is first to throw caution to the wind; she soars towards the rampant albino and ditches hooked claws in his strapping back. The gorilla roars but this time it's pain and frustration. His powerful right arm swings around at ferocious speed and clatters through the eagle's ribs. Thelma flies back and nose dives into the ground like a dropkicked sack of feathers. Her wings flutter momentarily before collapsing.

Eagles are tough birds, not fond of swallowing defeat, but Thelma knows she can offer nothing more while she's a pile of broken bones. The crippled officer drags herself through the mud with one claw, away from the danger zone, and leans against a wheelbarrow while she waits for medical assistance.

'*A spell in the city will do you some good,* she said.' Chico now recalls the wise words of his beloved aunty. 'Hell, we all gotta die someday right?' The monkey zips across the ground on all fours before flinging himself at Augustus. He manages to avoid a fearsome swing as a strong left arm whistles past the top of his head. Chico scratches, scrapes, and smacks the beast in a flurry. Yuriko provides support, biting on his white furry calf.

The gorilla is possessed with rage. He slaps Chico away like swatting a fly, then takes Yuriko's tail and swings her towards the sky. The helpless wolf crashes back down to ground; she's woozy for a second or two but then she comes around to her senses. She looks up at the two terrifying red eyes looking down. She can smell his breath, she can smell his stench, she's close enough to touch his filthy toes. The gorilla raises both fists; Yuriko closes her eyes and thinks of better days. But before he can crush the wolf, a 'frisbee' hits his chest and knocks him into a ditch. The block of wet timber is back in his hands.

Dazed and confused the gorilla stands and prepares to go again. This time he's facing Jake the Bear – better late than never. The polar detective was hoping the timber would settle the score, but he underestimated how resilient gorillas can be. They stand face to face and only yards apart - two fine warriors coated in white.

Yuriko crawls behind the bear, as does Chico. The pigs and Ruben are reluctant to move an inch from their cozy spots behind the barrier of cars; the closer to gates the better.

Jake rips off his shirt and reveals a map of scars across his body (the trousers stay on). Augustus removes his flat cap and chucks it towards the eagle, who remains propped up by the trusty wheelbarrow – but that's front row seating for the show's finale.

Jake cracks his knuckles, shakes his head from side to side, and moves forward in his preferred stance: left leg forward, arms up high to protect the face. Augustus prefers to swing wildly and hope for the best, but he only needs to catch you once and its most likely game over. Jake tries his best to avoid the barrage of attacks through weaving and side steps - an effort to tire the beast. Sensing exhaustion Jake then steps in and takes the opportunity to punish the mighty monster; a combination of stinging punches all land perfectly on the ribs before a sweet right hook nearly spins his chunky head around in a circle. Augustus isn't enjoying this and soon finds himself staring at clouds. Unwisely, Jake let's him recover and rise again- honor and pride over sense.

The gorilla grabs the timber and slams it against the polar bear's head sending him hurtling towards the edge and nearly into water. Luckily, Jake crashes in time to prevent an early swim. The stocky orphan is less willing to allow recovery time and chases his victim down. As Jake gets up, the gorilla pounds him in a furious display. Jake defends a few and lands a couple but his head is spinning and he's really struggling to focus. He catches Augustus again on the jaw but this time it doesn't drop him - it just raises the levels of anger. The gorilla smashes his head against the nose of the bear, and watches as Honeypaws sinks to his knees then slumps to the ground. Had there been a referee present, he would have waved to declare it over.

The triumphant king of the apes beats his chest, but Chico jumps on his back and tries a headlock. Yuriko isn't finished either and continues her attempt to chew on his stocky leg. The defiant albino warrior takes hold of Chico, choking his throat like he's squeezing a lemon until the monkey turns a nice shade of blue.

Augustus then feels something crawling up his leg, a tingle clambering higher and higher. If steam could explode from his ears, if balls of fire could be unleashed from his nose, then now was the time. A plucky rat has arrived on his shoulder.

'Sweet dreams, goliath,' screams Ruben, slashing across the eyes of the gorilla. Brawn by the bucket load, a foolhardy mind like a gnat, but who would've thought - a gorilla undone by a rat.

Chico wriggles free while the giant ape grabs his wounded face. Yuriko growls and attacks again, this time biting the throat. Augustus now wraps those large fingers around his neck, but it's not enough to prevent life dripping away. He staggers backwards and falls to one knee, coughing and spluttering, but now unable to roar. Darkness begins to fill the bloodshot eyes and a blur settles into his vision. He manages to rise one final time, but his legs are quick to give way and he plunges backwards, falling to a heartless ocean.

Ruben, Yuriko, and Chico stand at the edge, watching with crumpled faces as the white beast sinks without motion, descending to his watery grave. All that remains is a tarnished pennant, resting beside the drop.

An ambulance is warmly greeted as it parks outside the gates. A trio of sheep fall out the back and scatter towards the wounded, their medical bags clinking and clunking with every stride.

Jake is wincing and clutching his head but alive all thanks to his buddies. Yuriko helps him stumble back to the blockade of cars. Thelma is now *in* the wheelbarrow; a couple of pigs push her towards the ambulance.

'Thank you, Ruben. You saved my life,' says Chico, waiting for his face to resume a healthy color. 'Next time we face a gorilla, I'll know who to call.'

'Next time there's a gorilla, I'm switching to traffic duties, trust me. I'm done with heroics.'

With the help of a sheep, Lucas Panda rips off his muzzle and chains. He gently twists his head from side to side and strokes his aching neck, while he stares in disgust at the shackles. Then he's offered a red furry hand.

Chico pulls Lucas onto his feet, and then they shake. 'Detective Panda, I'm Detective Chico Monkey, pleasure to finally meet you. I know a penguin who might even break out a smile when he hears the good news.'

Lucas is head to toe in pain but manages to muster a smile 'Don't bet on it, monkey. Frank only grins at meal-time.'

As Chico moves aside, the panda spots a panther waiting to squeeze him tight. Eliana stands before Lucas with raindrops and teardrops gliding down both her cheeks. Before he can say a word, she dashes for the warmth of his arms. He decides to keep his lips sealed and instead plants a kiss on her head. Chico's work here is done – he nods and strolls away, allowing them their moment alone.

And then silence, a period of reflection and relief as they came to terms with what just happened, what they had survived. Some continued to breathe with a heaviness, some still shook and sighed, and some would lick their wounds for a long time yet (both physical and mental). They look upon one another, this band of law enforcing brothers, and nobody utters a word, for nothing need be said. It was chaos and they were fortunate, but they did what had to be done, and none of the good guys were lost. Whether or not justice had been served, was a question for another day. Now, they wanted a shower, a hot meal and a hard-earned spell of rest.

21

Fall Of The Damned

I t took over five years to build the Shepherd's Dam and thousands of workers - plenty of which sadly lost their lives during the feat of its construction. Standing as tall as thirty buses and stretching the length of a typical running track – it's not hard to see why it's a wonder of the world. All sorts of animals helped with the creation, but it was mainly a job for beavers; anything built to block water or help you pass over it, tends to be maintained goofy rodents. The dam is crucial to the survival of the city, not only because it holds off the Scarlet Ocean, but it generates power and tourism. If a deluded 'goat of the cloth' was able to destroy this most precious of shields then chaos, suffering, and casualties would certainly be hard to avoid.

Most of Noah's Kingdom have gathered for the annual parade but a bunch of beavers need to hang at the dam to ensure everything's sweet and dandy. One unfortunate beaver has been tasked with manning the main gate which leads you onto the site; they drew the short straw and get to spend their entire shift camped in a narrow hut.

Assuming a peaceful day lays ahead, devoid of thrills and spills, the lonesome beaver decides to put his feet up, grab a copy of The Chronicle, and skim through it's sporting headlines: *Jackson Cheetah wins the San Shem marathon for a third year running*. He's whistling so loudly and lost so deep in thought that he doesn't hear the police car chugging down the road towards him. It skids to a halt just short of the barrier before Frank rolls out on the double. The Chronicle sinks a whisker below eye level as the beaver peeks at his unexpected, and most unwelcome visitor.

'No tours today, buddy. Best you come back tomorrow,' shouts the beaver from his hut, without feeling it necessary to leave his comfortable seating position.

Frank leans into the hut, flashing his badge. 'Detective Frank Penguin. Any old goats swing by today?' he enquires with urgency.

'In case you hadn't noticed *detective,* this is a dam, not a retirement home,' replies the smug beaver, still enchanted by sporting glories: *Red Pegasus cruises to victory in The King Turkey Derby*. Frank tries to gaze up at the top of the dam without breaking his neck, then looks back at the unhelpful whistling beaver.

'There another way into this place? Different entrance, hole in the fence maybe?' says the penguin quizzingly. He ponders the easiest ways to gain access if you're a loony, hell bent on destroying the only plug between city and sea.

'Not that I know of, buddy.' He licks his finger and changes the page: *Horoscopes.*

'Well, I got reason to believe you got yourself an intruder, so I'm takin' a look around.'

'Ok, buddy,' mumbles the disinterested goofball.

'Jeeze, they chose *you* as head of security?'

'Sure did.' He picks up a corn on the cob and begins to gnaw while he checks out predictions for Scorpio: his love life should improve and there's talk of a prosperous endeavor, but no mention of friction with flightless birds.

'How do I reach the top? And don't say climb or to hell with the city. I'm done with steps.'

'There's a lift up ahead, can't miss it.' He points without taking his eyes off the news.

'*Finally*, a helpful answer.'

'You're welcome.'

'Now find your boss. Tell him there's a vicar on the dam, and he's thinkin' of blowing Kingdom to Kingdom Come.'

The beaver licks his finger again, but before he can turn the page there's a firm grip around his neck. The beaver's dragged off his cozy chair and pinned against the back of the hut. '*I said...find your stinkin' boss. Or we'll all be sleepin' with the fishes. Get it.*'

'Ok...ok,' says the beaver despite substantial pressure on his windpipe. The Chronicle floats out of the hut and drifts away. The half-eaten cob rolls into dirt.

Frank allows the beaver to breathe again then makes for the lift. The guard gasps and coughs, massaging his throat while he picks up a red emergency phone. This is usually nap time for the hot-blooded boss, but LeRoy Beaver will rise and shine when he hears about a showdown.

Father Goat looks out at the deep blue sea, his back on Noah's Kingdom. He stands alone at the top of the dam preparing for his plan's fruition. A white helmet rests at his feet; it's amazing the freedom you acquire in a place like this merely through dressing the part. The beaver at the gate had waved him through without a 'who' or 'why' –for an aged goat in a helmet and scruffy overalls just doesn't raise enough suspicion. Father Goat even arrived armed with a syringe full of sedative, but thus far had no need to use it. Entering the premises had been easier than he anticipated. The hardest part was carrying a backpack and bagful of dynamite but then he was never as weak or dainty as he'd lead the Kingdom police to believe.

Everything was ready. Red sticks, full of nitroglycerine, were neatly laid out along the top of the barrier, each connected to a lengthy fuse. All that remained was to plunge the detonator and Shepherd's Dam would be no more. The goat closes his eyes, raises his head to face the fading sun and breathes in the sea's salty air. He imagines the praise he'll receive from a grateful God.

'I hate heights, can't stand them. Make me *real* giddy.'

The goat's eyes slowly open and the head drops down; he recognizes the voice but wasn't expecting to hear it today, or ever again in truth. Frank is anxiously strolling along the dam with his wings tucked deep in his pockets.

'Do you know why rainbows appear in the sky, detective?' asks the goat, looking across to the penguin. 'A reminder of our covenant with the lord, our promise to live in harmony. A promise we've undoubtedly broken. This city's rotten to its core, and it is imperative we wash it away and start afresh. My orphans will grow a prosperous and peaceful new society. Or we face the wrath of God.'

Frank doesn't look convinced, but he stops strolling and stands his ground, ten paces away from the enemy – like two seasoned cowboys ready to draw.

'I was so sure it was Salvatore, so sure it was a dog,' says Frank rubbing his hands (it's chilly this high in the sky). 'Convinced myself this was all about money and amusements for The Swamp. Yet here we are. My partner kidnapped, joined by three damn beavers, all cause some gruff decrepit goat wants to play Noah.'

'I'm afraid such foul deeds were necessary,' says the goat, stroking his chinny beard. 'And a panda should know to choose his battles wisely, not meddle in other's affairs. They are after all…an endangered species.'

'What about the brothers? They adored you, they were on your side,' snaps Frank as he slides a step closer.

The goat checks a brown leather wristwatch clasped to his left arm: sixty ticks till noon. He turns to face Noah's Kingdom, almost shaking with nerves and excitement.

'Why the beavers?' hollas the detective, repeating his question till he gets a response.

'Absolute loyalty and devotion, until they discovered I'd sold The Swamp, *their home*, to that frightful bulldog. They failed to grasp the bigger picture, threatened to reveal my aspirations to the authorities. Augustus, my glorious white knight, saw to it that they divulged no secrets.' He checks the watch again.

'You do realize if the dam goes boom, you go boom, right? Unless you've hidden a canoe round here somewhere.' Franks teeth begin to chatter and a shiver takes hold of his body; he foolishly ignored his wife's plea that he wear a vest.

'Sacrifices must be made, detective. If I must perish for the sake of a brighter future. So be it.'

'What about the orphanage? Even a fancy new orphanage won't survive a tidal wave. You'll wipe out everyone you care for.'

'Oh, don't worry, detective. My flock will be just fine.'

'But *why*, vicar? Why blow up the dam? It's nothing but madness.' Frank takes another step forward.

'I grow weary of your questions,' snarls the old goat, taking a final glimpse at the watch. 'The time is upon us.'

'*Why*, why are you doing this?' asks Frank again, creeping closer to the goat, but not quite near enough to risk a leap and tackle. If he can stall the maniac for a little longer and sneak in a couple of strides, then there's a chance he could stop him and prevent disaster.

Wide eyed the vicar finally snaps, casting away his usual polite demeanor in favor of rage. 'The lord flooded the world….so tired he grew of humankind and all their wicked ways. He grants the animal a chance to inherit the earth, so long as we live in peace. But trouble was never washed away. We have failed him, just like man before us. We have betrayed the covenant,' he roars, with both arms flung above his head.

'The same black hearts and twisted minds still walk the streets. All I see each day is a hunger for greed, cruelty, and wrongdoing, but their end is nigh. What other choice do I have when anarchy reigns supreme? They've only themselves to blame, for that which must be done this day. What I do now, I do for God. We will sink this damned Kingdom and rise again, DROWN, DROWN, DROWN we must!!' Veins pop from the withering skin and his furious eyes look close to popping too, as he falls upon the detonator.

Frank winces, crouches, and covers his face as he waits for a bang and darkness.

But nothing.

The delirious goat pushes again, then again, but nothing. Aghast he inspects the fuse, only to realize that an unhappy beaver has bitten it right in half.

Not more than a stones-throw away was LeRoy Beaver, holding a perfectly ruined cable. He hasn't bothered with his white helmet for this task; he's kitted out in standard mucky denim and his favorite checkered shirt.

'No…no it can't be…it can't be,' quivers the goat attacking the detonator again, but his efforts are simply futile.

'For my brothers,' says LeRoy in a cold menacing tone, his head tilted forward like a bull about to charge. A flash of the gold tooth as he licks his lips. The second his lips are clean another beaver appears, clambering over the edge (climbing up and down the slippery walls of a dam is no sweat for experienced workers).

Frank takes a back seat and allows fate to do the rest.

The goat scrambles away from the two beavers on his hand and knees, but now they arrive from all sides of the dam. At least a dozen wet beavers emerge, all clawing their way to the battlefield.

'For our brothers,' they whisper in frightening unison as they form a circle around the goat. The vicar of North Beach - so confident of glory only moments before - now reduced to a bumbling wreck. His head spins and spirals as he tries to keep watch over all his approaching foes. He turns to Frank, both hands cupped, and desperately pleads for mercy. 'Penguin help…please…please penguin…help me!!' begs the vicar as vengeance draws closer and closer.

'For our brothers,' whisper the beavers, now close enough to hear each of the goat's panic laden breaths. His eyes droop and shine with tears. His bottom lip trembles. His hope fades.

Frank sighs. 'I'll be honest, father…they don't need any help.'

'No…penguin…NOOO,' screams the goat. The beavers clasp the goat and raise him above their heads, before silently carrying him into the misty far reaches of Shepherd's Dam, and he is never to be seen again.

The penguin walks away, not turning his head for a peek throughout the screams. With a shrug of the shoulders, rub of the hands, and a slight adjustment of his beloved fedora – he heads off to catch the parade.

****

The February parade always begins at Noah's statue, in a park at the heart of New Carnival. It then marches through Central, crosses the Boa River, and finishes at Paradise Valley where the celebrations continue till dawn. Lioness Annabella contributes most of the cost for the popular event but there's a zero percent chance she'll step on a float; she's quite content viewing proceedings from her lair at Emzara's Palace. The same, however, can't be said for her flamboyant assistant, Omar Tiger, who annually snaps up the opportunity to be heavily involved.

One of the little advantages of working for the Kingdom Police Force is that the parade passes right by headquarters as part of the route. Chief Vulture even encourages the squad to step outside and enjoy the show (maybe she does have a heart buried in there somewhere after all). But space is limited - even outside HQ. The whole street is buzzing with animals scuffling for the best view possible; volunteers and officer pigs battle for peace and order as all the floats begin their approach.

A local school has taken over the opposite side to the police station. A line of children with painted faces wave their colorful flags and dangle balloons as they simmer with anticipation. Jolly families and gangs of friends can be spotted in every direction, all unaware of just how close they came to a tragic end. And completely oblivious to the fact that their saviors now stand among them.

'You so silly, rat,' says Yuriko down to Ruben, worried he's cramping her style. Truly in the spirit of the occasion, the rat has chosen to decorate his face with white and pinkish stars

'What can I say, I like a party. It's never too late to dab a little glitter and color on your cheeks, Yuriko?'

'I'm ok thanks. Just don't let vulture see…or you be working traffic for long time.'

Battered and bruised but never willing to miss the show, the group of heroes have assembled to rejoice at their victory (except for Thelma Eagle who's recovering at Sheephaven Hospital but should be back in the air by next week). Two mysteries resolved in one day, and the culprits a worry no more. Inevitable silver medals to follow, and each fittingly carved with the word 'Gallantry'.

As is tradition Jake carries Squinty on his shoulders so she can feast her eyes on every creature parading. She twists and wriggles in an attempt at getting comfortable on top of the hairy bruiser, while whipping out ginormous binoculars.

'Careful you don't drop me, Jake,' she announces loudly, her claws clinging tight to his forehead.

'I got you, I got you,' says Jake confidently. He's still in a lot of pain following his rumble in the shipyard but much too stubborn to admit it - and would never ask Squinty to hop off given that she looks so joyous. 'Just tell me when you spot the turtles. Promised my boy I'd take a few pictures.'

'Why ain't he here watching?' asks Squinty, spying on the floats with her pair of lengthy telescopes.

'Outta town with his mother again. Poor kid.' Jake manages to punch the air with his fist while keeping hold of the clucking photographer wrapped around his neck. He's pumped by the sight of fire eating giraffes – so lanky they could singe the clouds. A troop of dancing flamingos are next - but they only make the bear groan.

The sound of chatter now soars into bursts of whoops, whistles, and wild cheers as the 'Simian Brass Band' boogies past the tight knit crew of jolly triumphant coppers; smaller apes at the front on trombones or sax, touch of woodwind in the middle, and a few gorillas on drums hovering at the back. Eliana and Chico have both been in the wars but rustle up an impressive cry of support for the popular musical primates.

'Jolly good...jolly good. Oh, aren't they just splendid? I do love a good parade,' gushes the persistently positive panther. Thankfully, the medics patched up the nasty bite mark on her neck and she'll soon be good as new. Chico's so relieved he made it out the shipyard alive and solved a curious case, that a few scars to remind him won't likely be a problem.

'What will happen to those dear little orphans?' asks Eliana, taking Chico's hand.

'A certain chinchilla arranged a few nights at the palace for them. Then back to their home on the hill, I suppose. If only there was someone kind and generous, *and* currently unemployed, who'd be a perfect fit to look after them?'

'Who, *me*? Oh, don't be daft. What do I know about caring for children?'

'I think you'd be great. You're smart, and you're scary...they'll learn but stay in line. Plus, I know a kindly ferret who'd probably lend a hand. You should think about it.'

'Mmm maybe I will, Mr Monkey. Maybe I will.'

'We couldn't have done it without your help you know,' says Chico, leaning in close to the panther's ear. There's so much commotion and amped up excitement around them that it's difficult to have a conversation, and the arrival of synchronized Komodo dragons twirling pointy spears does little to help.

'Don't be silly, Mr Monkey, I merely gave you a nudge. Without your *hunch* we'd be splashing around in a pool of doom right about now,' replies Eliana in her typical adamant manner. She won't hear any more talk of praise or thanks, preferring to focus on clapping the nifty troop of monstrous lizards.

'She's right.'

Chico looks around to see his partner waddling up behind him. 'Didn't have you down as a fan of parades, Frank?'

'And you'd be right, kid. Too much happiness...makes me uncomfortable.'

'Afternoon, Mr Penguin.' The panther blows a kiss.

'Eliana.' Frank bows his head and tips his hat.

'We heard about the dam,' she adds.

'Heard about the shipyard. *And,* the floating orphanage.'

'Quite a day.' Chico hopes his next case is less fraught with danger and lacking in hulking white brutes. Secretly he pines for a couple of simple burglaries before tackling his next batch of kidnappers.

'Is that...Omar Tiger?' asks Frank, distracted by the peculiar sight of a ferocious cat dressed as a frilly peacock. 'Jeeze Louise, I think that's Omar Tiger.' And so it was. Various staff from Emzara's Palace - including a slimmer Sammy Hippo - bow and wave regally to the crowds as they pass; each is stylishly strapped to a cape of bright feathers and drizzled in twinkling paint. Rolling behind them is a towering handmade sculpture of a lion - a blinding yellow tribute to their mysterious absent leader. It makes a nice change from Omar's usual day to day routine - a chance to let his hair down and finally have some fun. Frank's confused and mildly surprised but shakes his head a little, which is as close as he gets to a thumbs up.

But many have come today, solely for a sight of the next attraction.

'Mummy...mummy what's that?' shouts a shaken young toad, hiding behind her mother.

'The most dangerous of all creatures,' whispers mother to child, holding her nice and tight. Eyes open wide, hearts race, and cameras flash as a pitch-black truck gradually rolls towards them. The back of the truck is a sturdy long cage with thick steel bars, holding a guest of South-Central Zoo (not to be confused with South Central Prison).

'Make sure you catch this one guys,' says Jake excitedly like a thrilled child.

'Oh sure, like I'm gonna miss this,' snipes Squinty sarcastically. She gives the bear a cheeky little slap to the head.

'Room for one more up there, Jake?' shouts Ruben, stood on tip toes trying to catch a look at the cage; he's also cradling a box of toffee popcorn which is rapidly disappearing (and probably rotting his teeth).

'Look at its eyes. So wild and angry,' notes Yuriko. She reluctantly plants Ruben on her left shoulder for about the tenth time this week.

'Yikes, he does look angry...maybe I shouldn't look. My mother warned me never to touch one, said they love the taste of rats. And my cousin Louis, he tried to touch one once, nearly lost an arm.' Another handful of popcorn drops in his belly.

'Oh, I think they're fascinating. I could watch them all day,' adds Eliana, patting her hands together with sheer delight. 'Such a shame they're so close to extinction.'

'Not a shame if you ask me. Ugly things and stink o' garbage. Good ridduns to em,' adds frumpy Frank Penguin.

Chico has never seen one before. They don't tend to pop up in quaint little towns like West Bay. He's heard all the stories from Aunt Sally of course but seeing one up close is a different matter entirely. No words or thoughts are shared – he takes in the moment alone.

The prisoner shrieks and shakes the bars like he's completely possessed by a demon - unease takes hold of the crowd. A hairy gaunt face, pale scabby skin, and clearly in need of a meal. Thick brown brows cover manic bulging eyes and he never appears to blink. No shoes to warm his blistered feet nor garments to comfort his chest. The caged freak charges the walls of steel, trying as best he can to break himself free. He screams and scowls, dancing about with rage. Even the onlooking parents consider a run for cover.

For it is Man.

****

A silhouette watches the pomp and ceremony through a fourth-floor window of the police force building. The nosy shadow is in fact Chief Vulture - the only character to flap around on parade day in clothing fit for a funeral. She stares blankly at the gathering storm of enjoyment down below, until boredom wins her over and she promptly returns to her desk.

A folded copy of the Chronicle waits to be read. The headline is impossible to ignore: 'Mayor Missing'. She gazes upon a black and white image of a leopard which sits below the story. For a moment there's a strong feeling of guilt that she let this happen, that she had arranged for the delivery of a mayor to the clutches of a ravenous lion - but the day has not yet arrived when you question Annabella's wishes. Animals have office jobs, luxury homes and conversations over tea now, but deep down there's still a food chain and evolution has yet to knock lions off the top.

Chief Vulture gently sweeps the story into a basket beside her desk, trying to forget she's been complicit in such a horrible deed. But it's not the first time, and until the kingdom's true ruler adopts a healthier appetite, it shan't be the last.

****

Chief Vulture isn't the only one not congregating with all the hordes on the streets. Mason Gator is busy manning the barbecue in the gardens behind his restaurant: charred fumes can be smelt for miles. He may be the boss but he's more than happy to step up and cook the food, despite the fact he surrounds himself with plenty of world-famous chefs.

Fat Chinchilla to nobody's surprise, is deep in sleep beside the gator's swimming pool. The snoring chinchilla is sprawled across a sunbed, his drooling jaws wide open, and he's wrapped with a bright orange robe (worthy in itself of parading).

'Giddy up, veg is crisp and ready! Grab yourself a plate and tuck right in boys and girls!!' hollas Mason, turning over a few burnt carrots with his favorite spatula. The white apron makes him a tad less frightening, yet nobody is quite brave enough to utter the word 'overcooked'.

The bison twins, a certain naked mole rat, and a whole host of bunnies, hover around the barbie while Mason passes them grub. The gator and his mob plan to host a party tonight, but for now it's all about eat and relax.

****

Salvatore Bulldog stares longingly into his mirror, which is cracked and bolted to the wall of a prison cell (he can't find his glasses so it's all just a blur). Dressed in a less fetching orange outfit than the chinchilla, he shuffles back to his simple bed on the bottom bunk. The increasingly unhealthy dog lays there coughing and wheezing till the fox above him snaps and bangs on the side of the bed.

'I thought I told you mutt, quit making all that noise!'

Salvatore hasn't the strength to argue anymore. He fumbles under his pillow for the inhaler and takes a much-needed puff.

'Don't you talk to him like that, or I'll rip ya in two. Ya here me fox!!' Leonard Weiler rattles the bars of the cell next door, his thick head and wet black nose nearly managing to poke right through.

Hudson Rhino rattles passed in chains, with his chin sunk tightly into his chest, eyes fixed on the ground, and a couple of meaty guards to mind him all the way.

****

Beep. Beep. Beep.

Lucas Panda is desperate to sleep but his heart monitor keeps him awake; given more strength he'd probably switch it off. He's clearly been through the wars, poor thing, and fortunate it's beeping at all. There's a couple of cuts on his face, but none like the ones on his belly, or the various slits to his back - not to mention the numerous tubes, plugged in all over her body. But he's alive and on the mend, like the triplet of beavers on beds beside him – each wrapped in peach robes and healthy enough for tea and morning papers. There's two beds opposite, both empty, but this is Sheephaven Hospital which hides on the outskirts of town and isn't first choice for most of the sickly and wounded; that said, it's as good a place as any to recover, and all the staff are lovely. Fresh white jasmine pokes from the vase at Lucas's bedside and a calming sweet aroma fills the air.

A foxy nurse, with a radiant smile wrapped in cherry lipstick, scuttles into the room. She *clips clops* along, her black high heels making noise with every step. There's a bowl in one hand and glass in the other.

'How are you feeling, Mr Panda?' she asks, clad in spotless white.

'Better thank you, much better,' replies the panda, clearly still struck with fatigue.

'I've brought you some bamboo soup and warm milk. I'll pop it down on the table and you can have it when you're ready.' The nurse places the meal on the table beside the flowers, before placing a hand on the panda's head to check for a reasonable temperature. 'You have a delivery as well. Would you like me to bring it in?' she whispers, now inspecting the tubes. 'Smells like...*tuna.*'

'Yes please, send it in,' replies the smiling panda, reaching for the scrumptious soup.

****

'I knew I should've just gone home. I can't stand crowds and *whackos* on floats. What am I doing at a damn parade?' huffs Frank, struggling to get in the spirit of things. Panda's on chariots, carried by sweaty horses - are really not Frank's cup of tea.

Now came the arrival of 'The Tortoise' - one of few occasions where the tortoise leaves the Temple of Hope. Resting on a bed of fine pillows above a golden float, the ancient prophet can barely acknowledge the delirious reception due to his crazy age (next year he will be two hundred years old). Four elephants - also given the golden touch - proudly drag the float along as people celebrate the wisest of all. Maybe not the best time to offer an apology but Frank's seen *the old turtle* plenty of times so he doesn't hold back and turns to Chico.

'Listen, kid... about the goat. I shouldn't have doubted you. I was just...well I got history with the bulldog and...I messed up. *Ahem*, anyways look, you done well is what I'm trying to say,' he says grabbing the monkey by the arm.

'Thanks, Frank,' says Chico, trying to respond while 'tortoise watching' at the same time.

'So, what's next for Chico Monkey?' asks Frank, moving on from the awkward groveling apology as swiftly as possible.

'To be honest, I got unfinished business back in West Bay.'

'Oh...right. Of course– '

'I promised a pretty monkey I'd take her out for a drink and dance. And monkeys never go back on a promise.'

'Well, obviously I feel sorry for this poor lady, if she's stuck spending an evening listening to all your wise cracks and nonsense. But...ah...I suppose we did good, kid, me and you....and errrr, you know if you're ever back in town– '

'Soon as I'm done with milkshakes and waltzing, I'm back to work. Got this new partner who's bound to be lost without me.'

'New partner yeah...' Franks face lights up a little.

'Yeah, he's a grumpy old soul, sinks way too much coffee...*but* I think he means well, and to be honest, I'm probably lost without him too.' Most buddies would probably embrace at this point, but not when one of the duo happens to be an old school penguin.

'Monday morning then,' says Frank, now slipping effortlessly back into boss mode.

'Arctic Cafe.'

'Don't be late, kid. Walrus stops breakfast at ten.'

'I'll be there. And that's a promise too…Francis.' Chico can't help but sign off with a wink. The frosty penguin walks away shuddering at the sound of his name, but not before saluting his fellow detective.

Frank doesn't do hugs and long drawn out farewells. As the crowd applauds a blitz of fireworks, he takes his leave and slips down a nearby alleyway. His chariot awaits. He genuinely hoped to see the kid again soon, for underneath all his moaning was a growing respect for the plucky monkey and even his carefree ways. Chico had proven himself to be a promising young detective and a brave one at that (but Frank would never admit that to his hairy face).

'Gotta gold coin for a struggling ostrich, sir? Today's my birthday.'

Frank is startled, not expecting to find any company down a slender dark alley - but he's familiar with the voice and line of questioning. He turns to face the weary ostrich, who is sheltered beside a dumpster and rattling an empty can. Maybe the ostrich caught him on a good day, maybe it's a change of heart and fresh approach – but Frank digs deep in his pockets and flicks a coin for his fellow bird.

'Oh, thank you, sir, thank you kindly. Very generous,' he says, beaming at the coin with wide open eyes and delight.

'Happy birthday,' says Frank, swaggering towards the end of the alley.

Thanks to the parade all the back streets are empty - no snakes of traffic to cause delay, no scumbags to hold up his journey. The black and white sleuth crawls into his terrible excuse for a black and white car. He checks the mirrors and crushes the pedal. With a piercing screech he makes his getaway, leaving only a trail of dust. Full speed ahead as he swings round the corners and chews up the empty lanes, like a racing driver late for work.

Frank Penguin, renowned for a face like thunder, smiles with sheer delight. His wife was cooking fish pie for supper and he wasn't so far from home.

THE END

About the Author

J T Bird is an award-winning stand-up comedian from North London, where he lives with his wife and child. His humble abode sits neatly between the former homes of HG Wells and Robert Louis Stevenson...so there's no pressure to write something utterly successful and wonderful.

Lightning Source UK Ltd.
Milton Keynes UK
UKHW011952051120
372868UK00001B/162